THE MOTHER'S BOND

THE MOTHER'S BOND

The new, hard-hitting, emotional novel from one of the nation's favourite celebrities.

Kathryn Casey has a secret past. But these days she barely notices the little daily lies she tells to keep it hidden. She has a new identity now. All she wants is an orderly, predictable life that revolves around her beloved husband and children. Kathryn was once Kelly who lived on one of the roughest estates in the north and got pregnant as a teen. When she moved away, she left the past behind. Now there's a stranger in her kitchen, and he knows more about her than he is letting on. Will Kathryn finally have to admit to her family that she isn't who they think she is?

THE MOTHER'S BOND

by

Denise Welch

Magna Large Print Books
Long Preston, North Yorkshire,
BD23 4ND, England.

British Library Cataloguing in Publication Data.

A catalogue record of this book is
available from the British Library

ISBN   978-0-7505-4710-9

First published in Great Britain in 2018 by Sphere

Cover illustration © Christie Goodwin/Arcangel by arrangement with
Arcangel Images Ltd.

The moral right of the author has been asserted

Published in Large Print 2019 by arrangement with
Little, Brown Book Group

Magna Large Print is an imprint of Library Magna Books Ltd.

Printed and bound in Great Britain by
T.J. (International) Ltd., Cornwall, PL28 8RW

For my husband Lincoln for
loving me like no other.

For my sons Matty, Louis & Lewis
for making me laugh every day.

For my dad and my sister for being proud of me
– and my mum, Annie, whose memory
keeps me strong.

Acknowledgements

My nieces Olivia and Alex and nephew Wills. It's a joy watching you follow your dreams.

Jenny, my mum-in-law, who fills a place in my heart that was left empty.

Duncan, the 'little' brother I never had!

My best friends who never leave my side.

Gordon Wise at Curtis Brown, for taking me seriously.

Maddie West at Little, Brown, who asked for a second novel!!

And finally, Rebecca Cripps, who has been with me every step of the way and without whom you wouldn't be reading this book.

Thank you one and all xx

Prologue

As she wiped her feet on the welcome mat outside her front door, Kathryn Casey had no sense of the danger that lurked inside her house. Instead she savoured the feeling of coming home, as she always did, no matter where she'd been or for how long. This was her haven, her place of peace and safety – even when it was full of grumpy teenagers.

There was nothing grand about living in a modern red brick semi on a residential development just outside town. You couldn't swing a cat in the upstairs rooms, at least two of the taps were leaky and the paintwork needed redoing. But even after all the years she'd lived here, it still felt like a palace to Kathryn. Compared to the cramped, boxy flat she'd grown up in, it was a bloody mansion.

Brett was always saying that a home was more than bricks and mortar. It was part of his sales patter, but it was true. In this house on Totteridge Avenue, their family had blossomed, the kids had grown up and she had matured along with them. In some ways it had shaped them. Maybe its layout had even influenced the ties between the children – the boys in their side-by-side bedrooms and Flora slightly cut off. In turn they had changed its structure to suit their needs, by extending the kitchen and adding a sun lounge off the living room.

Would they be the same family in a different house? she wondered. Would there still be a room known as 'Flora's rabbit hole'? There was no way of telling. All she knew was that, after twelve years of Christmases, birthday parties and gatherings – after nearly a decade and a half of stories and dramas – who they were and where they lived seemed inextricably entwined, like a knot that could never be untied.

It only felt like yesterday that they had moved in. She would never forget the looks on the bairns' faces as they burst gleefully out of the back door into the garden. There had only been a small patio at their previous address, a house that Kathryn had never been fully able to consider her home. But when they moved to Totteridge Avenue, all of a sudden they had a lawn. They had trees and borders. They had space.

'Can we have a trampoline, too?' George had pleaded. Kathryn smiled at the memory. That boy never missed a trick.

Their new house had filled her with wonder. In the first days and weeks after moving in, she could happily have spent twelve hours a day at the kitchen sink, looking out of the picture window while she washed and dried the dishes, marvelling at their big green garden.

Twelve years on and I'm even more of a homebody, she thought, smiling again as she unlocked the door and stepped into the hall. Thirty-seven years old and already middle-aged, in attitude if not in years.

'I'm back!' she called out. 'Photos and all.'

She reached into her coat pocket and pulled out a small envelope. They were going to laugh at her latest attempt to get a decent passport picture done. This one was even worse than the last, a proper criminal mugshot, grim and staring, with mad eyes that looked almost black, instead of their usual dark blue. And was her hair really that straggly? It had looked so sleek and shiny brown at the hairdresser's the week before.

To her shame, she hadn't even said thank you to the Saturday girl-turned-photographer who had snapped her in a booth off to the side of the pharmacy. 'That'll do,' she'd said, pretending she was in a hurry.

'Are you sure?' the girl had said, sensing her dismay. 'I can try again if you like.'

'Don't worry, love. You know what they say – if you look like your passport photo, you're too ill to travel!'

Hers was even worse than most, though. Was there anybody in the world less photogenic? She knew what George would say. 'Mam, don't take this the wrong way, because you're not bad looking – you know, for a mam – but the camera definitely does not love you.'

She heard voices coming from the kitchen as she hung up her coat. Better get the tea on, she thought, glancing at a framed photograph of Brett's first wife playing with George and Flora in the garden.

'We're in here, love,' Brett yelled.

She made out George's voice and someone else's too, followed by a burst of laughter. She frowned.

15

'Is Steven home?' she asked. Steven was supposed to be poring over his maths books at a school study session.

More laughter. He'd better not have come back early, she thought, steeling herself for a row.

She felt a gust of cold air around her ankles and whipped around to see if she'd left the front door open. But it was firmly closed. So where was that draught coming from? She checked the downstairs toilet, but the window was shut, and by then the draught had disappeared.

Brett and George were in the kitchen, track-suits unzipped, beers in hand, faces glowing from cold air and exercise. Standing next to them was one of George's mates, who looked vaguely famil-iar beneath the shadowy rim of his baseball cap, although she couldn't see his face properly and God knew what his name was. The kitchen was always full of George's mates – it was hard to keep track of them all. It wasn't Steven, at least.

'Kath,' Brett said, coming over to kiss her. 'They won! They're finally turning things around, can you believe it?'

'And here's the reason,' said George with a boyish grin. 'Mam, this is Rory, our new coach, the man who is single-handedly turning the Steelers into champions.'

'Rory?' she said hesitantly.

Don't be silly, she thought, it couldn't be him – even as she realised it was. Her heart started pounding. Her cheeks felt flushed and hot.

'He's studying sports management at uni,' George added.

George's mate stepped forward and took off his

16

baseball cap in a gesture that could easily have been interpreted as old-fashioned politeness, if you didn't know what was really going on.

'Hello, George's mam,' he said, looking her boldly in the eye.

An electric charge of fear shot through her. She had dreaded this. It had kept her awake at night. It was a bad dream made real, a daytime nightmare. What was Rory doing in her kitchen, sharing a beer with her husband and stepson – as if he had every right to be here?

But I told you never to come to my home! she screamed silently.

Typically, Brett noticed something was wrong. 'Everything OK, sunshine?' he asked, putting his arm round her.

She tried to keep her face blank as she groped around for an excuse. She had to remember that George had asked Rory into their house. Even though he was an intruder in her eyes, to the others he was a guest.

By a miracle, it came to her. 'I've only gone and left my passport photos at the chemist,' she said, giving her forehead a light slap to emphasise what a wazzock she was. She looked at the clock on the wall. 'If I nip back now, I might catch them before they close. Nice to meet you, Rory,' she added, hoping that no one could detect the tremor in her voice, the suppressed swell of liquid terror.

She swayed slightly as she made her way back towards the hall. The shock of seeing him there, in the kitchen of her home, had left her punch drunk. She grabbed her coat and keys and swiftly got into the car. In a blind panic, she turned on the ignition, over revved the engine, shot along the road, braked sharply, opened her door, leaned out and was sick on the tarmac.

Rory had come to ruin her. He had come to destroy everything she had worked so hard to build, everything she held dear in the world. Somehow she had to stop him before he smashed her home and family to smithereens – if it wasn't already too late.

PART ONE

1

Kelly Callan wasn't surprised to hear a key turn in the lock, even though her nana wasn't due home for a couple of hours. She had been expecting a visit from Mo since the previous evening, when Jimmy Fry on the eighth floor had called her upstairs for a word, 'in private, like'.

As she'd climbed the grubby flecked stone steps to Jim's flat, she'd felt sure he was going to impart some news or other about her mam. He always seemed to know where Mo was and what she was up to.

Nana said he was secretly in love with her. 'Poor shite, on a hiding to nothing,' she added with a bitter smile.

Jim's complexion was the colour of the tab smoke that fogged up his flat. He stared flatly at Kelly out of eyes that looked like a couple of week-old fried eggs. Nana said he was in his forties, but to Kelly he looked about eighty. His yellowish white hair and jowly cheeks said it all, she thought. He wasn't long for this world. He was on the way out.

'I saw yer mam in town yesterday. I thought you should know,' he said, narrowing his eyes as he sucked on a roly.

Even though it was what she'd been expecting

21

him to say, Kelly's heart began to beat faster. It was her mam, after all. She hadn't seen her in months. 'Was she down the shops?' she asked.

He broke into a grin. 'You know Mo. Loves a gamble.'

'Hope she wasn't caught,' she said.

'If she was, she'll have given them the slip. That's all part of the buzz for her.'

Kelly didn't smile. Suddenly it felt uncomfortable to be discussing her mam's fondness for nicking stuff.

'Maybe we'll see her this time,' she said, with a hopeful note in her voice.

'If you do, tell her to come and say hello. Say Jim's got a present for her, something special.'

'OK.' She turned to go.

'How's the studies?' he asked.

She shrugged. 'The maths is hard, but I like geography. I'm applying to uni now.'

'What's the course?'

'Travel, Tourism and Hospitality Management.'

'Good for you.' He stubbed out his tab. 'Get away from this stinking pisshole and make a life for yourself.'

She stopped in the doorway of his flat. 'It's not so bad,' she said.

'You say that because you don't know any different, lassie,' he said. 'Now get back to your books and make good your escape.'

Kelly was trying to make sense of the Canary Islands' population statistics when she heard the scratch and rattle of a key in the lock. Next door had just stopped blasting Nirvana at full volume, otherwise she wouldn't have noticed.

Her pulse quickened as her mother came through the door carrying several bulging carrier bags.

'You see? I told you the bairn would be here to ruin our fun,' Mo complained, dropping the bags with a thud. 'Little Betty Bookworm, never leaves the flat.'

Kelly felt like she'd been slapped. Typical, she thought. The first words I hear her say in nearly five months and she's not even talking to me. Hello, Mam, she said silently. Remember me, Kelly, your daughter?

Mo had a bloke with her, as per normal, although he wasn't her usual type. She tended to go for men who had dark broody looks and short tempers to match, but this one was pale and pasty, with a moon face and soft mousy hair. So hopefully he wasn't her boyfriend, because there was nothing worse than watching your mam sloppy kissing her fella on the settee. God, it was gross. It didn't matter how many times she'd been there to see it, she couldn't get used to the sight – or sound – of it.

'What did I tell you, Paulie? She's like a piece of chewing gum stuck to the carpet,' Mo went on in her unmistakable rasp, the smoker's croak that Kelly would have recognised anywhere, even with her eyes closed.

Mo claimed it was a sexy drawl, a magnet for the blokes. 'Don't be daft,' Nana would say, creasing up. 'What kind of fool wants to go out with a frog?'

Kelly inspected her mam's face for signs of wear and tear. Mo could be quite pretty when she

23

didn't look like something the cat had dragged in – although she always had an unhealthy pallor. Even during the summer months her complexion was the colour of undercooked chips – and you could tell she wasn't one for eating vegetables, ever. Broccoli was for wimps, spinach was for tossers and if you offered her a simple glass of water she'd push it away and screech, 'Fuck off with that poison!'

Today she wasn't looking too bad. A bit tired and hollow-eyed, maybe – and her scraped-back hair ended in a choppy bleached ponytail that hadn't been near shampoo or water for a while – but it was safe to say that she hadn't been up for three days on some insane speed and cider bender. Still, anything could happen at any time, Kelly thought. She didn't doubt that today's bloke had a little something stashed in his wallet.

Mo started feeling around in her pockets for her packet of tabs. She smoked without restraint, like one of those small industrial cities in the former Soviet Union that Kelly had learned about in geography. 'How old are you now, our Kelly? Seventeen, eighteen?' she asked accusingly. 'Too young to hide away and shite, poring over your books. When I was your age, I was out on the town, having a laff, shagging myself silly.' She turned to the bloke and winked. 'I remember doing it in phone boxes when we couldn't find anywhere else. We all did it, didn't we, Paulie?'

Paulie squared his beefy shoulders. 'Phone boxes? Niver. Cramp my style.'

'Big man all over, eh?' Mo said, grinning.

Kelly winced. Seeing her mam flirt with a bloke

was almost as bad as seeing her snog one.

Mo lit a fag and jabbed a finger at her. 'Look at you, sitting there with a face like a slapped arse! Aren't you even going to say hello to your own mother?'

Kelly smiled, despite herself. 'Hello,' she mumbled.

Mo rummaged through a Tesco bag and pulled out a bottle of wine. 'Get some glasses. Let's have a jar to celebrate the return of the prodigal mam.'

Paulie sat down heavily on the brown velour settee, which creaked under his weight. 'Careful you don't break the fucking couch, man!' Mo hissed. 'I'll be sleeping there tonight.'

He smiled and sniggered. 'Room for two?' he asked.

'That'd be telling,' she shot back.

Kelly went into the kitchen, where she found two water tumblers at the back of a cupboard. She gave the cracked one to Paulie.

Mo's lip curled. 'What, no champagne glasses?' she said. 'And where's yours?'

'Not for me,' Kelly said.

'Whaa?'

'I'm studying.'

'Well, stop fucking studying.'

'Mam, I need to complete this module by to-morrow.'

Mo popped open the bottle. 'Go and get yourself a glass or I'll nut you.'

She obeyed, because you never knew with her mam. 'Is it real champagne?' she asked, holding out a pint jug that Mo had filched from the pub a couple of years back. She was being careful not

25

to use Nana's best glass goblets in case one of them got broken.

'As good as,' Mo said. 'Mouthful of bubbles. What's the difference?'

Kelly took a sip of the sweet frothy liquid and put her glass down.

Mo looked at her with narrowed eyes. 'You're a stuck-up little bitch, aren't you?'

Kelly said nothing. Had she already been drinking? It usually took more than half a glass to turn her nasty, but maybe champagne worked quicker.

Paulie took a small bag of powder out of his pocket and emptied it onto Nana's gleaming smoked glass coffee table. 'Blaster-bomber,' he said. 'Ultimate.'

'Come on!' shouted Mo, clenching her fists with excitement.

Using the edge of Mo's fag packet, Paulie tidied the powder into piles, rolled up a fiver, bent down and sniffed. Mo followed suit. 'Magic!' she said, offering the fiver to Kelly, who dumbly shook her head. Mo had been trying to force drugs on her for years, even though it was clear she wasn't interested. Her mam was like a great empty hole of darkness that she was constantly trying to pull people into.

She hasn't changed, Kelly thought, watching in silence as Mo dipped her head again and sniffed more powder off the table top. Why do I waste my time hoping?

She packed up her books and retreated into her bedroom.

That night Kelly had her old nightmare, her

'scream dream', she called it, because it always ended the same way – screaming her heart out until Nana came running. It wasn't your usual kind of nightmare filled with monsters and quicksand, the sort that left you gasping with relief when you woke up. Those she could have coped with, because she wasn't a nervous wreck or anything. You gritted your teeth and got through nightmares like that. No, the terrifying thing about this dream was the way it stuck to real life, forcing her to live through the hours and days she'd spent in Bobby's bedroom, locked up with a potty and a packet of biscuits.

It always began with a familiar feeling of dread. She and Mam would be climbing the stairs up to Bobby's room, and Mam would be giggling and saying, 'Do you want to see Bobby's bunnies, and all his lovely things?'

'Yes, Mam,' she'd say.

But at the top of the stairs, which seemed to go on forever, Bobby's room would be strewn with broken trains and mangled Action Men torsos – not a fluffy toy in sight.

'Where are the bunnies?' she'd ask, already fearful of what her mam might say in reply.

'Not bunnies, biscuits,' Mo would laugh, her eyes glinting with secret intent.

'No, Mam,' she'd whimper, as she felt Mo's hand slip out of hers and watched her dart out of the room. 'No!' she'd shout helplessly, as the bedroom door banged shut and she heard the key turn in the lock. She'd run to the door and hammer on it until she heard the front door of the flat click. Mam was gone.

27

Shuffling around to face the room, she'd notice a packet of fruit shortcakes on the floor and see Bobby in one corner, snot-nosed, smiling cruelly. And then she'd wake up drenched in sweat, screaming in terror until Nana ran in to comfort her.

Bobby and his dad were long gone, but they constantly returned in her dreams. Bobby's dad was called Si Crowther and he had once mistaken Mo for a prostitute in a pub on the Northumberland Road. Of course, Mo had turned round and given him so much jip *at the very fucking thought* that he'd finally bought her a drink to shut her up. They'd gone on to spend two nasty, drunken years together, fighting like bull terriers and boozing themselves rotten.

Si was a single parent, which was unusual for a man in those days. He claimed that Bobby's mam had upped and left the country with a Greek waiter, but Kelly had visions of him killing her and burying the body, because Si was the most frightening man she'd ever met. As tall as a doorway, with a sharp face and dark slit eyes, he had such a short temper that even the soft creak of a footstep on lino could send him flying into a rage. Kelly often imagined him towering over Bobby's mam and strangling the life out of her. More than once she'd seen him beat Mo black and blue, so murder was probably second nature to him.

Mo and Si used to shut the kids in Bobby's bedroom while they went down the pub. 'Council house babysitting,' Mo would cackle. 'Safe and fucking free.'

Mostly it was for hours, sometimes a whole day.

Twice – or maybe three times, she couldn't be sure – she had spent a whole weekend trapped in Bobby's spartan bedroom, cowering in fear behind his bed. She had tried to block out the memories – the whine of her voice as she pleaded with him not to hit her, the sharp kicks that dented her legs and left huge purple bruises, and the biscuits they shared in the miserable stretches between his bouts of viciousness. She still felt sick every time she saw a packet of fruit shortcakes.

Nana came running in. 'Bad dreams again?' she said. 'Don't fret, love, you're safe now.'

'Nana,' she sobbed. 'Sorry to wake you.' She inhaled a heaving gulp of air and her teeth began to chatter as the sweat cooled on her skin.

She had never told Nana what had happened at Si and Bobby's house. Mo had warned her not to, or Si would come after her, or she'd get him to adopt her and she'd have to share a bedroom with Bobby for ever. It was all drunken babble, but the idea of Bobby becoming her brother, with a licence to do what he wanted – and of Si being her dad – scared Kelly so much, even all these years later, that although she knew Si was in prison and Bobby had left Newcastle, just thinking about them set her teeth on edge.

I'll never tell, she thought, just in case.

Nana sat on the bed and put her chubby arms around her. Kelly sank into her cushiony softness. Nana was the person who made everything all right. You felt safe when you were near her. The world started to make sense again.

'Is Mam still here?' she asked.

Nana pursed her lips. 'She's gone out with the

fella – but says she's staying tonight, although there's not much more of the frigging night left now. I said, "Fine – you can stay on your own."' Nana went on. 'But I hope she doesn't come back – or if she does, that she'll be gone for good again soon. Even though she's my own daughter. I'm sorry, love, I know she's yer mam, but she's a wrecking ball, always has been.'

'It's OK,' Kelly said. She wanted to tell Nana that she felt the same, but she couldn't find the words. You were meant to love your mam, weren't you? Come what may? And she did. Only, it wasn't the kind of love she felt for Nana. It wasn't happy love, it was something more desperate, like having a lifelong crush on someone who didn't even like you, or longing for something you couldn't afford.

'Hush, now,' said Nana. 'Lie down again and I'll hold your hand until you fall back to sleep.'

'Reminds me of the storm night in Benidorm,' Kelly said with a sleepy smile, as her head sank into her pillow.

Nana chuckled. 'What a night that was! I thought the hotel was going to blow away. But we were still there in the morning, weren't we? Just like we'll still be here tomorrow, love. Nothing to worry about, Nana's here. We always get through.'

Kelly sighed softly and her breathing fell into a regular rhythm as she drifted off into a sunny dream about their one and only holiday abroad, in Benidorm, three years earlier.

Mo was flat out on the settee the following morning. Her mouth was open and she was gently snoring, loose strands of hair rising and falling over her face with every noisy breath. Her head was wedged in the crevice between cushion and settee back, her legs splayed and propped up over one arm. She hadn't bothered to remove the Lycra dress she'd been wearing and she still had her shoes on, a pair of red plasticky high heels.

Kelly popped her head into the lounge and scanned the floor for a sleeping Paulie, but he had obviously found somewhere else to crash, because he was nowhere to be seen. She wondered whether her mam had sent him away so as not to incur Nana's fury, or whether he had decided for himself that the chance of a shag wasn't worth the hassle. Kelly didn't care one way or another. She was just glad that there wouldn't be a scene about it.

As she washed up her cereal bowl in their tiny kitchen, she looked out of the window across a mass of grey houses and wondered where she would go when she finally left Byker. She had lived in Flat 74, Edison House for so long that it was hard to imagine what the world beyond held for her. But next year she would be leaving for good. First, to go to uni, and then, she hoped, abroad – somewhere carefree and sunny, where you could kick back in a clifftop bar at the end of the day and watch the sunset over the sea. Benidorm, maybe – although the travel rep who'd befriended her on their holiday had said that the Costa del Sol was a hectic place to start a career in tourism, and she should try other parts of Spain first, or one of the islands, like Menorca or Ibiza. Just the sound of their names set her off daydreaming.

Nirvana started up next door, vibrating through

31

the damp shared wall. Kelly heard Nana thumping her fists to get them to turn it down. She rinsed off the dishes. As usual, the foamy water wouldn't drain – the sink was bloody blocked again.

'Morning, love.' Nana came into the kitchen wearing her peach velour dressing gown and matching fluffy slippers, her hair done up in curlers. Somehow she always managed to look glamorous, Kelly thought, even first thing in the morning, even with her curlers in. It was a knack, almost a talent. If they had a version of Crufts for humans, Nana would win the 'best groomed' prize by miles – with a special commendation for her nails, which were amazing, every bit as pointed and polished as Joan Collins's.

'I've been through yer mam's pockets and found her front door keys,' Nana announced. 'I'm taking them back. I don't want her coming and going as she pleases any more, especially not while you've got exams to do.'

A tiny shock of fear went through Kelly. 'She'll go mad when she finds out,' she whispered.

'Not if she thinks she lost them last night while she was out on the razz. So don't say a word, love.'

Kelly saw a shadow cross the doorway behind Nana. 'Like a couple of old crones, you are. What are you plotting?' Mo asked.

'You up already?' Nana turned to face her. 'How's your head?' she added loudly.

Mo recoiled. 'Not too funny, Mam. I've hardly slept a wink. That settee's killed my back all night.'

'Oh, the settee, is it?' Nana said. 'Nothing to do

with those bottles of wine you were drinking, or the company you were keeping till the early hours?'

Nana was the one person in the world who could snipe at Mo without getting shouted at, or worse. But Mo couldn't help answering back. 'I said I've got backache, Mam, not AIDS or fucking liver cancer,' she said.

'And no headache at all?' Nana asked, raising her voice again.

Mo winced and narrowed her eyes. 'Backache,' she insisted. 'Anyway, I'll slip into our Kelly's bed now, have myself some cushty while you're out,' she added, as if it was her territorial right to take over her daughter's bedroom.

'You've forgotten that I don't work on Fridays,' Nana said. 'So I'll be here doing bits and bobs until our Alan comes to take me for lunch.'

Mo's lip curled. 'Big Al's coming over? The golden boy, the apple of everyone's eye? Doesn't my little brother work on Fridays, either? Lazy bugger!'

Nana smiled. 'He's his own boss now. He can work the hours he likes – and believe me, he doesn't shirk.'

Mo made a face. 'I could have had a great job too, if I hadn't been saddled with a bairn,' she said defensively.

'Yeah, you would have probably been a brain surgeon by now,' Nana said, nodding her head sarcastically. 'Only you gave it all up to be a mam.'

There followed a short silence, and Kelly wondered which of them was filling it with the darkest thoughts. The truth was that Mo had given up almost nothing to have her baby, at least when you compared her to other mothers. Kelly couldn't remember her infant years and a lot of the rest was patchy, but she knew what she knew, no matter what Mo sometimes claimed – her nana had brought her up.

Nana used to tell it like a fairy tale. 'Yer mam had you too young,' she'd say with a wistful sigh. 'She was a tot with a baby. You were just two bairns in the wood, lost and alone.'

Nana had saved them, the innocent children. But then Mo had gone astray, like the boy with the ice splinter in his eye in the Hans Christian Andersen story. That was the way Nana had originally told it to Kelly, anyway. In later years, when she thought Kelly was out of earshot, she'd tell people that Mo had 'always been a bad'un, from the day she was born'.

Kelly grew up worrying that an evil snow queen or fairy had put a spell on her mam. Which was probably better, she decided on reflection, than knowing that yer mam didn't want or love you. When she grew older and got into Catherine Cookson novels, she started hoping that the moment would arrive – perhaps when she 'came of age' – when Nana would sit her down and reveal that Mo was actually her sister, not her mother – and that Nana was mam to them both. But her sixteenth birthday had come and gone with no such announcement – and she wasn't sure it would matter by the time she was eighteen. After all, everybody apart from Mo agreed that Nana was her real mam, even though it wasn't a biological fact.

It helped that Nana had been at the hospital for her birth, and that she tenderly described their meeting just like a mother would.

'I fell in love with you on the spot,' she'd say with a nostalgic smile. 'You were the sweetest baby, so tiny and helpless that my heart swelled up every time I looked at you. There was something so familiar about your little face, something I don't think I'd even seen in my own kids. Was it traces of my mam? My own nana? I don't know, love, perhaps it was a mixture – but I do know that on the day that you were born, I swore to love and protect you for ever.'

'Like a fairy godmother?' Kelly would say.

That made Nana laugh. 'Yer fairy nana, love – that's me.'

From the other snippets she overheard, Kelly guessed that Mo had flitted in and out while Nana had been busy loving and protecting her. There had been a few times when Mo had come over all maternal and tried to make a go of setting up home with young Kelly, but then her man or her restlessness had got in the way, or the landlord had chucked her out, or she'd got drunk and stopped giving a fuck – it was never more than a few days – and then Kelly had gone back to Nana. She had never stopped hoping that Mo might suddenly turn into more of a mam – well, until now, perhaps – but had always secretly much preferred living with Nana.

'Well, I'll be asleep most of today, so say hello to our Alan from me.' Mo yawned and walked unsteadily towards Kelly's bedroom.

'Wait, Mam,' Kelly called after her, 'I just need

to get some books out of there first.'

'Don't mind me, you little swotbag,' Mo replied. 'I'll be dead to the world before you can say Mack the bleedin' Knife.'

2

Kelly dumped her shopping bags in the hall and rubbed her hands to bring the blood back to her palms. The lift was broken again, so she'd had to lug the weekly shop up seven flights of stinking stairs. Still, she was here now, with enough food to last her and Nana until next week, and a few quid left over, for once. The discount shelves at the supermarket had been fuller than usual and she'd happily stocked up on dented tins and battered packets of food.

Growing up with Nana had taught her that you had to stay on the ball when money was tight. You could never let up. You had to keep a constant count. Only then would the pounds miraculously stretch. Nana had an all-or-nothing approach to budgeting. She said you had to make it your way of life, otherwise you would end up in debt – and debt meant trouble. 'Just look at yer mam,' she said. She didn't have to say anything else. Mo had 'borrowed' fifty quid and disappeared about six weeks earlier.

In the usual run of things, Kelly handed the lion's share of her earnings from her Saturday job and waitressing shifts straight to Nana, who worked out their weekly budget in a little red book every Sunday evening. Nana liked everything to be organised. After she had put aside enough for bills, meals and fares, she would usually tuck around seventy pounds spending money in a chipped mug and hide it in the cupboard under the sink, behind the bleach. She had another roll of notes stashed somewhere in her wardrobe that she called 'our clothes account'.

Nana was more than generous with what she earned as a senior sales assistant in the daywear department at C&A – but it didn't amount to much after all the bills were paid. Over the years Kelly had become expert at calculating the supermarket shop right down to the last few pennies. Treats were few and far between and Nike Air Max were out of the question. But it was fine, it was all she had ever known. She wasn't one to sit and sigh over magazines showing off the lifestyles of the rich and famous, like her mam. Anyway, she preferred spending money on books.

She was just about to heave the shopping through the front door when she heard footsteps behind her.

'Greetings, our Kelly,' said a voice. She turned round and saw Uncle Al's bulky figure silhouetted in the stairwell. 'Let me take those bags inside for you,' he said.

As he picked them up, he started humming 'The Something I Want' by Sanctum, a local band that had shot to fame the year before.

'You're in a good mood,' she said, although it wasn't really something to remark on, since Uncle Al was nearly always of a positive frame of mind.

Nana liked to joke that if a ton of bricks landed on his head, he'd dust himself off and start building a house. 'He's very positive-minded,' she'd say proudly.

Uncle Al helped her unpack the shopping and stack it in the kitchen cupboards. When they had finished, he made her laugh by putting a bun in front of his face and singing 'the muffin I want' to the tune of the Sanctum song. For a moment, she had a vision of Uncle Al as a teenager, bright-eyed and fresh-faced, with hair. Then he stopped singing and reverted to her balding uncle again – kind of ageless and out of touch, but completely lovely.

'I didn't know you even liked Sanctum,' she said.

He laughed. 'I can't stand them, love! Especially that song – it's bloody everywhere.'

She smiled. ''Cos it's a great song,' she chastised gently.

'Oh yes, I forgot you were a fan,' he said. 'I suppose you'd like to go and see them in concert next week and all.'

Her smile turned rueful. 'No chance – it's been sold out for months and Nana said people are selling their tickets in the back of the paper for two hundred quid or more.'

He raised his eyebrows. 'So what would you say to a pair of tickets? A Christmas present from your Uncle Al?'

She looked up at his grinning face in surprise. 'Is this a wind-up?'

'No, lass,' he said, obviously relishing the moment. 'One of my clients gave them to me, because his daughter can't go.'

It still didn't quite sink in. 'You're bloody joking, aren't you?' she said. 'Why don't you sell them?'

He cocked his head, as if considering it. 'Now you mention it, I could, couldn't I?' He frowned comically. 'No, you daft thing! You think I'd prefer a few measly notes to the sight of your lovely face lit up with excitement? Although I can't think why anybody would get sparked up about that mardy lot. Proper bunch of wazzocks. What's the lead singer called?' He clicked his fingers as he tried to recall his name. 'The one with the massive jaw and the pudding bowl hair. Long Chin Silver, I call him – the Jimmy Hill of pop.'

Kelly rolled her eyes. 'Shane Moloney,' she said.

She was just about to ask him if he was really serious about the tickets when Nana walked into the kitchen, out of breath. 'Listen to you, our Alan. Anyone would think you'd been born in slippers, smoking a pipe!' She pointed a red-tipped finger at him. 'But I remember the pop posters on your bedroom wall. David Bowie in a pair of ladies' tights – and the rest!'

Kelly barely heard her. 'Do you mean, *really, really*, Uncle Al?' she asked. 'You're really giving me tickets to see Sanctum?'

'Yes, love,' he said, taking an envelope out of his inside jacket pocket and passing it to her.

She nearly screamed as she flipped it open. 'Thank you,' she said, bubbling up with happiness. 'This is the best present ever!'

'But there's one condition,' he said. 'You have to take me or your Nana with you.'

Her heart dipped, and she instantly felt bad

about it. 'OK,' she said brightly.

'I'm joking, love!' he guffawed. 'What do you take us for? Complete fucking killjoys?'

That made her laugh again. She loved Uncle Al's sense of humour. He always liked to twist things round to surprise her.

'You can take whoever you want,' he added.

Jamila, she thought, no contest. Jami was her best friend by miles, even though they'd only been friends just over a year. They'd met in the sixth form common room on the first day of the school year and instantly clicked, 'like a hip bone connected to a leg bone', Nana said.

Kelly could remember it like it was yesterday. A teacher had come into the room, clapped her hands and instructed the sixth formers to ask each other what they wanted to get out of their A Level years. Jami had turned to Kelly with one eyebrow raised, her haughty expression making her burst out laughing.

'A tin of biscuits, I think,' Jami said.

'A Madonna video for me,' Kelly shot back.

It was all they needed to say. They had been inseparable ever since.

Now Kelly rushed to phone her, but Jami wasn't at home. According to her grunting, moronic younger brother, she was going to a self-defence class after college and wouldn't be back until seven.

I can't wait that long, she thought, wishing she lived in a world where everybody had mobile phones.

As the afternoon ticked on, the waiting to tell almost killed the pleasure of knowing they were going. She was meant to be reading a book about the rise of leisure in the twentieth century, but she kept fixating on the idea of flying a helicopter over Newcastle, trailing a banner saying, 'Jami, we're going to the Sanctum concert!' Eventually, she ran into the kitchen and checked the cash cup, but there was only a tenner left in it. It was enough for a taxi to the sports centre later, where she could ambush Jamila with the news of the century, but of course she couldn't piss the last of the week's money away like that.

Eventually she got through to her, screamed it out and was out-screamed in reply. 'Are you sure it's next Saturday?' Jami kept saying. 'That's eight days, or seven – what the fuck are we going to wear?'

Kelly had already turned her wardrobe upside down. 'Jeans and a halter top, I s'pose. That's all I've got. Or the red Lycra dress me mam left behind the last time she did a runner, yeah, right. Do you think we'll be able to push to the front?'

'My bro says they don't let you do that any more. You've got to stay in your seat.'

'I bloody hope we're not too near the back, then.'

'Hey, we could dress up and blag our way to the front. I'll wear yer mam's red Lycra if you wear my little black dress.'

'Whaa! You'll look like me mam – and so will I.'

'It might get us past the bouncers, though.'

'No, I don't think so...'

'Come on, I dare you. Just this once.'

Kelly giggled. 'OK, just this once, then. You're on.'

They were seated six rows from the front of the stage. 'Wait till I tell that bastard brother of mine,' Jami kept saying. 'He'll be so jealous.' She reached into her bra and pulled out two miniature bottles of Jack Daniels. 'That door lady didn't squeeze my tits hard enough when she frisked me!' she said with a laugh.

Kelly screeched and gave her a hug. She wanted to bounce up and down in excitement, but could barely walk in the spiky heels Jami had insisted on lending her, let alone jump. Still, it didn't matter. Nothing mattered except soaking in the atmosphere of her first arena gig. There was so much anticipation in the air that she was just happy to be there, watching the crowd coming and going. She felt a part of something big and special – and she felt lucky, too, which was a totally new and brilliant feeling.

It was weird to think that practically the whole of Newcastle would have swapped places with her at that moment. There were people outside the venue literally begging for tickets. She and Jami had seen a lad brandishing a dummy dressed up like an old lady, with round glasses, a flowery frock and a grey wool wig. 'I'd sell my granny for a ticket to this gig,' he was telling anyone who would listen. He produced a plastic bottle and poured a stream of water onto the ground. 'For a front row ticket, I'll sell her down the river.'

He was caught on camera by a roving crew from the local news programme. Nana would have a few belly laughs if she saw it, Kelly thought.

Their seats were next to a boxed-off area where

two men were fiddling with illuminated panels, their faces lit up in the reflected glow of different coloured lights. 'What do you think they're doing?' she said.

Jami peeped over the wall of the box. 'Let's ask them.'

'Sound engineers,' one of the men said. He put his hand up. 'Sorry, can't talk now. The first act is about to come on.'

The support act was a group of soul singers. One of them looked a bit like Whitney Houston. She kept reaching for higher and higher notes, and when she finally made it to what sounded like the highest, purest note in the entire universe, Kelly found herself welling up. It surprised her that most of the crowd weren't even looking her way. Couldn't they hear the genius in her voice? But the people around her seemed distracted. They were still arriving, milling in and out of the auditorium, looking for their seats and shouting at their friends. There were groups further back cheering and whistling, but up front it was just Kelly and Jamila, whooping for all they were worth.

Towards the end of the set, one of the blokes in the sound box caught Kelly's eye and leaned over to speak to her.

'Fantastic, aren't they?' he said.

Kelly nodded shyly and grinned. 'They're too good to be a support act,' Jami chipped in.

'It won't be for long,' he replied. 'They're about to break America.'

The act ended. The stage emptied. The crowd quietened and Kelly and Jami started to feel restless. 'We could go and get another drink, but we might miss them coming on,' Jami said. They decided to wait.

Ten minutes later, the atmosphere changed and the audience began to stir, although Kelly couldn't see any reason for it. Nothing had happened on the stage – no announcements had been made – but there was a rustle in the air, a feeling of anticipation. Then people began to whistle and stamp. The lights went down and a spotlight roamed the heads of the crowd, revealing a sea of Shane Moloney mop tops.

'Do you think they all go to the same bleedin' hairdresser?' Jami giggled.

Kelly laughed and scanned the audience for Michael Kirkpatrick from her geography class, who was such a massive Sanctum fan that he had queued up overnight to buy his ticket, months earlier. She liked Michael. It would be nice to bump into him, she thought. Maybe they could all go for a drink together after the gig.

Rainbow colours flashed and flared as the band walked on stage. The crowd went mad and a tidal wave of human noise rolled from the back of the auditorium to the front, sweeping Kelly and Jami up with it. They stood up and started cheering themselves hoarse.

Shane Moloney swaggered onstage, arm in arm with his bezzie band mate, Conor Strachan. It was amazing to see them in person, Kelly thought – in the flesh, right in front of her. It was totally different to watching them on *Top of the Pops*.

Halfway to the microphone, Shane hooked Conor in a headlock and pulled him to the ground with laddish ferocity. A hush swept through the auditorium. Were they going to start fighting? Shane and Conor were famous for their show-stopping bust-ups. If they got into a scrap, the gig could easily be cancelled – it had happened in the past, more than once.

Please, no, Kelly silently pleaded. You could almost feel the audience praying for peace.

The band started playing and the mood changed again. Conor leapt to his feet and picked up his bass guitar. Shane grabbed the mic and starting singing dead on cue. Kelly wondered if the head-lock had been part of their act. They still looked like lads, but their performance was polished, and they blasted out hit after hit after hit from their first two albums with practised ease. The crowd began to sing along, swaying with emotion, and Kelly decided that Shane was actually quite gorgeous, although she'd never thought so before.

'There's a shedload of happiness in the air to-night!' he yelled out. 'We're happy to be home for Christmas, because you lot,' he added, 'every single one of you,' he shouted louder, 'you're all part of the inner sanctum!'

The audience roared back at him.

This must be what it feels like to be at a cup final supporting the winning side, Kelly thought blissfully.

All too soon, the main set was over. But the lights stayed down and the audience screamed for an encore, so she guessed the band were going to come on again – if they weren't secretly glassing each other backstage. She looked over at the sound box and saw the same man who had talked to them before. He called her over. 'Want

45

to come to the after show party?' he asked.

She shook her head and smiled, unsure if she'd heard him correctly.

He laughed. 'No? You don't want to come?'

She turned to Jami. 'What's he saying?'

Jami had a quick chat with him and grabbed Kelly by the hand. 'We're going. Now,' she said, dragging her away.

They pushed through the crowd to the side of the arena and a doorway with a gate in front of it, which was guarded by a couple of grim-looking bouncers. 'Geoff in the sound box says to meet him in the green room,' Jami said. The bouncers relaxed, smiled and pulled back the gate – and they were in. Jami squeezed Kelly's hand.

As they were escorted down a strip-lit white corridor, Kelly heard the crowd come alive again as the band reappeared onstage and started into the first bars of 'The Something I Want'.

'That's my favourite song,' she wailed at Jami, tugging at her to go back.

'Don't you get it, Kelly?' Jami said out of the corner of her mouth. 'Forget the last bit of the show. This is mega. This is the Sanctum after party – at their Christmas gig, in their bloody home town. We're going to meet Shane and Conor. Come on!'

The green room wasn't green – it was a wishy-washy grey – and it was empty, apart from a drinks fridge and a table stacked with bottles and glasses. Jami laughed nervously. 'Looks like we're early.'

The bouncer was gone before they could ask him if they could help themselves to a drink, so

46

they waited politely by the table to see if anybody else would appear. Ten echoey minutes later, during which a low rumble above their heads made them painfully aware of what they were missing on stage, two girls bounded in and grabbed a couple of beers from the fridge. Their black jeans, strappy tops and brand new trainers made Kelly wince with self-consciousness. She felt over-dressed. Or underdressed. Not enough dress, anyway. And too much heel.

'Is it OK to have a drink now?' Jami called over to them.

They turned and looked her up and down. 'Yeah! Why fucking not?'

'Magic,' Jami said, pouring out two glasses of white wine.

Kelly swigged her drink and cursed herself for agreeing to wear Jami's black mini dress and shoes. She felt silly and tarty, like the girls who hung around the plush bars in town hoping to hook up with footballers. The room began to fill up with people they didn't know, or recognise. She and Jami tried to keep a conversation going amid the rising noise levels, but it was hard to talk about nothing much with your best friend, especially when you had one eye on the door, checking for famous faces.

Geoff from the sound box walked past and Jami caught hold of his arm.

'Thanks for sorting us out,' she gushed. 'This is great. We've never been to an after party before.'

'Hello, girls,' he said with a grin. 'Glad you're having fun. I thought it was brilliant the way you cheered on the warm-up act.'

'Will Shane and Conor and the rest of them be coming in here?' Kelly asked.

He shrugged. 'I expect so, but you can never tell what that lot are going to do. Bunch of madmen, they are.'

'I hope they do,' Jami said. 'I've never met a pop star before,'

Kelly laughed. The wine was going to her head. 'Or even been in the same room as one,' she added.

Geoff stepped closer to them and tapped his nose. 'There's a rumour flying around backstage that there's going to be another party after this. Try and string along with someone. You'll have more chance of meeting them there.'

'Who's stringing along with you?' Jami asked, giving him a cocky smile.

Just then, a man in jeans and a black bomber jacket came to join them. His straggly, dark hair was slick with gel and he was chewing gum as if his life depended on it. 'All right?' he said in a London accent, his jaw springing up and down as he gave them the once-over. He punched Geoff's arm. 'Don't waste your time on this one,' he told them. 'Cinderella here always leaves in time to get the train home to wifey. The eleven-o-three from Newcy Central, isn't it, mate?'

'Correct,' Geoff said, and Kelly felt sorry for him. She imagined the crosspatch face of his wife at breakfast as she nagged him to be home on time, and his heart sinking at the thought of the fun he would miss. Poor bloke.

But he seemed unconcerned – happy, even – to be leaving, and smiled as his friend motioned towards the door with his thumb and said, 'Hop it, mate.'

After Geoff had left, they got stuck with the friend, who introduced himself as Micky and said he did 'a little bit of everything'. Chewing his gum, at high speed and turning his head every three seconds to see what was going on further afield, he talked about 'ducking and diving, a little bit of this and that', until Kelly had to start blinking extra hard to keep herself focused. She leaned against Jami – their getaway signal – just as a commotion on the other side of the room gave them an excuse to walk away.

'I bet that's them,' Jami said, pushing through the mass of people.

Shane, Conor and a few others had arrived and were surrounded by a throng of people. They were having their photos taken in various goofy poses and yelling, 'Howay, man!' and, 'Wey aye!'

At one point they squared up, fists out and ready to fight, triggering a frenzy of laughter and camera flashes. Kelly watched, mesmerised, until Shane looked her way and she felt stupid for gawping. But maybe it's OK to stare, she thought. Maybe he's still performing. Perhaps he likes a constant audience. All the same, she longed to tell him that she wasn't what she seemed on the outside. She wasn't an empty-headed slag looking for a celebrity shag – or any kind of shag. She was just curious.

Shane shook up a huge champagne bottle and spurted Conor with foam, then Conor chased him out of the room and they were gone. Kelly turned to Jami and was about to suggest one last drink when she noticed that Micky had come to stand directly behind them, still chewing furiously. She caught Jami's eye and grimaced. 'Pritt Stick's back,' she whispered.

He didn't notice. 'They're just kids, those two,' he said with a laugh. 'But they've got good hearts. They look after their own.'

'Have you met them, then?' Jami asked, suddenly interested.

He gave a nonchalant shrug and looked away into the distance. 'I drive them from time to time. In private, like.'

A couple of his mates came over and asked him about tickets to a match. One of them had a piercing green-eyed gaze that reminded Kelly of Ray Liotta; the other was blond and bland-looking, like a snooker player or something. After Micky had assured them he'd hook them up, they turned their attention to Kelly and Jami. 'All right, princesses?' said the one with gangster eyes. 'How's your night going?'

'Yeah, good,' Jami said. 'You?'

He grinned and danced around on his feet. 'The evening starts here,' he said, rubbing his hands together. He unclipped a beeper from his belt and glanced at it. 'Sanctum after party, yeah,' he said, giving Kelly a wink as he spoke. He reached out and pressed her chin between his finger and thumb. 'Just how I like them,' he added. 'Almost jailbait, but not quite. What are you doing later, princess?'

She frowned and stepped backwards, as if to remove herself from his magnetic force field. 'What are you on about?'

He smiled and raised his hands as if to say, 'Not guilty!' Then his mate dragged him away, muttering about 'business'.

Jami turned her attention back to Micky. 'Will you be driving the band on to the next party?' she asked.

He looked down at her with a sneering smile. 'Know all about it, do you?'

She shot a look at Kelly. 'Yeah, but we haven't got any transport.'

'And?'

'Can we get a lift with you?'

He stared at her. 'Eager little minx, aren't you?' he said. 'Wait here a sec. Let me see what's occurring.' He buzzed off.

They went back to the drinks table for a last glass of wine, but all the bottles had been cleared away. 'Grab a beer from the fridge, Kel,' Jami said.

'Wey aye, man,' Kelly joked. What with the booze and the high heels, she was feeling a little wobbly on her feet by the time Micky returned.

'I'm on duty until midnight,' he said. 'But those geezers you just met can give you a lift to the party. They've got room for one in each car. You'll have to get a move on, though. Quick, they're leaving now.'

'The guys asking you for tickets to the match?' Kelly said hesitantly.

'Where are they?' Jami asked.

'Out the fire escape at the bottom of the stairs,' he said.

Kelly grabbed her arm as they click-clacked down the staircase. 'I don't want to get split up. I want to go in the same car as you.'

'Don't worry,' said Jami. 'I'll sit on your lap if there isn't room.'

They emerged from the exit into darkness. There was no one around. 'We've missed them,' Kelly said, feeling a mixture of relief and disappointment.

They were discussing whether to go back upstairs to find Micky when they heard a whistle. 'Princesses!' a voice called out.

'Where are you?' Jami called back.

A figure emerged from the shadows, the green-eyed guy. In one smooth motion he put his arm around Kelly and propelled her into the darkness. 'Jami!' she called out.

'Right behind you,' Jami said, giggling.

'Where are we going?' Kelly asked, aware that she was slurring her words slightly.

'To the after party, of course.'

'My mate and I want to go in the same car.'

'No problem,' he said.

By the time they reached the car park, her left shoe was rubbing at her heel and she was certain a blister was forming. So when he opened the door of a metallic blue car, she gratefully sat down sideways, with her bare legs dangling to the ground.

'Get in, then,' he said. The electronic buzz of his pager started up again.

'Wait, I've just got to check my heel,' she told him. Her head swam as she bent down and she willed herself not to be sick.

'Get in, we're going,' he said firmly. 'This is the inner, inner sanctum. They've just paged the address of the party.'

She sat up. 'Who has? The band?'

'Yes, Shane fucking Moloney. Get in and shut the door.'

She peered inside the car. His mate was in the passenger seat and there was another lad in the middle at the back. 'Where's Jami going to sit?'

'She's getting in the other side,' he said. 'Shut the fucking door, or I'll push you out and leave you here.'

She pulled the door shut and sat back in her seat, feeling dizzy. The other door slammed and the car sped off. 'Jami,' she said, 'I've got a right blister.'

Jami didn't reply. Kelly looked past the lad sitting next to her and saw a boy of about her age next to him. Her heart jolted. 'Where's my mate?' she said, a feeling of panic rising inside her.

The green-eyed guy laughed. 'She changed her mind and got into the other car.'

'Turn back, I want to go with her,' she cried.

'Chill out, princess,' he barked. 'We'll see her at the party. You want to go to the party, don't you? You want to meet Shane and Conor?'

She sobered up in an instant. Why hadn't she checked Jami was in the car before she'd shut the door? She tried to breathe calmly, but her lungs could only manage short gasps. 'Not without my mate,' she said. 'Where's the other car? Pull over and wait for her, or I'm getting out.'

The guy in the passenger seat swivelled his head to look at her. 'Chill the fuck out,' he said softly. 'We're five minutes from the party. You'll see her there.'

No one else said anything and for the next few

minutes all Kelly could hear was the thudding of her heartbeat. The car sped past the hospital, took a few sharp turns and finally drew up in a residential street.

'Why are we stopping here?' she asked, looking out of the window at a scruffy red brick house. 'This can't be it.'

3

Kelly never told Jami what had happened that night. She was too embarrassed to admit that she could hardly remember anything. It was as if her brain had been hit by a winter storm and, in its wake, a thick layer of drizzle and cloud had dimmed and blurred her memory. An occasional flash of lightning lit up random moments, but the scenes they revealed were weird and disturbing. Why couldn't she remember more? Had she had what her mam called a 'blackout'?

Everything was clear up until a certain point. She distinctly recalled waiting for Jami outside the house. 'I'll come in when my mate gets here,' she'd insisted, standing by the front wall.

The green-eyed guy had tried to change her mind. 'It's icy out here, princess, you'll freeze to death!'

She gave him a stony look. 'Where's the other car? Shouldn't it be here by now?'

He shrugged. 'Probably stopped to pick up some booze.' He put his hands in his pockets and strode into the house. 'I'll leave the door on the latch,' he called from the entrance. 'Come inside if you see a limo draw up. It's going to be a lock-in after Shane and Conor get here.'

'They're coming?' she said in disbelief. 'Here?'

He looked at his watch. 'In fifteen minutes,' he said.

She shivered with cold as she waited for Jami to arrive. She couldn't understand how they had been separated at the last minute, silently, without a word of warning. Had Jami wandered off in the dark, or got into the wrong car by mistake? It seemed strange that she hadn't heard a footstep, or a giggle.

She looked up and down the empty street, willing Jami's car to appear before the band's limo drew up. Everything would be all right then. They could link arms and go inside the house together, bubbling with excitement. Being with her best mate gave her confidence – Jami could hold her own with lads, perhaps because she had brothers, whereas Kelly's inexperience made her feel vulnerable. The mini dress didn't help either. She couldn't help feeling that it sent out the wrong message.

The cold night air sapped her body of heat and she pulled her jacket tight around her. Why had the guys wanted to split them up into different cars? Did it make them feel manly to each have a girl in their midst? Or was it more about territory – one group of lads in one car and another group in another car, none of them wanting to change places and travel with a different driver? Men were funny like that. They rode in packs and were loyal to one leader, like dogs, or wolves. They had a pecking order and they stuck to it.

'Come inside, won't you?' One of the lads from the car was standing on the garden side of the wall, his eyes shining darkly in the reflection of a nearby street lamp.

'Not until my mate gets here,' she said.

'She's on her way,' he said. 'The driver just paged Neville. They stopped to pick up a case of beers.'

She didn't ask if Neville was the name of the guy with the green eyes. 'Is she definitely with them?'

A look of impatience crossed the lad's face. 'Yeah, why not?' he said. 'They wouldn't have left her behind. Look, why don't you come in? I'm freezing my bollocks off here.'

Kelly glanced at the house. A warm glow emanated through a sunset arch of coloured glass at the top of the front door. 'Go in, I'm not stopping you.'

'But I feel bad for you out here,' he said.

He sounded genuinely concerned, so she turned to inspect him properly. He was tall and rangy, with a soft round face and full lips. 'Thanks,' she said.

He raised his arm and offered her something. A small glass bottle glinted in the street light. 'Have a lug of this. It's whisky – it's meant to warm you up.'

She shook her head.

'Go on, you look frozen,' he insisted.

She took the bottle and twisted the cap. 'Proper St Bernard, you are,' she said with a shy smile, unsure if he would get the joke.

The whisky burnt her throat. She coughed and put one hand up to her neck.

He laughed. 'It's harsh at first, but it's like central heating after a few minutes.'

She waited for it to take effect.

'Maybe you need another nip,' he suggested.

'No, I think it's working.' She suddenly felt warmer.

The next thing she knew, he was standing in front of her, which was weird, because she hadn't seen him jump over the wall, and he couldn't have got to her so quickly by walking around and through the gate. 'Come inside,' he said, taking her arm. 'Your mate's about to arrive.'

She was going to say something, but then she found herself being led into the house, which must have meant everything was OK, or she wouldn't have been going, would she? Next she was in the front hall, holding on to her jacket. After that, she was upstairs, sitting on a sofa. It was blue and covered in a woven fabric.

Now the rain started to fall across her memory and she could only recall what came next in a murky half-light, apart from a few bright, disconnected images. Had she passed out? It would explain why her impressions were so patchy. All that was left were snapshots, with no sensory backup to make them feel real. It was like watching a slideshow of fuzzy paparazzi shots from somebody else's life. Except that she was the person in the pictures.

In one scene, she was glugging something from a bottle, in another smoking a reefer – two things she didn't normally do. Granted, she liked a pint of cider at the pub of a weekend – if she could manage to get served without showing ID – but she didn't smoke and wasn't one for getting wrecked like her mam. She wasn't a party animal. The final shot showed her naked on her back, with a bare-chested lad pumping away on top of her. She couldn't see him properly – he was silhouetted – but she could instantly tell he wasn't her type. Was there an older guy off to the side? With green eyes? She wasn't sure.

Could it really have happened? Her brain crunched and grated like stone against metal when she thought about it. She remembered nothing more of the evening.

She'd woken up in a strange bed, feeling cold, with a dull ache inside her head and a soreness at the top of her thighs. Thin winter light streamed onto the floor, through the crack in a pair of heavy green curtains, telling her it was morning. Her eyes were drawn to a solid wooden chair in the corner of the bedroom, which had Jami's dress draped over one arm and her jacket flopped over the chair back. She shut her eyes and opened them again, hoping she was dreaming. But the chair was still in the corner. Her thighs still felt sore.

Kelly got out of bed and put on the dress and her jacket. She felt sick. Her head was throbbing and she could barely swallow, her throat was so dry. She found her left shoe under the bed. Her right shoe was on a shelf, standing upright, like a trophy. She snatched it down and put it on her foot. One of the straps rubbed against a blister. She remembered the blister from the night before.

Where was Jami? Her heart began to pound.

She scoured the room for her underwear and found her bra between the bed covers. She tucked it down the front of her dress and slipped through the door, conscious that she wasn't wearing knickers. As she passed the doorway to another bedroom on the wide, carpeted landing, she peeked inside and saw two lads asleep on the floor, surrounded by empty bottles and overflowing ashtrays. She didn't recognise either of them.

It felt as if there were lead weights sliding around her head as she crept down the stairs, pleading with heaven that she wouldn't meet anybody on the way. She tiptoed towards the front door and quietly unbolted the lock, then stepped out into the bitterly cold morning air, leaving the door open, its arched sunset of coloured glass swinging in the icy breeze.

Her shoes rubbed and slipped as she headed along the street in the direction of the roar of traffic. She asked an old man walking a dog the way to the nearest taxi rank and followed his bony, pointed finger to a sign halfway along a parade of shops. A car with sloping plastic seats took her to Edison House. The driver insisted on coming up in the lift and waiting outside the door while she dug around under the kitchen sink for cash. Fortunately, Nana was having her Sunday lie-in. She paid the driver and stumbled to her bedroom, where she pulled off her clothes, put on clean pyjamas and fell into bed.

After half an hour of shivering and staring at the ceiling, she decided to run a bath. Ten minutes later, immersed in hot water and Radox bubbles, her bones no longer felt cold.

Her eyelids started drooping. She got out of the bath and wrapped herself in one of Nana's fluffy peach towels, then went back to bed and slept for most of the day, just like her mam would have done.

On the phone to Jami that evening, Kelly pretended that she'd taken a taxi home around two. 'You sounded proper out of it when I spoke to you,' Jami said. 'It was weird. You weren't yourself. I wanted to come and get you, but I couldn't get the address out of you. Anyway, you said you were having a laugh. Or, I think that's what you said. It was a fuzzy connection.'

She had no recollection of speaking to Jami the night before. 'Where did you go?' she asked, trying not to sound reproachful.

'I told you! We were at Francos in town, waiting for the band.'

'Did they come?'

'Shane did, but we didn't see him. He went into the VIP room and didn't come out.'

'Oh.'

'I know. Fucking typical.'

'But I just don't understand how we got split up. One minute you were there and the next you'd gone. It was like you'd vanished into the dark. I was really anxious about you.'

'And I thought *you'd* been kidnapped!' Jami exclaimed. 'Your car drove off before I could get in. But the other lads told me not to panic, because we'd be following you. So I bundled into their car and we ended up in town.'

60

'Weren't you worried?'

''Course. I kept asking them where you were and in the end I threatened going to the police if they didn't tell me. That's when they paged their mate and he rang back and put you on the phone.'

'I mean, weren't you worried for yourself?'

'No, I was too busy panicking about you. But I chilled out after I spoke to you. "Where the fuck are you?" I said and you said, "A rave in Fenham." You were slurring your words and giggling, but at least I'd spoken to you.

'Then one of the lads started sliding his dirty hands all over yer mam's red dress. Yer mam would probably have found it funny, but it did my head in and I decided to shake off that whole bunch of manky bastards. As I was leaving, I saw Michael from your geography class. He bought me a drink and then I caught the bus home. Oh yeah, Kel, he said he likes you.'

'Michael Kirkpatrick did?' she replied blankly.

'You OK? I thought you'd be well chuffed. Did you meet someone at the rave? Was it a laugh?'

She shut her eyes. 'No, it was dead boring. So I left.'

'I was bored at Francos, too,' Jami admitted. 'I couldn't wait to get home and watch telly. It was a great gig, though – and it really wound my bastard brother up when I told him we'd been to the Sanctum after party. Ha, bloody ha!'

Kelly laughed in response, but her voice sounded hollow, and she felt as if she was talking to Jami from the opposite end of the world. A massive sinkhole had opened up between them –

a vast oozy gulf – and she had a vision of being stranded down a sleazy back alley while Jami frolicked in a meadow of sunflowers.

'Funny,' she said.

In that moment she made a decision. She would never look backwards again. She would forget that she had got smashed and had sex with a complete stranger, with other men in the background egging him on. It was totally out of character. She couldn't understand what had made her do it. So she was just going to pretend that it hadn't happened. Not to her, not to anyone.

At first it was easy. She was used to shutting doors in her mind, so she could talk about the concert without unlocking the room that contained her disjointed memories of the rest of the night. The key was hidden, the keyhole blocked up. There wasn't even a pinprick of light.

Jami didn't question her. Why would she? She thought Kelly had gone home at two. Uncle Al was simply delighted that she'd been invited backstage. Nana was preoccupied with having a completely perfect Christmas. Only Mo seemed to sense that something had shifted in her.

'What is it?' she'd asked one evening, when she'd popped by, half-pissed, and sprawled herself on the sofa. 'Did some bastard break your heart, or something?'

'As if she'd tell you,' Nana snapped.

Nana turned her head to give Kelly a secret smile, and her eyes twinkled with mischief because she had noticed the phone calls from Michael Kirkpatrick and seen Kelly getting ready to go out and meet him.

Kelly smiled back, wishing she could feel more excited about Michael. She had every reason to be floating on air because it had gone really well both times they'd been out together. It was easy being with Michael. It was like being on an 'up' escalator. She especially liked his thick brown hair and big hands, and the way the skin around his eyes crinkled when he laughed. Not to mention the way her lips tingled when they kissed.

'So, are you falling in love?' Jami had asked her that morning at school.

She'd nodded uncertainly. It was flattering the way Michael made no secret of the fact he was into her. But she couldn't help wondering if it was her he really liked, or an invented version of her. She tried not to imagine what he would think if he found out about what had happened after the Sanctum concert.

Perhaps he'd be forgiving. It was hard to know, because they were so different. Michael came from a normal family – he had two younger sisters, parents who were still together, grannies who knitted and granddads with allotments. He lived in a house with a garden – and his mum cooked a homemade tea every evening. Three times a year they all bundled into their camper van and happily set off on holiday – to Scotland, Cornwall or France. It was everything she had dreamed of, growing up.

Her guess was that people from his sort of background couldn't imagine what it was like to come from a home like hers, a 'broken home'. So she hadn't told him much about her situation.

When he'd asked about her mam, she had optimistically described her as a free spirit – with her fingers crossed behind her back, hoping they would never meet. She was terrified of him meeting her mam.

'And your dad?' he'd asked.

'He's dead. I didn't really know him. I only met him a few times.'

She was used to people falling quiet when she told them this, too uncomfortable to reply. Then she would change the subject and her father would be forgotten, since there wasn't much to remember anyway.

Michael wasn't like other people, though. 'That's terrible,' he said. 'I don't know where I'd be without me dad. Do you miss him?'

She frowned. 'I never lived with him, or anything,' she said. 'Or not that I remember.'

'But that wouldn't stop you missing him.'

He was right, she realised. Something crumpled inside her. 'I'm not sure...' she said, her voice quavering.

He put his arm around her. 'I'm here if you ever want to talk about it, but I completely understand if you don't.'

Where had he learned to be so caring? She closed her eyes and leaned into him. 'I just want to be with you,' she murmured, without thinking.

'Do you?' he said, sounding surprised. 'Because that's what I want, as well.'

The following night they saw *Heat* at the cinema. While they were waiting at the bus stop afterwards, he swung from the roof of the bus shelter and made her laugh with his stories about his crazy nan. 'Is every family full of head cases?' he asked her.

'Only the interesting ones,' she said.

As if on cue, a couple came lurching arm in arm past the bus stop, drunkenly singing, 'Dance ti' thy daddy, sing ti' thy mammy'. Michael was leaning in to kiss her at that very moment, so she didn't give them a second glance, but he paused just before their lips met and sang softly, 'Tha shall have a fishy on a little dishy...'

She crinkled her nose and giggled.

'Come on,' he whispered, 'I'm not kissing you until you finish the verse.'

'I can't sing,' she protested. 'Don't make me.'

The drunken couple had crossed the road by now, but their reedy voices were still audible. 'Tha shall have a fishy when the boat comes in,' they chorused, before bursting into laughter. 'I'm a Geordie lass, deep to ma bones!' the woman yelled.

Kelly stiffened, almost certain that the voice belonged to her mam.

Michael brushed his lips against hers. 'They're having fun,' he murmured.

'Mmm,' she said, trying not to betray her feelings.

'Howay the lads!' came her mam's final shout, fading into the distance.

Kelly shut her eyes and launched herself into kissing Michael. Her mam – if it was her – had gone. It was a lucky escape. She prayed that fate would be on her side if it ever happened again.

4

Michael took Kelly home to meet his family in early January. 'At last we get to meet the famous Kelly,' his mother said, welcoming her into the kitchen. 'Honest to goodness, this boy doesn't stop talking about you.'

Kelly stared at the kettle in embarrassment.

'Stop it, Mam!' Michael protested, although he didn't seem all that bothered really.

She winked at Kelly. 'Just teasing, love,' she said. 'Actually, he's never even mentioned your name. Would you like a cuppa?'

Kelly laughed. 'Yes, please, Mrs Kirkpatrick,' she said.

'Call me Cathy, love. Take off your coat, sit down and make yourself at home. I want to know everything there is to know about you.'

This was typical of Michael's mam's whirlwind approach, she later discovered. 'Well, I can't stand small talk,' Cathy confessed. 'I've had enough discussions about the weather and late buses to last me a lifetime.'

In the absence of stilted chitchat, Kelly found it easy to open up. While Michael fixed a curtain rail in a bedroom upstairs and his younger sisters, Ella and Ruby, took it in turns to run in and out of the kitchen, stealing glances at her and giggling, she told Cathy about her plans to study business and tourism – and maybe one day to start her own travel agency.

Cathy seemed impressed. 'You can't lose, going into tourism, can you?' she said. 'The world and his wife goes to Lanzarote these days.'

'Yes, it's a growing industry,' Kelly replied, pleased to think she had chosen a promising future for herself.

They had shepherd's pie for tea, with apologies from Cathy for not preparing something special. 'It's just that the girls love it and they're so bloody fussy. But next time you come, I promise I'll make my spicy chicken curry.'

Ruby made a face.

'It was really good,' Kelly assured her. She held up her empty plate. 'I'll have some more, if there is any.'

Soon they were sitting in front of the box, summoned by the haunting melody of the *Corrie* theme tune, wondering if Maureen would go through with the wedding to Reg.

'She's a fool if she does,' Cathy declared. 'Reg thinks that much of the man in the mirror he'd be better off marrying himself! I say, marry Curly instead. He may be a bit wimpy, but he's loyal, and that's worth the world, in my experience.'

'Are you saying I'm wimpy?' Michael's father asked cheerfully.

Cathy bashed him with a cushion. 'Who said anything about you, Don, ya big lummox?'

Michael pressed his leg against Kelly's as they sat on the sofa together, drinking in the latest Weatherfield developments. 'I've something to show you, after this,' he said under his breath, during the ad break. 'Up in my room.'

'Great,' she said, trying not to laugh aloud.

She felt happy and excited to find herself in the midst of his family, but as the second half of the episode progressed, a sense of exhaustion swept over her and her eyes began to close. She tried blinking repeatedly and pinching herself, but it had no effect.

The next thing she knew, Michael was nudging her with his elbow. She came to with her mouth open and saw Peter Sissons reading out the headlines on the nine o'clock news. 'What happened?' she asked, through a fog of half-sleep.

'You nodded off just before Curly turned up to Reg's stag night,' Michael said.

That made her sit up. 'He wha'?'

Michael laughed. 'Yeah! And you've been asleep for more than an hour.'

She rubbed her eyes. 'Sorry, I don't know what's wrong with me – it keeps happening. My nana says it's winter weariness.'

'Winter weariness?' Michael said, turning to her with twinkling eyes. 'Is that an actual medical condition?'

She smiled weakly. She felt knocked out.

'What with your exams coming up, I expect you've been burning the candle at both ends with your studying,' Cathy said. 'They say teenagers need a lot of sleep.'

If only it was true, she thought. In the past few days, she'd fallen asleep every time she'd opened her textbooks. Maybe there was something wrong with her? Angela Mullen had dropped out of their class with ME, which she'd heard could be contagious.

'Dad says you're a snoozy Suzy,' Ella piped up.
'Rubbish!' Don said.

'Are you all right, love?' Cathy asked her. 'You look very pale.'

'I'd better get home,' she replied, standing up shakily. 'Thanks for the tea. It was delicious.'

Michael saw her to the bus stop and offered to accompany her all the way. 'No, I'm fine now,' she said. 'When can I come back and see that thing you've got to show me?'

He looked at her quizzically. 'What thing?'

She reached up to kiss him. 'You know, that thing in your bedroom.'

He grinned. 'Oh, that thing! Is tomorrow any good?'

'It might be,' she said coyly. 'Ask yer mam first – and then tell me at break.'

But the next day she woke up feeling so heavy and tired that she couldn't drag herself out of bed. 'I keep thinking I'm going to be sick,' she told Nana, when she came into her bedroom with a cup of tea.

Nana diagnosed a bug. 'Best stay in bed, love. Ring the doctor if it gets any worse, but the chances are that it'll iron itself out by the end of the day.'

After dozing for most of the morning, she suddenly felt fine. But on the bus on the way in to school, she felt nauseous again and turned back. Two days later, she went to the doctor.

Dr Wingfield-with-the-posh-voice was on duty that day. She was Nana's favourite GP and Kelly had known her for years. 'Is there a bug going around?' she asked her. 'When I'm not feeling

69

sick, I'm falling asleep. I can't study or concentrate.'

Dr Wingfield wrote something on a pad of paper. 'Do you know the date of your last period?' she asked gently.

Kelly looked back at her, mystified. 'I can't remember,' she said. 'It's not like I write it down in my diary.' She laughed nervously.

'Have you experienced any tenderness in your breasts recently?'

She shook her head. 'No.'

'Well, if you think there's a chance you might be pregnant, it might be worth doing a test. We can do one now, if you like.'

'Pregnant?' she said, shrinking back in her chair. 'Are you joking? No, definitely not. The last time I ... you know ... was last summer.'

With Nick Lightman, she thought, who loved his skateboard more than he loved me – until I dumped him, ha.

'Are you sure?' the doctor said, leaning in towards her.

'I ... yes, absolutely certain,' she said.

A memory flashed into her mind, of walking along a parade of shops wearing Jami's dress and no knickers underneath. Don't, she told herself. Don't look back.

She got up to go. 'Maybe it's just winter weariness, like my nana says.'

Dr Wingfield shrugged. 'You can always change your mind about having a test. It's available any time – it's confidential and free.'

She looked around the consulting room, taking in the family photograph on Dr Wingfield's desk

70

and the breastfeeding poster on the wall. 'I don't need a test, but thanks all the same,' she said. 'What do I do if it's a sickness bug?'

The doctor smiled at her. 'Not much, I'm afraid, except stay away from greasy foods and wait until it's out of your system. If it lasts more than a week, come back and see me.'

A fresh wave of nausea washed over Kelly. 'OK, thanks, bye,' she blurted out, turning to leave. She hurried past the waiting area, through the surgery door and out into the street, where she dry-retched into the nearest litter bin.

5

Kelly stopped feeling sick after a couple of weeks. 'It was a right bad bug,' she told her friends when she went back to school. 'I couldn't move from my bed for days.'

'There's a lot of it about,' everybody agreed.

'You look prettier,' Michael said, when they met in a break between lessons.

'How do you mean?' she asked.

He broke into a grin. 'I mean, *even* prettier, of course.' He grasped a strand of her hair. 'And sort of shiny.'

She felt pleased, and a little embarrassed. 'Are you saying I should be poorly more often?'

''Course not,' he replied, checking there were no teachers around before he leaned in to kiss her. 'It takes the fun out of getting off with your girlfriend if you think she's about to be sick all down you.'

She pushed him away with a laugh. 'It was never that bad!'

She liked that about Michael – he made her feel special without ever getting soppy, and then turned it into a joke so that neither of them felt awkward.

'I know,' he said, pulling her close again. 'Hey, remember I had something to show you? At my house? Well, Mum and Dad and my sisters are going away next weekend and I was thinking it might be a good time to come over...'

Her heart skipped a beat. 'Why aren't you going with them?'

'I've got to study,' he said, pretending to look sorry for himself. 'But I'll need a break on the Saturday night. Will you be free?'

She gave him a coy look. 'I might be.'

'Yeah?' The tip of his nose was touching hers.

'I'll let you know nearer the time.' She flicked her hair back, trying to appear cool despite the hot and cold currents playing beneath her skin.

She didn't need to hide her excitement from Jami, though. 'I think it'll be good with him,' she said, as they walked to the bus stop after school.

'What are you going to do for protection?' Jami asked.

She frowned. 'I was thinking about the pill, but will I be safe by next weekend? Or do you have to take it for a month first?'

Jami had been taking a combined pill to regulate her periods since she was fifteen. 'You're safe if you start on the first day of your cycle,' she said.

'Oh,' Kelly said, wondering when her body would start working properly again.

At the walk-in clinic in Byker, she told the nurse that she was expecting her period any day. And then, luckily, she got it that Thursday, although it was only very light, hardly a period at all – not that she was complaining. It was a good omen, she thought, as she popped her first tiny orange pill out of its foil wrapper. She'd be safe by the time she went to Michael's house.

'You don't need that,' she told him the following Saturday week, as she lay next to him on the hall floor, ten minutes after he had answered the door. His T-shirt was off, her top unbuttoned, and there was an unopened condom packet in his hand.

'How come?' he asked, grazing his cheek against hers.

'I'm on the pill,' she said – and giggled, because it seemed like such an adult thing to say.

His eyes widened. 'Yeah?' He chucked the condom packet over his head and she heard it skim across the parquet floor.

She lost herself in their next kiss. When he finally pulled away and his face came into focus again, she could see that his eyes were filmy with desire. She shivered slightly in the cool air of the hall. 'Wouldn't it be warmer in your bedroom?' she asked, hoping it didn't sound like too much of a come-on.

They made it as far as the landing, and then to the stretch of carpet outside his bedroom door. Eventually they went to sleep beneath the tartan duvet on his springy single bed. The next morning, he brought her toast and orange juice on his mam's favourite lacquered tray.

'How was your weekend?' Jami asked on the Monday morning. 'Were you right? Was it good?'

'Fucking brilliant,' she said, and they looked at each other and squealed.

It was Mo who noticed Kelly was putting on weight. At least, she was the first to mention it outright. 'Getting proper fussy, aren't you?' she said, on one of the countless evenings she out-stayed her welcome after 'popping in' for a coffee earlier in the day. She took a deep drag on an expensive-looking, gold-tipped cigarette, which seemed out of place between her grubby fingers, with their chipped scarlet nail polish. It wasn't her usual bargain brand and Kelly thought she'd probably 'found' a stray pack in a club, or got a carton cheap off the back of a French lorry.

'Wha's happening?' Mo said, looking her daughter up and down as she exhaled. 'Did you win a year's supply of doughnuts, or something?'

'Lay off!' Nana snapped. 'She's fine. She's developing natural female curves, just as I did at her age.'

'I am eating more, though,' Kelly admitted.

She'd been wondering for weeks whether being in love did something to your taste buds. Sally Milman in the year above claimed to have lost her sweet tooth and her virginity in the same month – and Sally was sure the two were connected, or so she told the lower sixth girls one Thursday dinner-time, as they waited together in the second sitting queue. 'I used to love trifle,' she said, wrinkling her nose up at a tub of jellied fruit and whipped

74

cream. 'But since I slept with Calvin, I can't stand the friggin' sight of it.'

Kelly's taste buds had gone the other way, though. Since she'd been going out with Michael, her appetite for food had surged, especially for sugary snacks between meals, and there was a near-constant fluttery sensation in her stomach. Her sweet tooth was sweeter and her clothes felt tighter, especially her bras – she couldn't work out if it was love, sex or the pill that was doing it. Maybe having a boyfriend could crank up your appetite, she thought, although she'd never heard of it. Girls in books usually pined and starved when they fell in love. They didn't gollop down mountains of pasta and sweets.

'You look great,' Michael assured her, when she told him what her mam had said. He put his arm around her. 'I don't care how much weight you put on...' He chuckled. 'As long as it all goes to your bust!'

She gave him a playful punch. 'Think you're funny, do you?'

'I don't mean to pry, but are you on the pill, love?' his mam asked, when she mentioned her surging appetite to her. 'Because I ballooned when I started on Microgynon. It was right bad. Eventually, I realised that I had a choice between fat safe sex or slim risky sex – which is how I ended up with three children instead of two.' She started giggling. 'No regrets, mind,' she added. 'But after Ella arrived I had my tubes tied.'

Kelly stared at a saucepan, too embarrassed to respond.

'Of course, you don't want to know all my

intimate details, do you, love?' Cathy said with a laugh.

Kelly looked at the floor.

'But I'd suggest going back to your GP to see if you can change to another pill. Maybe oestrogen-only would be better for you.'

'Michael's mam says it could be the pill,' Kelly told Jami the following day, undoing the top button of her hipster jeans and breathing out. 'I'm hungry all the time, even though I feel totally bloated.' She flopped down onto a pile of brightly coloured cushions on Jami's bedroom floor. 'Apparently, it can do that to you.'

Jami was flicking through an issue of *Cosmopolitan*. '"Appetite out of control? Stop valve not working?"' she read out. 'It says here that the answer is to give your body a short, sharp shock by fasting for three days, to reset your metabolism.'

'Let's see.' Kelly got up to look over her shoulder and quickly scanned the page. 'Bananas and grapefruits? I could do that.'

She stocked up on fruit at the next weekly shop, but fasting made her feel dizzy and she cracked halfway through the second day of the diet, wolfing down half a fresh bloomer in a matter of minutes. Bread had never smelled or tasted so delicious in her life. She wanted to savour every crumb, but her hunger was so overwhelming that she barely chewed it before swallowing it down and tearing off another mouthful. What's happening to me? she thought, scanning the kitchen like a stray dog. Her appetite was starting to frighten her. Why wasn't her stop valve working any more? Why did ordinary food taste so completely delicious all of a sudden?

At the weekend she'd had a pint of cider with a flavour so intensely appley it had freaked her out. 'Does this taste funny to you?' she asked Michael.

He took a sip and shrugged. 'Just normal cider,' he said. 'What's it taste like to you?'

She laughed. 'I dunno, like falling into a massive vat of crushed apples, or something.'

'Yeah?' he said, giving her a strange look. 'Shall I get you a lager instead?'

Now, as she pounced on Nana's packet of Rich Tea biscuits in the kitchen, she felt a ripple of movement cross her belly, and yelped. Something was definitely wrong. She wondered if it could be tapeworm. John Ashworth in her geography class said that parasites could grow to eight feet long in your gut. She tried to recall if she'd eaten any dodgy pork recently. But I'd be losing weight if I had a tapeworm, wouldn't I? she thought. It had to be something, though. Her stomach flipped over and the fluttering started again.

She heard the front door buzzer and went to answer it. Jimmy Fry from upstairs was standing in the doorway. She hadn't seen him for weeks and he looked thinner and paler – less likely than ever to survive to the end of the week. She remembered that Nana had said he'd been in hospital. She wondered what was wrong with him. For once in his life, he didn't have a fag in his hand.

Jimmy looked her up and down and took a startled step backwards. 'I thought you were yer mam for a moment there!'

'Go on!' she said. 'Don't tell me I look like me mam. She's ancient.'

'Ah, but I'm talking about from years ago, when she was around your age.'

'You knew her then? Before she had me?'

He smiled ruefully. 'Funnily enough, I met her when she was expecting you, when she looked just like you do now.' He raised his eyebrows. 'It's not a case of history repeating itself, is it, love?'

'What do you mean? Me nana says I'm nothing like her.' She bit back a cutting comment about Mo, because in Jimmy's eyes her mam could do no wrong. 'She's not staying here any more. Nana won't let her,' she told him.

'Oh.' He looked crestfallen. The lift shaft rumbled behind him, as if in sympathy. 'Will you be seeing her at all? I'd like her to know I'm back at home.'

'She's in and out all the time,' Kelly said. 'I'll tell her to come up when she's next here.'

Just then the lift doors opened and Mo stepped out. Her timing couldn't have been better if she'd actually been answering Jimmy's silent wail of longing. Today she was wearing a sludge green vest dress that showed off a blue lacy bra underneath. Slung over her shoulder was a massive string bag, stuffed with clothes. Her swag bag, Kelly thought, noting the bruises on her shins. Waltzing Matilda waltzes in – after a scrap.

Mo took one look at Kelly and burst out laughing. 'All right, fatty!' she said. 'How are you, Jim?'

His face lit up. 'Still alive. Ready to fight another day,' he said gamely.

'You look half-dead to me,' Mo snapped, and his smile dropped away. 'But what do I know, eh,

Jimmy, lad? I'm as thick as shit – as the bairn and her nan are always pointing out.' She turned her gaze to Kelly. 'That said, I knew full well when I was up the stick, plain as day. I didn't need three A Levels to fathom that one out.'

Kelly felt a lurch in her stomach.

'Wha' the fuck,' Mo added with a shrug. 'You can always get rid of it. Just don't leave it too long.'

'Have you got a minute, Mo?' Jim asked. 'There's something I'd like to show you.' He cocked his head and made a clicking sound with his tongue. 'Upstairs, like,' he added.

'Yeah?' Mo said disdainfully, dropping her bag. 'Go on, then.' She walked over to the lift and pressed the call button. 'Our Kelly'll still be here in fifteen minutes, won't you?'

Kelly nodded automatically. She shut the front door of the flat and went into the kitchen. Her appetite was gone. The ravenous hunger of a few minutes earlier had turned its teeth inwards and was gnawing on every anxious bone and sinew within her body.

She opened the cupboard under the sink and took a tenner out of Nana's emergency fund. Ten minutes later she was at the counter of Hallways Chemist, buying a pregnancy test. Five minutes after that, she was in the Burger King toilets, tears streaming down her face as she stared at two horizontal red lines in the tiny window of a plastic test stick. It was the bleakest view she had ever seen.

Kelly had to wait an hour for Dr Wingfield-with-the-posh-voice to squeeze her in for an appointment. 'I haven't told anyone. I've come straight here from doing the test,' she said, sitting opposite her.

Dr Wingfield gave her a reassuring smile. She and Nana were about the same age, according to Nana – but in Nana's words, the doctor was 'much better preserved'. It wasn't true, though, Kelly thought. They just had totally different looks. Dr Wingfield, with her glossy black hair and well-cut trouser suits, was the polar opposite of her peroxide and velour-loving nana.

'Would you mind lying down on the couch so that I can examine you? Let's see if I can feel anything.'

Please let this be a nightmare, Kelly thought, as the doctor softly pressed her fingers onto her exposed belly and pelvis.

'Well, there's no mistaking it, Kelly.' Dr Wingfield's tone was gentle, but firm. 'You're definitely pregnant.'

'But I can't be. I'm on the pill,' Kelly whispered. 'And I had a period recently. It wasn't much of one, but...'

'It may have been what we call "spotting",' the doctor said. 'And I'm afraid the pill isn't always a hundred per cent effective, especially among young women,' she added. 'Why don't you come and sit down again, so that we can have a chat?'

Kelly got up off the couch, pulled down her top, did up her jeans and put on her shoes. She felt floaty and weightless as she walked the few steps back to her chair.

'The baby feels quite big and I'd estimate that you're in the second trimester of the pregnancy,'

Dr Wingfield said, once she'd sat down. 'That means that you're more than twelve weeks pregnant, in my opinion – probably several weeks more than that, even. But I'd like to make sure – and have you and the baby checked, if you don't mind. Would you be able to go along for a scan at the RVI today? There's also counselling available to you there, in case you have mixed feelings about the pregnancy.' She smiled at Kelly, but there was sadness in her eyes.

'I've got a boyfriend...' Kelly said weakly. There was a pause while Dr Wingfield waited for her to finish. But the words wouldn't come. She hung her head.

'Are you worried this lad won't be supportive?' the doctor asked eventually. 'You may be underestimating him, you know.'

Kelly bit her lip. Her eyes filled with tears. She looked up at Dr Wingfield. 'But I've only been sleeping with him for two months,' she said, her voice cracking as she spoke. 'What if he's not the dad?'

An image sprang into her mind of a bare-chested lad on top of her, his hips thrusting against hers, and a green-eyed man in the background, braying, 'Go on, nail her good!'

Stop it, she told herself. Shut it away.

Her sense of weightlessness left her. Now her mind felt as if it was slowly filling up with molten metal, blurring her thoughts and making her head heavier by the second. She desperately wanted to get back on the couch and go to sleep.

Dr Wingfield leaned towards her. 'I can tell you're upset, dear, and I expect it's partly the shock. It's not the end of the world, though – even if it feels like it is right at this moment.'

Kelly shut her eyes tightly. It was the end of Michael, if not the world.

'You have options, Kelly – that's the important thing to remember,' Dr Wingfield said. 'No one is going to make you do anything you don't want to. But look, I'd rather you didn't leave the surgery unaccompanied, not while you're feeling this shaky,' she continued. 'Is there somebody you could contact to come and pick you up? A friend – or your grandmother, perhaps? You're more than welcome to use the practice telephone.' She gestured to the phone on her desk.

Kelly nodded, speechlessly. Tears streamed down her face. The doctor was being so nice. She wasn't judging her at all. 'My nana,' she blurted out. 'She'll be leaving work in an hour.'

Nana! she pleaded silently. *Help me, now.*

Dr Wingfield picked up the phone. 'Do you know the number?' she asked.

'Off by heart,' she said with a sob.

Nana came with her to the hospital, and took her home afterwards, and sat and cuddled her in the evening as she cried over her lost dreams. She was eighteen weeks pregnant, according to the scan and various measurements taken by a tall, serious, blond doctor who barely spoke. Having done GCSE biology, Kelly knew exactly what that meant. It meant that there was a half-grown baby inside her. Not a creature the size of a grain of rice or a kidney bean, but a semi-formed human being with hands, feet and a brain. There was no way she could get rid of it.

She called to mind the January day she'd been to see Dr Wingfield about her upset stomach. Why hadn't she listened to the doctor's warning? Why had she been deliberately deaf and blind?

Because of Michael, she thought, although he was only part of it. In fact, if she'd listened to the doctor that day, perhaps she wouldn't have to split up with him now. But it was over with Michael. There was no getting round it. She couldn't expect him to take responsibility for another lad's child, a baby with an unknown dad. His family might have offered to help her if it had been Michael's baby, but it was nothing to do with Michael. She'd been pregnant with someone else's kid on their first date.

'A lad put a pill in my drink,' she said in a muffled voice, her face buried deep in Nana's fleshy shoulder. 'I blacked out and I can't remember what happened afterwards. Except, when I woke up, I knew I'd been–' she searched for words that would lessen the horror '–taken advantage of.' She started sobbing again, clung tighter to Nana and dug her face further into her shoulder. 'It's so unfair,' she whispered. 'I'll end up like me mam now. Just like me mam.'

Nana's body stiffened. She pulled away from Kelly and took her firmly by the shoulders. 'Don't talk such nonsense – you're nothing like yer mam,' she said sharply. 'You're not going down that path – you're not the type – and certainly not as long as I've got breath in my body, by heck. You've been violated, my angel. By wicked, despicable men.' She spat the words out.

'But you can't let it defeat you – and you won't. We'll bring those bastards to book and you'll finish your studies too, love, baby or no baby.'

Kelly shook her head in despair. 'How can I?'

'We'll manage, love. We'll find a way. I'll scale down my work hours to give you time to study. You're an ambitious lass. You'll get where you want to go. I'll help you.'

'But I just can't see–'

'You're still alive, angel,' Nana interrupted. 'You survived that night and you'll go on surviving. You're Molly Ross's granddaughter, never forget it. You're from a long line of fishermen's wives, from strong, sturdy stock – and we don't give up.'

'Me mam did,' Kelly said.

Nana squawked. 'She's a Callan, love. Soft in the head, like your grandpa. There's not a drop of Ross blood in her – or not that you can see. Whereas you're a Ross, every inch of you; you're a Ross, through and through. Don't worry, love, we'll cope. Nothing can beat us, as long as we're together.'

Kelly leaned forward and rested her head on Nana's shoulder again, knowing she was right. She had a guardian angel, a fairy godmother, right by her side. She had Nana. They would get through this. Together.

6

Kelly was poring over an example maths A Level paper when Nana came home, looking pleased as punch. 'How's the studying?' Nana asked, beaming at her.

She grimaced. 'My brain's a bit muzzy, but I'm getting there. I keep forgetting which formula I'm supposed to be using.'

'Don't worry, it's normal,' Nana said. 'I had a right brain fog when I was expecting yer mam. I lost everything, forgot everything – I thought I was totally losing it. But I was sharp as a tack again after the baby came.'

Kelly sat back in her chair and gave her belly a rub. She was more than six months pregnant now – and it showed. 'What were you looking so happy about when you walked in?' she asked.

Nana tapped her nose. 'Now that would be telling.'

Kelly stood up. 'What is it? Have you got something for me?'

Nana's grin grew so wide that you could practically see all her teeth within the pearlised pink frame of her lips. She was never happier than when she was giving gifts. It gave her twenty times more pleasure than receiving them. 'Well...' she said, her face lighting up like a pixie's. She paused.

'Yes?' Kelly instinctively mirrored her expression – eyes wide, eyebrows raised – and they stood facing one another like two pantomime elves who had forgotten their lines, until eventually she burst out laughing. 'Aren't you going to say anything?' she asked.

Nana frowned and shook her head. 'Sorry, love, my mind went blank for a moment there.'

'Come on, Nana, anyone would think you were pregnant too!'

Nana blinked hard and rubbed one of her eyes. 'That'd be a stretch, at fifty-five. Not unheard of, mind. It seems to happen a lot in India, according to the papers.'

'I'd love it if you were,' Kelly said wistfully. 'We could bring our babies up together.'

Nana snorted. 'We'll have our hands full with just the one! Although they're easy to care for when they're tiny, just as long they don't have colic, touch wood.'

'Fingers crossed,' Kelly agreed. 'So then,' she added, changing the subject, 'what's the big secret?'

Nana stared at her vacantly. 'What, love?'

'Have you got a surprise for me?'

'Oh yes!' Nana said, perking up. 'There was a flash sale in the baby department today. My girls had a little whip-round for you – and our supervisor used her staff discount to buy a few things for the little 'un. Look!' She went over to the door and picked up a C&A bag.

Kelly watched her in amazement. Her eyes filled with tears. 'I don't believe it.'

'Wait until you see what it is,' Nana said excitedly.

86

They sat together on the sofa and Nana opened up the bag of goodies. First, she took out a new-born-sized cotton all-in-one, embroidered with tiny rattles – blue for the boy she'd been told she was having, at the last scan.

'Oh!' Kelly clapped her hands to her mouth. 'It's so diddy – and so soft.' As she picked it up she felt a movement inside her. Suddenly it was that much easier to imagine holding a tiny person in her arms.

Next, Nana produced a matching vest and bib, two weeny blue hats, a set of cot sheets and a striped cotton blanket. 'All you need now is the Moses basket,' she said gleefully.

Kelly bit her lip and stared at the floor. Everyone was being so kind. Jami had offered to come with her to the hospital when she went into labour. Uncle Al was going to put some money into a savings account for the baby. Her teachers and friends at school were behaving as if it was entirely normal for her to be putting on weight one minute, pregnant the next – and still planning to take her A Levels and go to college. And it wasn't just the people she knew who were being nice. Old ladies had started smiling at her in the street and random strangers kept offering her their seats on the bus. Kids asked if they could stroke her tummy. Mams with older kids spoke wistfully to her of the joy ahead and told her to make the most of it, because 'it'll be over before you know it'.

And now this – Nana's friends at work chipping in to buy baby things. They had done it because they loved Nana, of course – it wasn't so much about Kelly as a testament to Nana's popularity and good-heartedness. But it was further proof that babies brought out the best in people. Just the thought of them made people nicer to each other.

It made her want to cry with ... what was it? Not happiness, exactly – although that was a part of it. More a sense of wonderment at life. Everything's different when you're pregnant, she thought.

It was odd how the nightly news on telly made no sense any more. All the bad stuff that was happening in the world seemed a million miles away from Edison House, as if it was taking place in another universe. She managed to brush aside the headlines, just as she had banished – again – the memory of the night she had conceived the baby. It had come out of its box when she'd found out she was pregnant and Nana had persuaded her to reveal it, first to a nice, grey-haired counsellor called Daphne, later on to a young policewoman with flinty blue eyes. Hardest of all was telling Michael – baldly, haltingly. But now it was back in the dark again, behind a closed, sealed door, hopefully for good.

Nana had got her through those first bleak days after the pregnancy test. She'd been her shining star, her guiding light – she would have been totally lost without Nana. Revisiting what had happened had been torture, like having her fingers broken one by one. She hadn't been able to stop replaying the images in her head, especially the terrifying moment she had woken up in a strange house, with a head like a block of concrete and no memory of the night before. Nana said that she'd been brave not to panic or scream when she realised what those men had done to her. She said it showed how strong she was, mentally.

She wasn't sure if this was true. 'I just wanted to get home,' she told Nana. 'I would have done anything to get back here.' But Nana's words reassured and comforted her, all the same.

She had said goodbye to Michael in the White Horse, 'their' pub, on a Monday afternoon. She had hardly been able to speak for shame and self disgust – she hadn't met his eye as she'd stammered out the sentences.

'I can't see you any more, I'm sorry. I'm pregnant. I was raped. I'm keeping the bairn.'

She couldn't blame him for looking stunned, as if she'd nutted him or something. 'What are you saying?' he asked, shaking his head as if to say, This can't be true. But there was no mistaking her words.

She stole a look at him. His expression was dazed. 'I'm sorry,' she said again. 'I didn't know I was pregnant. I wasn't even sure if I'd been raped.'

'How come?'

'I was drugged. I couldn't remember. And I did my best to forget.'

She could see that he didn't know what to say. She wanted to make it easier for him, but couldn't think of anything to say either. The only thing she could do was stand up and leave.

'Wait, that's it?' he said, reaching out to grab her wrist. At last she met his gaze, which was full of questions.

She hesitated, wondering for the hundredth time how he would react if she said, 'Unless we got married and brought the baby up together? I've thought it through. We could make it work.'

In her daydreams he'd say, 'Kelly, I want to be with you until the day I die. I'll do anything to be with you and make you happy. I'll love the bairn as if it were my own. I'll get a job and support you both.'

But she knew it wouldn't be like that – and she didn't want to risk seeing a sneer cross Michael's face, or cruel words dropping like lead weights onto her already bruised heart. Michael wanted to study international relations at Manchester University. He wanted to become an aid worker and go to Africa. Why would he give up his dreams to live in a tiny flat in Byker with Nana, Kelly and a bairn?

She turned her back on him and walked out of the pub.

Nana came into the lounge wearing her apron. 'What shall we have...?' she asked.

'For tea, you mean?' Kelly said.

Nana moved her lips, soundlessly.

'What are you doing?' Kelly asked in surprise.

Nana's lips went on moving.

Kelly laughed. 'Nana?'

Nana winced and shut her eyes. Kelly stood up. 'What is it? Are you all right?' She rushed over to her and put her arm round her. Nana shook her head and seemed to be about to lose her balance, so she led her slowly back to the sofa and helped her to sit down. 'Feeling dizzy?' she asked. Nana nodded. One of her eyes twitched, and twitched again. She put her head on one side. 'OK, take a deep breath,' Kelly said, her heart racing. She clasped Nana tighter and then thought better of it. If Nana was feeling faint, she needed space. She rubbed her shoulders, slowly and gently. 'There, you'll feel better in a minute. Put your head down. Keep breathing.'

They sat in silence for a few moments that felt like a lifetime, Nana breathing in gasps, Kelly massaging her shoulders and back. At long last, Nana spoke. 'Funny turn,' she rasped. 'Eyes blurry all of a sudden.'

'Don't worry,' Kelly said, relief washing over her. 'At least you can talk now. I thought you were trying to make me laugh or something, but it was scary.'

Like watching a ventriloquist in reverse, she almost said – mouth moving, no sound.

Nana managed a weak smile. 'I don't feel well, love,' she said.

Kelly's heart started up again. 'Do you need a doctor? Shall I call an ambulance?'

'Oh, no, it's not that bad.' Nana put one hand up to her forehead. 'I just need to sit here for a little while and gather myself again. I'm afraid I'm not going to be up to making the tea.'

'I'll make the tea!' Kelly exclaimed. 'You should have said if you were feeling tired. I would have done it like a shot. Now, what do you fancy?'

Nana patted her on the knee. 'I know you would, love. I just didn't think...'

'You were fine up until a minute ago, weren't you?'

Nana gave her a worried look. 'I've been feeling a bit poorly all day, actually.'

91

'You sit down and take it easy, then. How about I make bacon and pease pudding? Or macaroni cheese?'

Nana nodded. 'Whatever you like, dear. They both sound...' She raised her eyebrows.

'Good?' Kelly said.

Nana nodded again. She closed her eyes slowly and lowered her head.

Kelly frowned. It was weird seeing Nana poorly. She was never ill, never. She wondered if she was coming down with the flu, or some kind of summer bug. 'You look knackered. Would you be happier going to bed for a bit?' she asked.

'No, I'll be fine,' Nana assured her. 'I'll sit here while you get on with the tea.'

'I'll put the telly on, shall I?'

Nana sighed, as if she didn't care one way or the other.

'I'll put it on low, shall I? Just for a bit of company.' Nana didn't react, so she switched on ITV. The six o'clock news had just started and the newsreader was reading a report about the rise of male rape. She switched over to a programme about fishing on BBC2 and headed into the kitchen.

A few minutes later, she popped her head round the lounge door. 'I decided to make macaroni cheese, because it's your fav–' She stopped mid-sentence. 'Nana!' she screamed.

Nana was lying awkwardly on her side. Her eyes were open, her tongue lolling out of her mouth, and Kelly knew instantly that she was dead.

The emergency operator talked her through CPR

and mouth-to-mouth resuscitation. She frantically pumped Nana's chest and breathed air into her lungs.

'Please wake up!' she begged her. 'Please!'

She did everything she could, but Nana just lay there, lifeless and odd-looking.

The baby boy inside Kelly moved restlessly around. 'It's no good,' she told the operator, dropping the phone to the floor.

When the paramedics arrived, she was sitting quietly, holding Nana's hand, echoing Nana's comforting words and singsong lilt all those nights she had shooed away Kelly's monsters.

'It's all right, Nana, everything's fine, I'm here to keep you safe, Kelly's here to look after you...'

As the paramedics knelt beside Nana, the baby kicked hard, several times, as if he was trying to bust out of her body and escape, to run as far away from this mess as he could get. He understood the trouble they were in. He realised the cold truth. Where would they be without Nana? How would Kelly cope alone with a baby?

She kept hold of Nana's hand in the ambulance and Uncle Al met her at the hospital, where they said goodbye to the most important person in their lives in a small, bright room next to the hospital mortuary. Nana looked like a statue of a woman sleeping. There was no life left in her at all – no sense of fun or compassion. But now that she was lying down and her eyes had been closed, there was an air of dignity about her. She looked at peace.

Uncle Al's face was as white as the walls, his lips bloodless with tension. 'I can't believe it,' he kept saying. 'Me poor mam. It's so sudden. It doesn't seem real.'

He put his arm around Kelly and she stood stiffly next to him, feeling the weight of it across her shoulders. She was relieved when he took it away, because she wasn't ready to be comforted. It was too soon for hugs and tears. It was too soon for anything but disbelief.

Shock buffered her through the hours and days that followed. Uncle Al did all the official stuff and broke the news to Nana's friends and colleagues. It took ages to find Mo, who laughed herself into a wheezy coughing fit and then marched around town demanding free drinks from anyone she even vaguely recognised. 'I'm a poor orphan now,' she told people. 'I'm all alone in the world.'

Uncle Al took care of the funeral arrangements, which were shockingly expensive. When Kelly told him about the cash stashed in Nana's wardrobe, he took a portion for the funeral and gave the rest to her. 'But don't tell Mo,' he warned. 'I've said that me mam was skint. There was no money in the bank, after all.'

Kelly blinked slowly. 'What about the flat?' she asked. 'Can I go on living here?'

He looked at her with sad eyes. 'It would have been yours if you were eighteen, love. But you're too young to transfer it into your name. Unfortunately, it looks like our Mo's going to put in a claim. She'll get it, too – Jimmy upstairs knows someone in the housing office. But I'll make sure she keeps a bedroom for you … and with a bit of luck you'll get a place of your own when the bairn arrives.'

He smiled and squeezed her arm and she tried to smile back, but all she could think about was Mel Macpherson on the fourth floor, who'd got a flat when she'd had her twins, a year before. At school, Mel had been one of the sixth form golden girls, and a prize-winning gymnast. Kelly remembered seeing her rehearse in the school gym, her face lit up with daredevil pleasure as her body miraculously arched and coiled, vaulted and sprang across the floor. But Mel had lost her bounce now – and the fire in her eyes. She spent her days trudging around Byker with a buggy containing bairns that shrieked and bawled all day long.

Kelly had helped her to get them up the stairs one day when the lift was broken, a couple of weeks before Nana died. She couldn't help noticing the dark bruises on Mel's arms.

'Good luck to you,' Mel said dully, when Kelly told her about her plans to go on studying. 'I truly hope you and the bairn make it out of here.'

A week after Nana's death, Mo moved into Edison House. She bagged up Nana's clothes and put them down the rubbish chute. 'This place is mine now,' she boasted when Kelly got home from school. 'You can keep your room, for the time being, but I'm telling you now there's no fucking way I want to live with you and a screaming bairn.'

Kelly stared at her blankly. Who are you? she thought. I don't know you at all.

Uncle Al helped her put in a housing application to the council. 'But I can't see how you'll be able to stay at school,' he said. 'Have you talked to any of your teachers about it?'

95

She shook her head. Her geography teacher, Miss Jewell, had asked her to stay behind after class the day before, but she'd made up an excuse about having to rush away for a doctor's appointment. Her head was too full of Nana to think about how she was going to look after and support a baby. She kept telling herself that she would manage somehow. At night she slept with the baby clothes Nana had given her under her pillow.

Nana's funeral was held on a sunny Wednesday afternoon in Chester-le-Street, in the ancient church where Nana and her husband Malcolm had got married. Nana had often spoken of the town where she'd lived when she'd first left Scotland – about half an hour's drive from Newcastle – but Kelly had never been there until now. It looked like a nice place, she thought, staring through the tinted windows of the people carrier that drove her smoothly along the main street. It seemed a lot calmer than Byker, although it was hard to tell what anything was like from inside her dream world of shock and grief.

The car slowed to let a blonde woman in a pink tracksuit cross the road. Kelly half-closed her eyes and pretended for a moment that the woman was Nana, even though Nana was lying flat in the car in front, sealed up in an oak coffin. Only it wasn't Nana in the box – it was just her body. And the woman in pink wasn't Nana either – she was just someone crossing the road. So where was Nana now? Had her spirit gone somewhere? Was she all right? Perhaps the woman in pink had been sent as a sign. Maybe Nana had somehow prodded the woman in pink to cross the road in front of the line of funeral cars, so that Kelly could see her and know that Nana was all right.

'Are you OK?' Jami asked, interrupting her thoughts. She reached out and touched Kelly's arm.

Kelly turned to look at her friend. 'Yeah, just... I don't know,' she said. 'Thank you.' There was so much she wanted to thank Jami for, not least for buying her a Nana-pink scarf to wear with her black dress and shoes. Nana would definitely have approved.

Jami stared glumly back at her. 'I loved your nana. She was family to me.'

'You can't have known her very well, then, love,' chipped in Mo, who was sitting in the row in front.

'Stop it, sis,' Uncle Al said. 'Now is not the time.'

The car drew up outside the church. 'We're here,' Kelly said, unnecessarily.

Jami stayed close as they walked inside. The pews were packed out with Nana's friends. 'Everybody loved her,' Jami whispered as they walked down the aisle to their seats near the altar. Kelly clutched her arm and squeezed it tight.

Mo followed them into the church a few minutes later, having hung back to have a fag outside. 'Budge up,' she said as she sat down next to Kelly, who fought the urge to scream at her to go away. Instead she pressed her shoulder against Jami's and Jami pressed back, and suddenly she was trying her hardest not to giggle. Her world was teetering on hysteria. Everything seemed absurd. It *was* absurd – her mam had the mental age of a twelve-year-old and Kelly was carrying her grandchild. Wherever Nana's spirit was now, she was probably thinking she'd had a lucky escape from her fuckwit daughter and her pregnant fuckwit granddaughter, not to mention the unborn child – who knew what *he* would be like? Tears streamed down her face. She bit her lip. It wouldn't make a difference, anyway. The poor bairn had no chance of being normal coming into a family like theirs.

The funeral passed in weird flashes. Uncle Al was the head pallbearer. After he set Nana's coffin down at the altar, he squeezed himself between Mo and Kelly, sat down and put one arm around each of them. The vicar had a gentle voice and seemed genuinely saddened by Nana's death, even though he didn't know her. Nana's best mate, Betty, managed not to cry as she talked about her kind, bubbly friend. 'Nothing was ever too much trouble for her. The world has lost an angel,' she said.

The congregation was subdued after the vicar's final blessing. They left the church in silence. Nana had died too young. Everyone felt the unfairness of it. Jami steered Kelly into the churchyard. 'Cathy's here. Michael's mam,' she said.

For a moment, Kelly thought she meant that Cathy was buried in one of the graves outside the church. She frowned. Cathy was dead, too?

Suddenly, she came face to face with her. 'Hello, love,' Cathy said, her head tilted to one side, her eyes full of compassion. 'I'm so sorry for your loss. Your nana was a wonderful woman. Everyone says so.'

Kelly blinked several times. Her eyes felt itchy.

'Did you know her?'

'I didn't, love, but I wanted to be here to support you today. I wanted you to know that your friends are thinking of you. Jami here told Michael what happened, and Michael told me. He would have come today, but no one wanted to upset you.'

'Thank you,' Kelly said. Her lip began to tremble. She lowered her head and stared at the ground. 'It was nice you made the effort.'

Cathy launched at her and gave her a hug. Kelly shut her eyes and tried to pretend it wasn't happening. 'If you ever need someone to talk to, the door is open,' Cathy said. 'Any time, love. If you need to talk...'

Kelly nodded, but wouldn't meet her eye. She wrapped her arms around her belly in a defensive gesture. 'Thank you.'

In the car on the way to the wake, Mo produced a can of Special Brew from her shoulder bag and started swigging thirstily. 'Everyone's asking how you're going to manage with a bairn now,' she said. '"I know," I keep saying. "She should fucking forget it and give the bairn away."'

'Not now,' Uncle Al said sharply. 'We're saying goodbye to our mam today. That's what today is about. Everything else – and I mean *everything* – belongs to tomorrow. So lay off Kelly. She knows what she's doing, anyway.'

Kelly watched trees and fields fly by out of the car window. I don't, she thought. I haven't got a clue. But I'm keeping my baby, no matter what.

7

Kelly balled her hands into fists and clenched her jaw to stop herself from crying. It was 3.25 a.m. and Mo was 'partying me tits off' through the night again, blasting Run DMC and Aerosmith at full volume for the fifth time in a row. Kelly wished to God that her mam had died instead of Nana. She wished to God that her mam would drop dead right now.

Reaching behind her favourite framed photo of Nana, she found a loose wad of cotton wool that she kept by her bed for moments like these – and there had been many in the month since Nana had passed. She rolled up two balls, stuffed them into her ears and eased herself back onto the mattress. She had a pillow between her legs and another under her belly – there wasn't a third pillow to lay her head on, so she did without. The smell of cigarette smoke seeped under her bedroom door and filtered into her nostrils as she tried to get herself comfortable.

She heard someone knocking at the door. Her mam's party pals often tried to get in to talk to her on these nights, when they came back from a pub or club to shout, dance and take drugs. The locked door made them curious – they wanted to see what was on the other side. They wanted to chatter away to someone new, tell tales of drunken exploits and say profound things about birth and death. 'One door closes and another opens,' they'd pronounce sagely, nodding at her bump.

In this world of theirs, where they drank all night and to hell with tomorrow, the future, though they damned it, was bright and bouncy. But by morning it had floated off and popped like Fairy liquid bubbles.

The knocking continued. She was glad of the lock that Uncle Al had screwed onto the wall after Mo had moved in. She picked up a few muffled words. 'Kelly Kel ... little chat ... just a li'l minute...'

'I'm asleep!' she yelled and shut her eyes.

The knocking stopped and she hoped that her would-be visitor had gone. She rubbed her stomach and flexed her fingers. What would happen when the baby was born? Would he be disturbed by the noise of Mo's parties? Would he be harmed by the smoke seeping in from the lounge? Jami had seen a programme about the dangers of passive smoking. She said there was scientific evidence that Mo's tabs could already be hurting him.

She wished she could go and live with Uncle Al, but he couldn't have her. It wasn't just that he only had one bedroom in his dockside flat, it was also that he worked all hours building his business, often through the night. He needed to live alone, in peace. And maybe there was a new girlfriend, too. She sensed there was someone.

Al wasn't optimistic about her chances of getting her own place. 'Technically, you need to be homeless first,' he said. 'Stay friendly with Jimmy upstairs,' he advised. 'He might be able to influence his friends at council housing.'

But Jimmy only had eyes for her mam. He seemed more besotted than ever now she was living in the building. She often saw him hanging around the lobby, near the lifts. He'd feign surprise when he 'bumped' into Mo, but he was a terrible actor, totally unconvincing.

'Uncle Al thinks you might be able to help me get a flat,' she said to him one day when she came in with the shopping.

He shook his head. 'It's not that easy any more. There's a new supervisor,' he told her. 'How's yer mam doing? I haven't seen her for a couple of days.'

Aside from Al and Jimmy, there was no one to turn to. She tried to feel grateful that she and her boy would at least have a roof over their heads. Jami's mam said that the baby would fit around her life, and studies. 'She says you'll be OK until he starts crawling, which gives you six months, maybe eight,' Jami said.

Mo went on urging her to give him up for adoption. 'What sort of mam can you be to a bairn when you're seventeen years old and you haven't a pot to piss in?' she kept saying. 'You've no daddy to pay the bills and yer free babysitter died in June. You'll end up hating the bairn and wanting to kill it. I know. I've been there.'

Kelly usually managed to keep calm no matter what Mo said. She'd find a spot on the wall to stare at and only half-hear what she was saying. But sometimes it wasn't possible to block her out. 'I won't!' she snapped. 'I'm not like you. I'd never hate my own bairn.'

102

'You would, if it turned into a grumpy, pregnant lump of mush, living under your roof and cramping your frigging style!' Mo yelled back.

Style? she thought. That's a joke. And it's not because I'm pregnant. You've always hated me.

'First chance I get to move out, I will,' she said as calmly as she could.

She went to East End Library and took out two books on pregnancy. The bairn was the size of a pineapple now; she had seven weeks to go, maybe more if he came late. Walking home – waddling, more like – she went past a junk shop and saw a solid wooden cot in the window. She imagined a baby lying inside it on a soft white sheet, gurgling and moving its little arms around. Sweet and safe and sound.

Inside the shop, she asked how much the cot was. 'Fifteen pounds,' said the woman sitting behind the cash counter. 'It's a good one,' she added. 'And it looks like you might need something sturdy, love. You're getting big. How many weeks are you?'

'Thirty-three,' she said, feeling embarrassed about her size. Her appetite was massive. There was no denying she'd been eating for two – or three. She'd been through a mountain of crisps and chocolate bars in the past few weeks.

The woman broke into a grin. 'Snap,' she said, rising from her chair to reveal her own protruding belly. Only difference was, there was no fat on her body. Her limbs were slender and balletic; she almost looked as if she'd stuffed a cushion under her short pinafore dress for a laugh. 'I'm Zoe. Which hospital are you at?'

Kelly instantly found it easy to talk to Zoe. On the surface, they had nothing in common. Zoe was ten years older than Kelly and married to Paul; she came from Wolverhampton and had only just moved north. But as they discussed hospitals and antenatal classes, aches, pains and swellings, Kelly felt a warmth and familiarity grow between them. So when Zoe nodded at her belly and asked, 'Is there a dad, love?' she didn't feel too awkward about shaking her head and saying, 'No, there isn't.'

Zoe leaned back in her chair and smiled. 'Well, it means you won't have to share the bab', doesn't it? You'll have him all to yourself. There'll be no bothersome man hovering over you, trying to interfere.'

Kelly struggled to hold back her thoughts about what might have been if Nana hadn't passed away. She bit her lip. She wanted to open up about her loss to Zoe, but couldn't bring herself to say the words. She was too worried about breaking down.

The shop was quiet, so Zoe made them a cup of tea and they went on chatting about insomnia and swollen ankles. Suddenly Zoe said, 'Why don't I ask Paul if he can deliver the cot to you at home later?'

'Are you sure?' Kelly never ceased to be amazed by the kindness of strangers. 'I need to pay for it first. Is there a cashpoint around here?'

'That's fine, you can give the money to Paul when he delivers it,' Zoe said with a waft of her hand.

Kelly wrote down her address. She pictured

Paul saying, 'Edison House? Are you kidding? I'm not going there. Not in a million years.'

But evidently Paul thought himself a bit of a hard nut – or Zoe had pleaded with him – because he rang the buzzer at seven and brought the cot up in the lift. Luckily Mo was out and they didn't have to suffer her sweary commentary from the sofa as he carried it through into Kelly's bedroom. 'There you are, love,' he said, nudging it into a corner. He looked around the small room. 'Nice and cosy.' She thought she saw a trace of pity in his eyes. 'Just give us a tenner, Zoe said, and she's the boss.'

'Really?' Kelly said, not knowing what else to say. 'It's so kind of you to bring it here, an' all.'

She rifled around in her chest of drawers to find the twenty-pound note she'd stashed in a sock the day before. She found the sock, but it was empty; she shut her eyes in disbelief. Mo had been complaining about being brassic before she left for the library – she should have known she'd rummage through her room. Why hadn't she been more careful? 'Me mam's twocked it,' she blurted out. 'She's been going through my things again.'

Paul frowned. He shrugged and gave her a don't-know look, a not-my-problem look. She felt her cheeks heat up with shame.

'Do you mind waiting a couple of minutes?' she said. 'I'll pop upstairs and get a tenner from our neighbour.'

He glanced at his watch. 'Maybe you could drop it in to the shop on Monday?' he suggested. She could tell he didn't trust her now. Why would he? She could easily be lying.

'I'll just go up and see if Jimmy's there,' she said. 'You could wait – or come with me?'

He shifted from one foot to the other. 'Nah, look … I'll go. Bring it to the shop sometime.'

'Please!' she begged. 'You've been so kind. I don't want Zoe to think … anything bad of me.'

But he wouldn't have it, and she wondered whether he thought she was trying to lead him into a trap – that he would follow her upstairs and get mugged and beaten by her boyfriend, have his car keys stolen. She couldn't blame him. Edison House looked like the kind of place where something like that might happen.

'I'll drop by the shop on Monday, then,' she said.

'Cool,' he replied, looking pissed off.

After he left, she went and got the money from Jimmy anyway. 'It's for me mam. She says she'll pay you back tomorrow,' she lied. 'I'll make sure she brings it up herself.'

He smiled and his eggy eyes shone. 'OK, love. Tell her to come at dinnertime. It'll be pan haggerty and kippers.'

'Right, I'll pass that message on to her.'

She wondered if he thought there was a cat in hell's chance of Mo appearing at his door for Sunday dinner. There were so many reasons why it wouldn't happen. First, Mo would have to know what time of the day it was. Second, she would have to be hungry at an actual mealtime. Third, she'd have to want to sit down with Jimmy and eat his food. Fourth, she'd have to be prepared to pay him back money that she didn't technically owe him – although, admittedly, he didn't know this last bit. Fifth, well, the reasons were endless. Basically, you had to wonder whether Jimmy wasn't a little bit demented even to suggest it.

Mo got home at nine with two blokes in tow. 'I needed that twenty quid you stole out of my room to pay for a cot,' Kelly told her. 'So I borrowed it off Jimmy and now you owe him.'

Mo turned to her mates. 'This is what I have to live with!' She turned back to Kelly. 'Fuck right off, I don't have a clue what you're talking about.'

Kelly went to her bedroom and locked herself in with three packets of Wotsits, a bumper bag of fruit jellies and the two library books about pregnancy. Halfway through reading a section about nutrition, she dozed off.

She woke up to the sound of someone knocking on her door. A sudden blast of music filled her ears. Then it went quiet. There was more knocking. The music started up again, the thumping chords of 'Eye Of The Tiger', punching holes through her drowsiness.

'Leave me alone, I'm trying to sleep,' she called out.

She heard a whiny male voice complain, 'She won't let me in! Says she's tryin' to sleep.'

'She's no right to have a lock on her door,' Mo squawked. She sounded dead drunk. 'This is my flat now. I say who goes where and who doesn't, not Missy Tight-arse.'

Kelly grasped a pillow and hugged it. It would be unbearable to live without the lock on her door. She prayed that Mo hadn't decided to rip it out.

'I could knock it down for you, easy,' a deep

voice said.

'I bet you could,' Mo laughed. 'But why do you want to go in there, you wazzock? It's not Bluebeard's dungeon. It's just a fat beached whale sobbing into her pillow.'

'I'm curious,' said the whiny voice. 'Locked doors bring out my nosy side.'

'Well, we could smoke her out,' Mo suggested. 'There's nothing the bairn hates more than the smell of tabs.'

Kelly heard the click of a lighter. The sickly sweet scent of marijuana curled its way over to her bed – they were blowing it through the cracks in the door. She hugged the pillow tighter and tried to picture Nana sitting on her bed. 'Ignore them, love,' Nana would say. 'They can't hurt you. I won't let them. And don't worry about the smoke. Babies have thrived in far worse conditions. It's nothing to the smog we had to brave in the fifties.'

The knocking started up again. 'I'm fooking just gonna kick the door in,' said the man with the deep voice.

'You pay for the damage if you do,' Mo warned him, but she wasn't telling him not to.

Kelly heard a loud thud, followed by the sickening sound of splintering wood. She shrank against the back wall of her room and curled herself into a ball, her arms clasped protectively around her belly. The door swung open and a hulking figure appeared in silhouette in the doorway. 'No problem, see?' he boasted.

'Oh, it's just a bedroom with a bed and a hump of flesh in it,' a voice said behind him.

'What did I tell ya?' Mo screeched.

Drunken laughter filled the air.

'Mmm, nice cot!' said the whiny voice. A gangly figure pushed past the hulking silhouette. 'I could do with a sleep.' He launched himself into the cot, flipped himself over and landed heavily on the thin mattress, where he lay on his back with his legs in the air, making goo-goo noises.

In the semi darkness, Kelly stared him in horror. What if her little boy had been sleeping there? He would have been squashed and likely killed.

It's not safe here, she thought. I have to get away, now, for the sake of my baby.

8

August and September 1995, Byker, Newcastle

Kelly ripped three tissues from the box on her lap in quick succession, crushed them and pressed them against her eyes. 'I'm too young to be a mam,' she told the social worker. 'I'm seventeen.' She swallowed hard. 'There's no daddy and I've no money or any idea of how to look after a bairn. You need to live first, don't you? It's no good if you're still a bairn yourself.'

The social worker's name was Helen. She nodded sympathetically and pushed her glasses up the bridge of her nose.

'I wanted to get away from Byker and study to

become a travel rep,' Kelly went on. 'I was hoping to live abroad for a while. That was my dream.'

There was a long pause. Kelly stared at the only poster on the wall of the consulting room. It showed two hands – one small, one large – fingers touching.

'Did your dream include having children?' Helen asked.

She started to cry. 'Not now,' she said. 'I wasn't going to make the mistake me mam made in having me so young. But I was halfway gone when I found out I was pregnant. It was too late for an abortion.' She gave Helen a pleading look. 'Still, I might have done it anyway, you know, if me nana hadn't said not to. I mean, the daddy...' She faltered.

She tried again. 'You see, the father...' But she couldn't say it. She couldn't say that her baby's daddy was a rapist. 'There isn't a father,' she said finally.

'You won't be naming him on the birth certificate?' Helen asked.

'I can't, I don't know his name,' she mumbled.

Helen wrote something on a piece of paper. 'And now you're thinking about having your baby adopted,' she said.

It wasn't a question. It was a statement, and she could simply have said yes, I am. But she wanted to explain.

'I was going to keep him. Nana said we'd work it out. She was going to scale down her hours at C&A and look after him so that I could study. She talked me into it, really. I think they would have given me an abortion at the hospital, but I

110

already felt so bad...'

'About being pregnant?'

She looked at the floor. She still couldn't say it. 'I s'pose,' she replied. 'Then I found out it was a boy and felt him moving inside me.' She brightened a fraction. 'He started to become real. It changed how I felt about him, no matter how he was...'

Helen sat forward. She turned her head, as if straining to hear the next word. 'No matter how he was...?' she echoed.

Kelly blinked. 'Nana said children are the greatest gift of all and it doesn't matter where they come from. And she was right, although it depends on the circumstances, I'd say. Anyway, I went along with it. I started to think about my bairn and all the things I could do for him. I used to lie awake at night thinking about him, and after a bit I began to look forward to having him...'

It was painful to remember how happy those imaginings had been. It was all there in her mind: dressing the baby in soft, warm clothes; giving him milk and rusk biscuits; bathing him, singing to him, tickling and comforting him and teaching him how to walk and talk. She'd pictured his tiny fingers and little smiling mouth, imagined him gurgling and crying and looking up at her with adoring eyes.

'And ... I prayed to God I would be a good mam to him,' she said. 'The sort of mam he could depend on, like my nana was to me, even though she wasn't my mam. And I don't even believe in God, but I did believe for a few weeks, as I watched my belly grow and I thought about my baby. Maybe this is God's plan for me, I thought. Maybe things will work out, with Nana by my side. She said the bairn was a blessing, a silver lining.'

She paused, before going on. 'But then everything crashed,' she said, 'and I realised there is no God, just an evil being up there stamping around on people's lives. And I didn't know why I was stupid enough to hope that things would turn out OK. Just OK, mind, not fantastic or anything – I wasn't expecting miracles.' Her voice trailed off and she stared at the floor again. 'But of course things weren't going to be OK. Not for me, anyway.'

'Did something happen?' Helen asked.

Her shoulders crumpled. 'Nana had a stroke,' she mumbled. 'She passed.' She ripped some more tissues out of the box and pressed them against her eyes.

'Oh. That must have been very hard,' Helen said, with genuine feeling in her voice.

'It changed everything,' Kelly said. 'Overnight.' She frowned. 'And you know what? I hate God for doing it. For taking her so young, when me and the baby needed her, and she had so many friends, and we all miss her so much. It wasn't fair. Why did He do that to me? To Nana?'

Helen clasped her hands together. 'Is your mother around?' she asked gently. 'Can she offer any help or support with bringing up a baby?'

Kelly looked at her suspiciously. 'You're joking, aren't you? She drinks Special Brew when she gets up of a morning and rolls her eyes and calls me a silly fucker every time I say something. She's the one that keeps telling me to have him adopted.'

'And is it what *you* want?' Helen said. 'Really? I ask, because it's possible to arrange to have him taken into care until such a time as you feel you're able to look after him. We do everything we can to keep families together.'

Kelly gave her a defiant look. 'I've thought about this a lot in the past few weeks,' she said, her lower lip trembling. 'I've thought about the life I want for my bairn and the actual life I can give him. I want him to have a normal home, with a mam and a dad, lots of toys and a garden to play in, and maybe a swing or a climbing frame. I want him to have a happy childhood, a smart school uniform, a gang of friends and holidays by the sea, building sandcastles.

'I want my bairn to have everything I didn't have when I was young. But I've no chance of giving any of it to him, even if I get away from me mam. And I tried that – I went to the housing people a few weeks back and after a lot of hassle they offered me a flat on the seventeenth floor of Bell House. But everyone knows those flats are that damp and clammy they've got mushrooms growing under the floorboards. All the kids who live there have coughs and asthma – even me mam said I'd be mad to go there, and she wants shot of me. So I made up my mind and I'm not changing it. I want my boy to go to a safe, warm home, where he's loved and wanted.'

'You sound very sure,' Helen said.

'I am.'

The words lingered in the air. I'm sure, I'm sure, I'm sure, Kelly told herself, inwardly battling a swarm of doubts and fears.

The silence in the room began to feel oppressive. 'I don't want to give him up,' she burst out suddenly. 'I don't even know if I'll be able to let him go when the time comes. But I have to keep reminding myself that I'm doing it for love.' She covered her eyes with her hands. 'I feel I know him already, you see. I've given him a name and he's a proper character – I can tell by the way he bounces around in here all day.' She tapped her belly. 'Do you think it's possible? To know someone who hasn't been born? To love him?'

Helen smiled. 'A mother's bond is very strong,' she said.

'I think it must be,' Kelly said miserably. 'Because I love him so much.' She clenched her fists. 'So, I want to ... have him ... taken in...' she went on, struggling to get the words out, '...by a couple who live in a nice house in a nice street, who can't have their own children.'

She pulled herself up in her chair and raised her chin. 'By a couple who are desperate for a bairn, and they'll love him and care for him and give him all the best things in life,' she said. 'My boy, my baby Ross.' She looked at Helen through the blur of her tears and gave a determined sniff. 'So that's why I'm here. To do the right thing by him.'

The contractions came two weeks early, at the beginning of September. Pain wrapped around Kelly like an All Star wrestler trying to squeeze her to death. Her instinct was to dig a hole for herself in the corner of her bedroom, line it with pillows, throw a duvet on top and hide. Instead she left a message for Helen and called the hospital to say that she was coming in. She ordered a taxi and went through her hospital bag, which was a present from Jami and had a cute picture of kittens on the side. Inside it were her pyjamas, trackie, some underwear and a novel about teenage girls living rough in London. She added her toothbrush and wash bag.

'He's in the breech position, sunshine,' said Sally, the midwife on the maternity ward after she'd examined her. 'We'll have to proceed *pretty* carefully.'

The next contraction gripped her. They were coming every five minutes now. She gasped. An arrow of pain shot across her back and the low ache in her pelvis exploded into cramping, searing shards. Her knees buckled. Her whole body shuddered. She struggled to stay on her feet.

'I can't have a Caesarean,' she insisted, as she clung on to a chair back for support. 'I need to leave here and forget, without a scar to remind me.'

'We'll do our best, love,' Sally said. 'Keep breathing. You're doing very well.'

It was just the beginning.

An hour later, Jami arrived, carrying a large bag of grapes and two bars of Dairy Milk. 'I can't even look at food,' Kelly told her. 'I feel that sick you could put a pistol to my head and I still couldn't eat a thing.'

So Jami fed herself chocolate with her left hand while Kelly squeezed her right. They walked up and down the ward a hundred times. 'Can you keep still for a minute?' Jami asked.

'I can't,' Kelly said. 'It doesn't hurt so much if

I move.'

Hours passed, then more hours, and the pain kept up its onslaught. Jami went home for the night. A doctor came and tried to turn the baby into the birth position, manually. It was agony. He went away, saying never mind, it rarely works at this late stage, but still, it was worth a try.

Get lost, she thought. I hate you.

In the morning, Jami returned with two magazines and her maths homework.

Uncle Al arrived some time afterwards. Kelly squeezed his hand and looked at him with frightened eyes. He stared back at her helplessly. They were both thinking of Nana. Jami finished her homework and went off to school.

The hours turned into days – maybe months, years, even. Time swirled around her. She was the eye of the storm. All she wanted to do was push, but Marie, the midwife who was now in charge, said she mustn't. She had to wait, resist, hold off and breathe and breathe. Doctors came and went. They kept saying well done and keep going. Well done for enduring torture. Keep going through more and more pain.

She was a train without a piston, wanting to push, push, push. She longed for that moment of pushing. It would be better than seeing daylight again after years locked in a dungeon, better than eating ice cream in the desert when you were dying of heat and thirst. But when Marie finally said, 'You've reached ten centimetres. Let's try a push,' – and she did – it didn't bring the relief she'd been hoping for. Instead, her tender pelvic bone felt as if it was cracking in two. She heard her screams rip though the air, knives flying out of her heart.

She was dying – she knew it – but no one heard her cries for help.

Except Jami, outside the room, who was insisting, 'She doesn't sound OK to me. Can I go in and be with her?'

'Not just now, love,' said a voice. 'Give it a minute or two.'

A minute, a month or a millennium of pain – none of the nurses cared.

'She's my mate and she's in trouble. I'm going in,' Jami said.

'Wait, love! You can't. It could harm her and the baby.'

'Jami!' Kelly called frantically.

'Here he comes, the little footling breech,' Marie announced with a chuckle.

I'll kill you, Kelly thought.

If she didn't die of pain first, she would smash the teeth out of Marie's chuckling mouth. Nasty, smug cow – what was there to smile about? 'I hate you!' she shouted – and something slid out of her, all tangled up in cord and covered in mush and gunk.

I meant the midwife, she thought. Not the baby.

She stared in bewilderment as Marie fiddled around in the mess, gathered it up and took it away. The pain subsided. Finding she could move again, she dragged herself up onto the bed and lay on her side, breathing heavily. Thinking, Fuck, oh, fuck, oh, fucking hell.

Two more midwives came into the delivery room. There was a flurry and a hushed confab.

The only words she picked out were, '...hold it for an hour...' and, '...not sure what the instructions are...'

Was there a baby? That slippery lump of blood and mess – was that it? Misshapen, malformed, like something out of a horror movie? Where was it now?

A sense of detachment suffused her, as if a cool wind had swept through her brain and blown away her feelings. Maybe she'd dreamt it. Maybe there wasn't a baby, after all.

She watched numbly as Marie walked over to her, carrying a bundle of pale purple blankets. Suddenly the midwife loomed above her, as though she'd jumped forward through time and space. She took her right arm and shaped it into a crook, then placed the bundle onto it. Kelly glanced down and saw a tiny, red, wrinkled face, flecked with yellow dust. This was baby Ross. Here he was. She felt nothing.

Time passed.

'Hiya.' Jami was at her side. 'Look at him!' she said. 'So diddy. You all right now?'

'Yeah,' Kelly said. 'Hold him?'

'OK.' Jami went to take him from her.

Marie intervened. 'You've washed your hands?' Jami nodded. She lifted the bundle from Kelly and gently positioned it on Jami's arm.

Jami stared down at the baby. 'Sure you're all right, Kel?' she asked. 'You were screaming like a crazy woman.'

'It was the pain,' Kelly said dully.

'Are you OK, now, though?'

'Yeah, why do you keep asking?'

'You looked spaced.'

'How long have I been here?'

'Ages, nearly three days.'

'What? I need to go.'

'You coming to ours?'

'I'll go home first.'

'You're not going anywhere yet, young lady,' Marie said. She turned and looked directly at Jami. 'But *you* are. I suggest you go home and wait for a call from your mate here. We're not finished, not by a country mile.'

Jami lowered her head. She hated being bossed around.

After Jami left, the hours passed in a blur. Kelly went through the motions of whatever she was asked to do: she held the bundle and gave it back again. She expelled the placenta, someone stitched her up. She rested for a few minutes, or a fortnight – it was impossible to tell. She woke up feeling like a robot and took the baby again. She held it stiffly, in a trance, waiting.

Eventually some people arrived. Helen, the social worker, was among them. She came into the room, shut the door and sat on the bed. She talked to Kelly about how she was free to change her mind about the adoption, whether it was today, next week or in a few months' time. 'You won't be giving your formal agreement for at least six weeks,' she reminded her. 'Then it's another three months until the adoption order can be granted, so there's plenty of time to think it over.'

'We've already talked about it,' Kelly said. 'I want him to go to his family today.'

'That's fine,' Helen said. 'Just let me know when

you're ready. There's no hurry, by the way.'

She got out of bed. Her limbs felt heavy. 'I'm ready to go,' she said.

Helen gave her a puzzled smile. 'I mean, when you're ready to say goodbye to your baby. We don't mind you having more time with him. We don't want to rush you.'

'It's OK.' Kelly shook her head. 'I don't know,' she admitted. She felt frozen. 'I guess it's now or never,' she added, without any sense of what now or never might mean. She signed some forms and held the bundle again.

The baby's little eyes opened and he stared at her intently. You can't let me go, he seemed to be saying. You're mine. I'm yours. You can't break the bond.

She stared flatly back at him, and then Helen took him away.

Jami's mam had said she could stay at theirs for a few days after the baby was born. First, though, she needed to go home and pick up her stuff. Although it wasn't home any more, she realised, as the front door swung open. It was Mo's place now. The flat that Nana had lovingly furnished, with bits and pieces she'd saved up for and paid for by instalments, had all but disappeared under a layer of Mo's trash and dirt. There was a crack in the veneer side table; the framed pictures had been taken down; half the carpet had been ripped up; Nana's best glasses had been smashed. The place was returning to its concrete boxiness, its basic council flat layout, with bare, flimsy walls and falling-off fixtures and fittings. There was nothing stylish about it any more, no pride in it. It was a functional apartment again, not a home.

She took all of this in after her three days in the hospital, but it didn't touch her. She didn't care. She went to her room and lay down. Something was wrong with her, she knew. She had just had a baby and given it away, but she only felt soreness and tiredness. Emotionally, there was nothing. Her thoughts were moving at a snail's pace. The bed seemed to sway beneath her and she noticed a dark shadow falling over her, like a net.

She didn't have the energy to pack another bag. Jami's house seemed a thousand miles away, a journey full of hazards and obstacles. Roads. Traffic. Noise. She couldn't face any of them. The idea of making a cup of tea exhausted her. She didn't even have it in her to undress before she got into bed – it was enough of an effort to haul herself under the bedcovers.

She fell asleep, surrounded by darkness.

She didn't go to Jami's, not the next day or the one after. There was no particular reason, apart from dullness and a lack of energy. She wanted to feel something. But no feelings would come.

She tried to describe the emptiness on the phone to Jami, who said, 'But me mam's made up a bed for you and everything.'

Jami's mam had gone to a lot of effort, but Kelly couldn't drag herself over there.

'I need to rest, I think. There's been a lot of bleeding. I'll see you back at school.'

'You could have rested here,' Jami said. She sounded put out.

Kelly didn't care. Nothing stirred her. Nothing

121

made a difference. Someone could have thumped on the front door and yelled, 'It's the end of the world!' and she would have shrugged as if to say, So what? Or they could have presented her with a first-class plane ticket to the Bahamas and a top travel job on Paradise Island – and still she would have padded back into her bedroom and stared at the ceiling. The feeling was the same, whatever happened – whether Mo grabbed her, shook her and told her to, 'Snap out of it, you silly cow!' or ignored her while she partied with her mates all night.

Her days passed lifelessly. Weeks went by. The past was vague and hazy. Did it happen? she wondered. Was I pregnant? Was I raped? Did I have a baby? Nothing seemed real – not the now, not the then.

But it must have been real because two social workers came round and she signed an agreement form to start the adoption process for baby Ross. 'Are you getting back on your feet again now?' Helen asked her.

'Yes, I'm getting back on my feet now,' she echoed obediently.

'This place could do with a tidy, perhaps,' Helen ventured.

She looked around the lounge. There were old teacups on the coffee table and ring stains where other cups had been. There were tea towels and discarded clothes on the floor, and crumbs every-where, and a broken dinner plate. It was a right mess, she realised, although she hadn't noticed it earlier. 'Yes, it could do with a tidy–' she started to parrot.

'Feck off, ya bloody do-gooders!' Mo called out from her bedroom. She came into the lounge wearing her dressing gown. 'Shoo!' she screeched. 'You've got what you came for. Now leave us the feck alone.'

Helen looked at her watch. 'Look, we've got another appointment,' she said, standing up hurriedly. 'I'll give you a call in about a week, Kelly. See how you're doing. OK?'

Kelly nodded. She didn't care. There was something wrong with her, but Helen didn't seem to have noticed. Too busy, she guessed. Not bothered.

Once a week, she left the flat to go shopping, but seemed to have lost her head for totting up discounts in the supermarket. Sometimes she came home with just a packet of cornflakes and a pear, forgetting everything else on her list. She stopped washing her bedclothes and when she got into bed her sheets felt slightly shiny, filmed with sweat and grime. On good days, she took them to the launderette and sat and watched them slosh around in the machine. Then she'd lug them home wet and hang them around her room, where they dampened the air and took days to dry.

She didn't study, didn't go to school. She couldn't remember why she'd ever been drawn to read books. She watched TV, but favourites like *Corrie* had lost their appeal. She could just as well have been down the launderette, watching her washing go round, she thought. Heartbreak, death, deceit on TV: it was all the same to her. The only thing that caused her pain was her inability to feel. She hated the deadness inside her. She was desperate to feel normal again.

Coming back from the shops one day, she walked into the flat to find a bloke in the kitchen, standing on a chair, holding a screwdriver. Recognising him as one of Mo's mates, she turned around and headed towards her bedroom. 'Aren't you going to make me a cup of tea?' he called after her. She turned back. His blue eyes were twinkling. 'I've just fixed yer mam's cupboard door.'

She stepped obediently back into the kitchen. 'Have you?' she said, and put the kettle on.

'I'm very handy with a screwdriver,' he told her, as she made his tea. 'I was a talented sparkie back in the day. Could have had my own business and people working for me, but I didn't want the responsibility. I was young and just wanted to have fun. I'd probably be living in a house with an electric gate now if I'd stuck to it.' He sighed. 'That's life. You make your choices.'

'What do you do now?' she asked, out of politeness.

He gave her a wink. 'This and that.'

She wondered why he didn't just go back to being an electrician, if it was so well paid. Perhaps it wasn't that simple. She put his mug of tea on the table and turned to leave.

'Kelly, isn't it?' he said, lighting a tab. 'You're Mo's bairn. She says you never go out, never have any fun. Is that right?'

She stared at the floor.

'What's wrong with you?' he asked, not unkindly. 'When I was your age, I didn't stop. Now, you're a good-looking lass – well, not bad, anyway – why don't you get out there and have a laugh with your friends?'

She guessed he didn't know about the baby. 'I don't know,' she faltered. 'Life doesn't feel real at the moment. I'm not myself.'

'Well, why didn't you say so?' he said, feeling around in the pockets of his jeans. 'The name's Bazza, if you're wondering. I think I've got something that will help.'

'Help?' she said.

He took a tiny envelope out of his wallet, opened it, tipped some white powder onto the kitchen counter and used his bank card to divide it into lines. He rolled up a five-pound note and held it out to her. 'Try this,' he said.

She stared at the note. 'But I don't...' she started saying. She shook her head.

'You look awful, love. Believe me, this will make you feel better.'

This will make you feel better. The words encircled her like a spell. She was desperate to feel better. Bazza showed her how to press her finger against one nostril and inhale the powder through the other. Seconds later, the fog in her brain began to lift. Within a few minutes, she was feeling nearly normal again. Her brain felt like a machine starting up after a winter of idleness, an old car sputtering back to life or a boiler firing up.

'That's all it takes – a tiny bit of gear?' she said.

'Time for another,' he said cheerily, about fifteen minutes later.

After the second line, she was on the verge of phoning Jami to say sorry and could she come round? But then Bazza started dropping hints. If she wanted more, she would have to return the favour, 'blow for blow', as he laughingly called it. Dismayed, she made an excuse about having a doctor's appointment, got her coat and left the flat without ringing Jami.

Outside, although it was cold, she felt invigorated. Night was falling as she looked at the shapes of the world: gnarly tree branches against the darkening sky; towering blocks of flats crowned by fluffy cloud wigs; aeroplanes arcing through the atmosphere; a helicopter hovering over the estate. She had been stuck in the flat for too long, she thought. It was time to get back out, into the world, into life.

But then her heart began thumping, knocking, asking for something she couldn't give it, and she rushed back to the flat, half-hoping that Bazza would still be there. He wasn't. Instead, her mam was sitting on the sofa, alone, drinking cheap Spanish brandy. 'Have you been out?' Mo asked her. 'Did you see Bazza?'

The words came out in a torrent: 'He gave me some coke and it made me feel better than I've felt since in ages, but now my heartbeat's gone weird and my brain is swooping all over the place. I feel terrible. I don't know what's happening to me.'

Mo held out her glass. 'It's the comedown, you daft fucker,' she said. 'Knock some of this back and you'll level out.'

Kelly swigged the brandy. Her heart slowed. Her paranoia started to dissolve. She slumped onto the sofa.

Mo took out a small paper envelope. 'Look at you. You're all over the place,' she said. 'Have some of this. It'll get you feeling normal again.'

9

25 September 1998, Byker, Newcastle

'The fucker's taken off with me last tenner!' Mo squawked. 'I knew I should never have trusted him, the dirty, scumbag junkie. How dare that minging lowlife come into my home and steal the last of me hard-earned money?'

Oh God. What is it now? Kelly thought, although it hardly mattered, because with Mo there was always something, a daily drama. Mostly, she had learnt to ignore her.

From her bedroom she heard the sound of something crashing to the floor – a box, or a body, even. 'Where the fuck is my breakfast coming from now, then?' Mo yelled. 'I need a drink! I need me brew.' There was another crash. 'Ooh, I'll kill him. I'll rip the skin off his body and eat it in front of his eyes. I'll bite off his nose and eat that too – you see if I don't. He won't ever be able to snort a line again. Just watch me.'

For God's sake, stop blathering! Kelly thought. She reached for the glass of water by her bed, but it was lying sideways, knocked over in the night, its contents long since spilled and soaked into the carpet. If she'd had the energy, she would have

127

gone to the kitchen to refill it, but her head felt that heavy she didn't think she could lift it more than an inch. As she fell back on the pillow, her brain seemed to sink into jelly, like a pickled medical specimen in a jar of gloopy preservative.

She wished Mo hadn't woken her up. She needed more sleep to get rid of her headache, otherwise the day ahead would be impossibly bleak. After a heavy night, the darkness always seemed thicker and blacker, the deadness deader – and she'd definitely overdone it the night before. One line too many, one drink too many, trying too hard to push the shadows away.

These last few weeks it had got so bad that she'd started to think about suicide again. Not if, but how – the best way to do it, where and when. She'd mulled over different ideas. How to get a gun and find the sweet spot at the back – or side – of her head. Whether to jump off a bridge against – or into – the wind. Which combination of booze and drugs would be gentlest? She was planning to go to the library and look it up.

Somebody who hadn't experienced it might think that feeling numb would be painless. But it wasn't, it was unbearable. And at some point, she knew, she would choose a way out. It might even be today. It was comforting to think of the torture ending soon.

Would she go to hell? She knew there were people who still saw it as a sin to take your own life. But they didn't understand how it felt to search for a glimmer of hope every morning. They didn't have lives that felt lifeless and joyless. They laughed and cried and loved – as she remembered doing, once upon a time. Only, it seemed so long ago, so distant, so achingly remote.

She stared up at her bedroom ceiling, thinking about Nana, about her baby. Beside her, Bern made a snuffling noise and flung an arm over her. He was a deep sleeper; Mo's rant hadn't even caused a flicker of wakefulness. But soon enough her mam would be marching in to try and rouse him. Mo reckoned she'd been clever matchmaking her daughter with one of her drug dealer mates. It brought the party home. It eased her supply route. Or so she'd thought.

In fact, to this day Bern hadn't broken his golden rule, which was never to deal on a promise. So Mo could beg, plead and spin every tale in the book about where she'd be getting her next wad from, but if she didn't have the cash up front, she didn't get the gear. Bern never wavered. It was cut and dried with him. And Mo couldn't shag him for it either, because he was going out with her daughter. Still, it didn't stop her trying.

Kelly wasn't sure how long she'd been seeing Bern, but thought it was probably about two years. They'd got together one evening when he'd come over with a tenner of skunk for Mo, and ended up staying to watch *Corrie.* Mo had been coming down off a mega bender that day. She kept calling to Kelly to come and meet Bern, but Kelly had kept to her room. Soon Mo had nodded off and Bern was left with no one to talk to.

When Bern had knocked on Kelly's bedroom door ten minutes later, she was sitting on her bed, staring into space. 'I'll be off then,' he said, unnecessarily.

129

'OK.' She barely glanced at him.

'Unless I can tempt you with a line,' he added, flicking his tawny fringe away from his eye.

An hour later, they were naked in her bed, and he was tapping joint ash into the dregs of her coffee mug. 'I'd like to get to know you,' he told her. 'I can see you're sad, but you're deep too and I like deep girls. Plus, I've got a thing for blue-eyed brunettes,' he added. 'You look like a girl from Paris I used to know.'

Bern was a far cry from what Nana would have called a catch, but he was kind to her, in his own quiet way, and that counted for a lot when you had no friends. His line of work added to the appeal, of course. His parka was a medicine cabinet of pills and powders that made her feel human again. And there was an oddball magnetism between them, too. She couldn't explain it, because if she'd seen him in the street she wouldn't even have noticed him, and their conversations were never about anything much more than what was on the telly. But he suited her, despite his hangdog eyes and small, stocky frame, his skin as white as salt – and apparently she suited him back, in a low-energy kind of way. In their separate clouds, of smoke and darkness, they watched daytime TV together. They were like companionable ghosts, she mused to herself – insubstantial, only ever half there.

In the evenings, Mo had her mates over, a rotating cycle of lowlifes. The volume changed, the bottles of spirits appeared, the drugs came out. Kelly was used to the rhythm of Mo's life now. She knew what to expect, and sometimes she joined in, because it was an escape, a dis-

130

traction that pulled her out from the shadows.

And so the months and years had passed in darkness. Missing Nana. Missing her baby. She turned over and lay facing the wall, trying to block out her thoughts.

Mo put the radio on. Robbie Williams was singing about the millennium, a year and three months too soon. 'It's 10.42 on Friday, the twenty-fifth of September,' the DJ cut in, 'and we all know what that means...' A tinny roar came out of the speaker. 'It's six hours and eighteen minutes until the weekend starts,' he yelled excitedly.

Oh God, it's my birthday, Kelly thought with a jolt. I'm twenty-one today.

Kelly got dressed, helped herself to a half-gram wrap from Bern's coat pocket and took the bus to Chester-le-Street, where she spent an hour sitting on a pew in the church where Nana's funeral had been held three years earlier. She didn't pray. It would have been a joke to pray. But she allowed the peace of the church to seep into her bones, and kept herself steady with the occasional finger dab of coke.

The sense of calm stayed with her on her way back to town. She got off the bus outside the hospital and made her way to Leazes Park, where she found a bench by the lake and sat down. Touched by a breeze, the leaves on the yellowing chestnut trees around the lake rustled and swished. The sky was a deep cobalt blue. The air smelt crisp.

A flock of Canada Geese flew overhead. If I hadn't been raped, she thought, as she watched them, I would have graduated from uni now. I'd have a job. I'd be leaving, flying away.

A sudden surge of anger swept through her. It scared her, because she hadn't experienced a feeling so strong for years.

How could anyone be that evil? she thought. Why did they pick on me? I didn't do anything to deserve it.

She put her head in her hands. Where's my baby? she thought. The pain was overpowering. She groped around her pocket for the wrap of coke, looking for a way to shut it down.

Moments later, she heard a familiar voice. 'It's Kelly, isn't it? I haven't seen you for a long time. What's wrong, love? Is there anything I can do to help?'

Looking up with a start, she saw Cathy, Michael Kirkpatrick's mother, standing next to a bicycle.

'Oh, I ... hi Cathy! Not really,' she said. She managed a weak smile and looked away shyly.

Cathy had a happy, healthy glow about her, as if she'd just come back from a holiday abroad. She propped her bike against the bench and sat down beside Kelly. 'Hope you don't mind, love. I won't stay long. But it's been a while, see, and it would be nice to catch up.'

'Yes...' A sob caught in Kelly's throat. She dug her nails into the palm of her hand.

'What's your news? Are you still living in Byker?' Cathy asked. 'With your mam?'

She nodded. 'I can't escape,' she whispered. 'That flat is like my coffin. It's like I died the day I had the baby, like I lay down and never got up.'

She saw a flash of shock, or horror, in Cathy's eyes. 'That sounds terribly bleak, love,' she said.

Her mouth drooped in sympathy and she touched Kelly's arm very lightly. 'But I wouldn't be a bit surprised if you've found it hard to pick yourself up, love. You were dealt some tough old cards – too many for a young lass like you – and they all came at once. I felt so sorry for you when your nana passed. We were all very sorry. And having to give away your baby, too. What terrible times, love. It's hard to imagine what you've been through.'

Kelly rubbed her eyes and leaned back on the bench. She could feel the slats through her coat. 'How's Michael?' she asked, changing the subject to give herself a moment to breathe.

'Michael? He's great. He's got his degree now and he's off into the world. He's digging wells for Voluntary Service Overseas, in India – and loving it, according to his letters. Not that we've had many, mind.' Cathy sighed. 'But that's boys for you.'

Kelly chewed her lip. 'India,' she echoed. She tried to picture it. 'Wow.'

'And what about you, love?' Cathy asked. She looked her up and down. 'There's nothing left of you! What's happened?'

Kelly shook her head. She couldn't bear to go into any more detail, couldn't bear to describe her life of hell. She shook her head again and looked down at her lap.

'I just want to put the past behind me,' she said eventually. 'I want to live again.' The words took her by surprise. They sounded ... positive.

'You need to get on and make a future for yourself,' Cathy agreed.

133

A door slammed shut in her mind. 'But I can't,' she said.

'Why, what's stopping you?'

'I'm trapped. I've got a ... drug problem.'

'You? Taking drugs? That beggars belief!' Cathy grimaced. 'You struck me as too sensible for that kind of thing.' She looked out at the lake for a few moments. 'Not that anyone could blame you for it, of course – not in your position, after all that's happened. But drugs aren't a solution, are they, love? I'm sure you know that by now. Have you thought about seeing someone, a drugs counsellor, maybe?' she asked. 'There's help out there. The council have started several new initiatives, I've heard.'

Kelly looked at her with pleading eyes. 'You don't understand. I need the drugs; I have to take them. I can't find any other way to feel normal. That's all they do – they help me feel just about OK, stop my mind from plunging into hell. Otherwise, I'm living in darkness. I can't do anything.'

Cathy frowned. 'But I think it's pretty simple, love. If you want to stop – if you want to move forward – you should speak to someone who knows about these things.'

'But–'

'I'll find out what's available, if you like. I'll make an appointment for you and come with you.'

'But I might not be able to leave the flat,' Kelly said. 'I get panic attacks and then I can't go anywhere.'

Cathy gave her a reassuring smile. 'You're here now, aren't you?'

'I know, but...' She didn't like to say that she

had only been able to go out after twocking a wrap of Bern's cocaine. It was shameful. Cathy would think she'd turned into a thieving druggie.

'Shall we give it a try?' Cathy pressed. 'You never know, it might make the world of difference.'

'I'm not sure. I'm scared...'

Cathy looked thoughtful. 'Well, it's up to you, love. You were the one who said you wanted to change things.' She rummaged in a cloth bag and found a pen and a scrap of paper. 'You know where I live. Here's my phone number. If you need my help, give me a ring.'

Kelly stuffed the piece of paper in her coat pocket. 'Why are you being so kind to me?'

'You're a great girl,' Cathy said simply. 'I'd hate to see you waste your life away.' She put her arm around Kelly. 'Now, listen to what I'm about to say: it's important. *There is always a way out.* You just have to take the first step.'

'OK.' Kelly's eyes filled with tears. 'It's so weird. I mean, I can't believe I bumped into you – today, of all days.'

'Is it a special occasion, then?' Cathy looked intrigued.

'Just ... my birthday,' Kelly mumbled.

Cathy's eyes lit up. 'Today? Oh, love!' She pulled Kelly close. 'You must have a guardian angel looking out for you up there in heaven.'

'A guardian angel?' She doubted it.

'And meanwhile, down here in toon, you've got me, love, and I'll do my best to help you.' Cathy gave her a squeeze. 'But you've also got to try to help yourself, Kelly. I can't get better for you.'

A few minutes later, as she watched Cathy

wheel her bike across the park and out of sight, Kelly wondered if she had been hallucinating. When she played back their conversation in her head, it seemed unreal and dreamlike. Had it actually happened?

She put her hand in her pocket and felt around for the scrap of paper Cathy had given her. Her fingers searched frantically through old bus tickets and sweet papers. Finally she found it, after emptying both pockets and sorting through the contents on her lap.

'Ring me,' the note said, above Cathy's name and number. 'You can do it.'

She stared up at the sky, looking out for birds. Could she? She wasn't so sure.

Kelly made the call on Monday morning, after a weekend spent silently praying to Nana for courage.

'Kelly, love!' Cathy said. 'I didn't know if I'd hear from you.'

They went to see her GP the following day. Dr Wingfield-with-the-posh-voice was full of concern. She diagnosed Kelly as having a chemical imbalance that had a probable link with post-natal illness, and prescribed a course of anti-depressants.

'When will I feel better?' Kelly asked, not really believing that she ever would.

'In about six weeks, hopefully,' Dr Wingfield replied. 'Try to hang on as best you can until then.' She added some anti-anxiety pills to the prescription.

On Wednesday, Cathy went with her to the drug

rehabilitation day centre behind the library, where she enrolled on a programme that required her to attend group therapy every other day from ten to two. 'Whatever happens, try and get here for your slot,' advised Maeve, one of the younger counsellors. 'Just getting here will kick-start your recovery.'

Kelly never missed a session, even if, most days, she needed a line of Bern's coke to be there on time. It was a crazy deception, but nobody seemed to notice, and the centre was a lifeline for her. She desperately needed somewhere to go, away from the flat, away from Mo. Although she didn't really identify with the other addicts on the programme – who took drugs to lose their inhibitions and block out their feelings, who wrecked family weddings, danced on tables and got arrested – it helped her to be around people who were trying to change their lives, as she was. And she heard stories that made her upbringing seem like *The Waltons* by comparison, which made her feel less alone in the world.

When she passed the library, she still sometimes thought about slipping in to look up the best ways to commit suicide. But somehow she didn't get round to it, and then the darkness began to lift, two months after she'd started taking Dr Wingfield's pills. It was a gradual process, but there was a moment – she would never forget it – when she was out having a cup of tea and cake with Cathy, and she laughed. That's all it was, a simple laugh, but it was light as air, with nothing weighing it down, and in that moment she realised she was getting better.

'It's not you, it's me,' she told Bern, the following day. 'You've been a good mate, but I need to focus on getting out of here. Hopefully I'll be working a lot, and I'm giving up the gear. I want to live a clean life from now on.'

Bern took it on the chin. 'There's a silver lining,' he said, toking on one of his endless joints. 'I like you, Kelly, but I've had enough of your mam. She gets on my wick, mon, with all that shouting. I can easily do without her.'

Kelly bought a simple lock and a screwdriver from Nigel's Hardware and attached it to her bedroom door. She bought an old cricket bat from a market stall and told Mo that if anyone tried to force their way into her room at night, they'd get a crack round the head. She got a job at the Cream Tea Café in Grainger Street, working from eleven to four, and a second job at Pizza Crust in Heaton, starting at five. At weekends, she served canapés and white wine at private parties and functions organised by a company called Silvertree Events. She opened a bank account and slept with her chequebook and cash card under her pillow. Every night she had dreams about the baby she had given away.

At first, Mo didn't seem to notice the change in Kelly's schedule. When she did, she demanded a share of her earnings. Kelly compromised by putting spare change and the odd note in a beaker under the sink, which seemed to satisfy Mo, who no doubt thought she was getting one over on her daughter every time she emptied it. Kelly didn't care. She stayed away from the flat as much as she could, to avoid Mo's chaos. Her goal was to earn enough to get away from her for good. It was hard, though. The money went out as fast as it came in, because life was much more expensive the moment you stepped out into the world. Sitting on a sofa in your trackie all day didn't cost a lot, but now she had to buy new shoes, a coat, a black skirt, two white shirts and some essential make-up. She had her hair cut and stopped biting her nails.

Once she looked halfway decent, she started to put every spare penny towards saving up enough for a rental deposit on a flat. But however strictly she budgeted, she soon realised that it was going to take months. The landlords of some of the nicer flats wanted the equivalent of six weeks' rent as a deposit, plus four weeks' rent in advance. It was even more expensive because she didn't want to share.

'You know, it might be good for you to have someone else around. As long as they're nice,' Cathy said.

But Kelly wanted a flat to herself, because she was planning to fetch her baby out of care. He would be three now; he would have blown three candles out on his last birthday cake. What was a three-year-old like? All sweetness and squidge, smiles and dimples – she'd seen it in the little ones who toddled into the Cream Tea Café, hanging onto their mammies' hands, chubby little angels.

She longed for her son. She hated herself for letting him go. She wanted him back, as soon as possible.

'I don't understand,' Cathy said, looking

puzzled, when she confided in her. 'You gave him up for adoption, didn't you? I don't think it's a decision you can reverse.'

Kelly smiled. 'But I remember the social worker saying I could change my mind any time.'

'No, love, I don't think that can be right,' Cathy said. 'Not unless you've been getting regular updates from them. When did you last see a social worker?'

'I'm not sure. But I would have had to sign papers, wouldn't I? And I never signed a thing.'

'They didn't visit the flat? You didn't go to the office?'

'No,' she said. But her sense of certainty began to crumble. A memory scratched her brain, like a tiny kitten batting for attention. She frowned. 'I think they did come to the flat once. But it was years ago.'

Cathy looked at her sadly. 'Oh, love.' Her tone of voice said it all. Kelly's eyes filled with tears.

That night in bed, she went through it all again. If she'd been ill when she signed the papers, they wouldn't be valid, would they? Dr Wingfield had said she'd been suffering from serious depression, which was a mental illness. So she wouldn't have been fit to make decisions, would she? Especially not life-changing decisions like giving your baby up for adoption. Which meant she had a case for fetching him back, no question. Right?

She kept returning to the moment when she'd held him in the hospital, just before they had taken him away. She would never, ever, not as long as she lived, forget the way her baby had looked at her. His eyes had burnt words into her soul. Don't leave me. You're my mother. I'm yours.

He belonged with his mam – they belonged together – it was only natural, she thought. She bit into her fist to stop herself screaming it aloud. I want my bairn! I want my baby.

Kelly wasn't able to see Helen, who was 'on leave' for a few months, she was told. Instead she was given an appointment with Andy, a balding man of around thirty, who met her plea for the return of her bairn with barely disguised amusement. 'I'm sorry,' he said with a smirk, 'but are you saying that after coming to us when you were pregnant to arrange your child's adoption, and after signing the papers giving your legal consent to that adoption several months later, you are now trying to get your child back, *after three years?*'

'Yes, but I was ill when I signed the papers,' she insisted. 'I had post-natal depression and wasn't in a position to consent. Helen and the other social worker must have realised that. I was like a sleepwalker. I didn't know what I was doing.'

He sat back in his chair. 'Post-natal depression,' he mused. 'What *is* it?' It was almost as if he'd never heard of it before.

'Don't you know?' she asked.

He stroked his chin. 'I'm asking you to tell me what *you* think it is,' he said.

She swallowed nervously. She had expected sympathy, at the very least.

'It's not the same for everyone, but I know what it did to me,' she explained. 'It turned me into a ghost. I was totally lost, half dead, surrounded by fog. Everything was darkness. I couldn't see the

141

wood for the trees. My brain felt as if it had shut down. My memory was really patchy. Some days I wasn't sure if I'd even had a baby. It was the weirdest feeling. I can just about remember Helen coming to the flat, but I don't remember signing any papers. So I don't think I can be held responsible for my actions – that's what I'm saying. It doesn't matter if my baby was legally adopted or not, if I can prove that I wasn't in a fit state.'

'You think you can prove that?' His voice dripped with scorn. 'Were you medically diagnosed at the time?'

'Not at the time, but my GP says she's sure that's what was wrong with me. I've only recently gone on the anti-depressants, which is why it's taken me so long to make it here.'

'Oh, your GP says so,' he said dismissively. 'And she's prepared to stand up and swear this in a court of law? And you've got the money to fight this all the way?'

She nodded. 'Yes, I think she would, and I'm prepared to pay for a lawyer.'

She saw a flicker of surprise in his face. 'So you're actually serious about this?'

'Yes,' she said, gritting her teeth and glaring at him. I hate you, she thought. You're just like all the rest of them. She wanted to yell the place down, or leap across the desk and nut him. Something. Anything.

'Excuse me a moment,' he said, and he left the room. Five minutes later, he returned. 'I've just been having a word with my supervisor,' he explained – and she thought she heard a note of sincerity in his voice that hadn't been there before

142

– 'and she raised a very good point,' he went on, 'which was that, aside from the expense involved in a case like this, not to mention the upset it would cause to everyone concerned, would it be in the best interests of your child to take him away from the people he knows to be his mother and father, rightly or wrongly?'

She sat on her hands and looked at the floor, trying to pick apart his lengthy question. 'What do you mean? I'm his mam,' she said eventually. 'If he'd been mixed up at birth, wouldn't the authorities be legally responsible for returning the right bairn to the right mam? It's a similar situation, isn't it?'

'Because you were mixed up?' he said, reverting to the smirky tone he had used earlier.

'I was confused, because I was ill. I think it's called "diminished responsibility".'

He closed his eyes and shook his head, as if frustrated by her sheer ignorance. 'And I think you might have been watching too many detective dramas. That's not a term that would apply in this case. It just doesn't make sense.'

'It makes sense to me,' she said.

He snorted. 'But you're not a lawyer, are you?'

She pressed her lips together. 'I'd like to speak to your supervisor, please.'

'Really? Why?' he sneered.

She felt tears pricking her eyes. 'I just would. I don't think you understand anything about me.'

'Of course I do,' he said crossly. 'You're by no means the first person to regret a decision you made as a teenager. But there's nothing you can do about it, don't you understand? You think the

143

authorities would contemplate taking a legally adopted child away from a stable, happy home and placing it with a single mother who might change her mind about having him back at any moment?'

'I wouldn't change my mind!' she protested. 'I was ill, but I'm a lot better now. And I can support him.'

'Please don't raise your voice again,' he said coldly. 'Or you will be asked to leave.'

'Can I see your supervisor?' she asked.

'No,' he said. 'You can't.'

'You mean, not now – or ever?'

He took a deep breath. She was trying his patience. 'You can try and make an appointment with her if you go through the appropriate channels. But it might be a long wait. Her caseload is extremely full. Look, I would forget about–'

'I don't care what you'd do. You're a complete twat,' she said, standing up to leave. She was trembling with anger.

'Right, that's it,' he snapped. 'I will be reporting you for verbal abuse of a member of staff.'

She hesitated, tempted to tell him where to stick it. But her longing for her baby took over. 'Please help me!' she begged him, bursting into tears. 'I want my bairn back. You've got to believe me. I didn't mean to let him go. I was ill. My GP says so. And I'm totally clean now. My life is different ... please...'

He didn't react. He looked at his watch. 'This interview is now concluded,' he said. 'I won't report you this time, but I will tell you now that if you have a history of using drugs, you'd better just forget about taking this any further. I mean, you haven't a chance. Not a chance. It will be thrown out of court – if it even makes it that far, which I doubt – and will be a waste of your time and money, as well as everyone else's. I'm sorry.'

But she could tell by the thin-lipped expression on his face that he wasn't sorry at all.

10

Kelly got in from work, late one Thursday night, to find her bedroom had been turned upside down. Horrified, she dropped to the floor and sat there with her head in her hands. She knew immediately what it meant. Mo needed money. And pretty badly, judging by the state of her room. She'd even taken a knife to the mattress, to check if there was cash hidden within.

She thought back to one of the lessons she'd learnt at the day centre, which was that having a car crash for a mother didn't make you a car crash. She and her mam were separate people who made their own choices. So whatever Mo did had nothing to do with her – except, of course, in terms of the impact it had. She tried to reassure herself with this thought, but it didn't make her feel any better.

She spent the next two hours restoring order to her tiny bedroom. She tidied, hoovered and threw away handfuls of mattress stuffing. Then, just as she was getting into bed, she heard Mo come in –

and as usual there was someone with her. She looked at her watch. It was two a.m. She checked the lock on her door.

A few minutes later, she heard a fight erupt. It started with shouting, followed by banging, crashing and the sound of slaps against bare skin. 'Help!' she heard Mo scream. 'If you're there, Kelly, come quickly. He's gonna kill me!'

Pressed against the door, Kelly didn't move. She felt frozen with fear – and also confusion. How could she help? She didn't know how to fight. Did she even want to help? A huge part of her didn't care what happened to Mo. But if he killed Mo, would he come for her? Was she safer in her room? Was it better to come out?

She went on waiting, paralysed, thinking, If I could get to the phone to call the police, then it wouldn't be up to me any more.

She heard a movement outside her door. 'Don't kill me, please don't kill me,' Mo was whimpering. 'Let me go. I'll get your money, I swear it. On my daughter's life.'

Kelly held her breath. Her heart was pounding. So this was about money, which meant the heavy on the other side of the door could be someone really nasty, someone who wouldn't think twice about murder. She'd heard stories about loan sharks who tortured people who didn't pay them. They pulled off fingernails and stubbed fags out on their skin. She felt cold with fear. What should she do? Could she run for it? Would she get away? She cursed herself for not trying to leg it earlier. She would have had a better chance then. Now, she was trapped. She edged over to her wardrobe and silently took out the cricket bat.

'Please don't, you're hurting me,' she heard Mo beg pathetically. 'If you're listening, Kelly, don't try anything silly. He's got a knife to me throat.'

Kelly unlocked her door and came out of her bedroom. A lad with a buzz cut and spotty cheeks was standing behind Mo. He had her arms in a lock behind her back and was holding a long knife under her chin. Mo looked terrified, her mascara smeared, her hair uncombed and straggly, her mouth gaping like a fish's.

'How much?' Kelly asked. There was a tremor in her voice.

'Two ton,' the lad said.

'Will you take a hundred? That's all I can get out in one day.'

He nodded. 'I'll drive you to the cashpoint.'

'No,' she said. 'I'm not getting in your car. I don't know you. I'll get a taxi. You can follow.'

When she got back to the flat, it was four a.m. Mo was crashed out on the sofa, snoring. I've got to get out of here, she thought. I can't live with this madness any more.

The next day, she begged Cathy if she could move in with her temporarily. Cathy looked unsure. 'Well, maybe for a few days,' she said. 'Let's say a week, shall we? I wish I could offer you somewhere more permanent, but we've only got Michael's room and I'm expecting him back in a few weeks.'

'A week would be enough,' she said, relief flooding over her. 'I just need a safe place to think about what I'm going to do.'

A week was all it took for her to understand once

and for all what she had missed out on in her life. There was so much love in the Kirkpatrick home. There was also peace. Nothing ever seemed to happen, or if it did, it happened happily, with banter and joyful shrieking. The house was quiet by ten-thirty at night. It sprang to life at seven in the morning. Breakfast time was jaunty and full of hope for the day. Tea was a meal spent chatting about how things had gone. The girls took mugs of hot chocolate up to their rooms after *Corrie*, did their homework and came down again for a chat before bed. They talked about their friends and school projects, mainly – as well as Michael, their adored older brother, of course.

This is the life I wanted for my bairn, Kelly re-called. She could almost forgive herself for giving him up for adoption. She had only wanted the best for him.

She found it hard to sleep the night before she was due to go back to Byker. She desperately wanted to ask Cathy if she could stay a few more days, even though they had agreed to a week. Cathy hadn't mentioned her departure. She hadn't said, 'Well, tonight's your last night,' or, 'Have you thought about what you're going to do when you get back to your mam's?' Yet she knew that Cathy would expect her to stick by the agreement. It had been very specific.

'It's really hard to go,' she said the following morning, as Cathy busied herself with last-minute tidying before she hurried off to her part-time office job. It was a shameless hint, but she couldn't help herself.

Cathy turned from the pile of books and maga-

148

zines she was stacking and stretched out her arms. 'Oh, love!' she said, giving Kelly a hug. 'It's been great having you – I hope it's been helpful in sorting your head out. Ring me in a couple of days? And we'll arrange to get together for one of our iced bun and tea sessions in town.'

Cathy was kindness itself, but Kelly couldn't help feeling rejected. She bit back the tears, hoping Cathy wouldn't sense how unwanted she felt. 'Thank you,' she said. 'I'm more grateful than you could ever imagine.'

'Our pleasure,' Cathy said. 'I know you'll find a way out of your predicament, love. Best of luck.'

She cried for the rest of the day, on and off, at the unfairness of life. When she got back to the flat, she could hear Mo shagging someone in her – in Nana's – bedroom. She smashed her hands over her ears and went straight to bed.

In the morning, she walked into the kitchen to find a naked man making coffee. 'All right, lass,' he said. It was the lad with the buzz cut who'd threatened her mam with a knife. She turned and went back to her bedroom.

Moments later, she heard Mo guffawing with laughter. She shook her head in disgust and started to cry. So the knife scene had been a set up, just another of Mo's schemes to get hold of drug money. What a mug she'd been, what an idiot.

She got dressed and grabbed her coat. She wasn't due at work for another couple of hours, but she just had to get out of the flat. On her way out, she saw one of her hair bobbles on the lounge floor and, stooping to pick it up, noticed a brown envelope peeping out from under the sofa. Something prompted her – curiosity, perhaps, or a nudge from above – to turn it over and see who it was addressed to. It was a surprise to see her name and address printed in black letters, and above them, the words, 'This is not a circular.'

Her heart started beating faster. Was it from social services? Something about the bairn? She stuffed it into her bag and hurried out of the flat.

On the bus into work, she opened the envelope with trembling hands and unfolded the piece of paper inside. It wasn't from the council. It was a letter informing her that she had won a sum of money on her Premium Bonds – bonds that had been purchased for her by Mrs Molly Ross. Nana. There was a number to call.

In a daze, she got off the bus at the next stop and went into a phone box. She'd had no idea that Nana had bought her some Premium Bonds. The phone box stank of piss and the receiver had been hacked off. She had to walk half a mile to find a phone that worked.

She rang the number that was printed on the letter. A woman answered. Kelly reeled off her name, date of birth and address. Moments later, the woman told her that she was the lucky winner of a twenty-five-thousand-pound prize.

'Congratulations!' she said. 'How would you like to receive the money, by cheque, or in person?'

PART TWO

11

21 January 1999, Chester-le-Street,
County Durham

She changed her name on the journey to Chester-le-Street and was Kathryn Blake when she got off the train. It felt like the name of someone older and more responsible than anyone called Kelly Callan could ever be; it made her feel safer, more distant from Mo. As soon as she was sure it suited her, she applied to change it permanently and officially, by deed poll. It took nine weeks to process and send off for a passport. She did casual bar work to tide her over until she'd become completely new.

Through a lettings agency, she found an airy studio flat in a red brick Victorian block in the heart of town, paid a deposit and two months' advance rent. She decided to stay in Chester-le-Street until the paperwork was finished. After that, she wasn't sure, but it didn't matter. The future was hers to decide, as and when.

Every morning brought a fresh sense of exhilaration. The flat felt like heaven and sometimes she had to pinch herself when she woke up to the silence and tranquillity of her own space. No doors slamming, no vicious effing and blinding, no scuzzy dishes piled up in the sink or cups rolling on the floor. No Mo, simple as that. Con-

153

sidering that she might never have found the brown envelope under her mam's sofa – considering how easily she could have missed it – she couldn't count her blessings often enough. At long, long last, she'd had a lucky break.

The flat was only part furnished, so she spent her weekends browsing antique and bric-a-brac shops in Durham, looking for things to make it more homely: a white bedside table; a blue rug for the lounge. She bought a second-hand 'cookbook for one' and taught herself to cook, dancing around the kitchen with the radio on loud while she experimented with soups and sauces. She ate her pasta at a table by the large window in the lounge, either staring at the trees and sky outside or watching *Corrie* on her brand new telly. On her days off, she went swimming at the leisure centre, to the cinema in Gateshead or did a section of the Heritage Trail across town.

There were moments of loneliness – it was natural, she told herself – and a great, gaping hole where her little boy should have been. Sometimes she had to fight the urge to ring someone from her old life, just for a chat: Cathy, Uncle Al or even Jami, with whom she'd lost touch years before. But the spectre of Mo always held her back, because if Mo ever found out where she was, or learned about her windfall, she'd be done for. All the nastiness and evil surrounding her mam would descend on her again. She couldn't risk it.

She had read somewhere that the past was another country, so she tried to think of herself as having emigrated into the future, taking nothing with her but the few remnants of Nana that she had packed into a bag when she'd popped back to Edison House for one final visit, while Mo was crashed out. Now, to keep herself busy, she accepted every bar and pub shift she was offered. She didn't have an urgent need for money, but her plan was to leave what remained of her Bonds win untouched until she used it to put a deposit on a flat, once she'd decided where to settle down. Or maybe she'd just blow the whole lot on a back-packing trip around the world. She could do anything she wanted, she told herself. The choice was hers. It felt like such a luxury.

The day her new passport arrived, she went for an afternoon reccy, looking for inspiration as to whether she should stay in Chester-le-Street or go elsewhere – searching for a sign from above, she thought wryly – because she was in two minds about what to do. She had chosen Chester-le-Street for its connection to Nana, and the feeling that it was a world away from Byker, even though it was just down the road. It was a friendly town, with a strong sense of community and lots of character. It felt relatively safe and she liked it – but was that enough? It was hard to know what else to take into account. Potential growth? GDP? She smiled to herself. She could barely remember all that stuff she had learned in geography.

Walking down Front Street, she saw a balloon in the distance, drifting above a line of trees, a ribbon trailing beneath it. Maybe it was sign she should cut loose and float free, she thought. She could go abroad if she liked. She could move to Spain and live in the sunshine. She tried to picture herself getting off the plane in Alicante,

155

not really knowing where to go next. Perhaps not. She wasn't ready to emigrate yet; she needed to get up a bit of courage for that. Going south was another option and there would be more job opportunities there, but ... London would probably feel just as foreign as the Costa del Sol, and no one would understand what she was saying there, either.

Maybe she didn't need a sign to help her decide, she thought. She was happy enough where she was, for the time being. She could always change her mind. She searched the sky for the lost balloon, but it had either bobbed out of sight or popped.

Settling down meant getting a steady job, but there wasn't much on offer at the Job Centre. 'I've had enough of bar and restaurant work,' Kathryn told her advisor, 'so I was thinking about working in an office or a shop.'

He sighed and scrolled down his computer screen. 'We haven't got a lot at the moment.' His eyes flickered. 'Wait, there's a vacancy just come up for a general assistant at Sharma's Chemist. It's central, off Front Street. Does that sound like something you'd apply for?'

She bit her lip. 'I'm not sure. What would I have to do? I don't know anything about medicines.'

He smiled. 'Why don't you go and have a chat with the owner?'

Mr Sharma, who interviewed her in a room off to the side of the pharmacy, seemed to take an instant shine to her. Tall and rangy, with legs like stilts and a Colgate-bright smile, he wore a white coat and held tightly onto a clipboard. 'I'm look-ing for someone sensible, polite and neatly turned out,' he told her. 'Someone who can think for themselves, if need be. And you, my dear, appear to fit the bill. So I have high hopes that you will be joining us on Monday. You can start on Monday, can you?'

'Have I got the job, then?' she asked hopefully.

He looked down at his clipboard. 'I have seven candidates to see. The first was absolutely useless.' He shook his head emphatically. 'You are the second on my list. So you have a one-in-six chance of coming to work here. In percentage points, that's—'

'Sixteen-point-six, repeating?' she said.

He beamed at her. 'Exactly right, my dear!' He looked down at his clipboard and frowned. 'You know your maths, but you have no previous experience of working in a chemist's shop?'

'I'm a quick learner, though,' she said.

She was pleased when the jobs liaison adviser informed her that she'd come out ahead of the other applicants. 'I wish it was always this easy to place people,' he said despondently.

The following Monday morning at eight-thirty, Mr Sharma greeted her with a grin. 'Welcome to Sharma's Chemist,' he said. 'You were by far the outstanding candidate!'

She smiled back gratefully. You wouldn't be saying that if you'd known me a year ago, she thought.

The shop was modern and uncluttered, with a glass door that beeped every time it opened and closed and two central rows of shelves leading down to the pharmacy and till. Her job was to keep the display stock tidy and dust-free, to price every item individually and to keep a record of sales and orders. Mr Sharma was very particular about how things looked. 'It needs to be spanking spotless at all times, with no gaps or holes on the shelves,' he told her. She was also to assist Tabitha behind the till.

Tabitha arrived at ten to nine, dressed smartly in tapered black trousers and a cream shirt. She was in her mid-twenties, Kathryn guessed, or maybe a little older. Her dark hair was cropped around her face in an asymmetric cut and she was striking, rather than pretty, with inquisitive blue eyes.

Mr Sharma introduced them. 'Kathryn will be finding her feet for the next couple of days,' he told Tabitha. 'If you could show her the ropes with your customary patience and grace, I'm sure she will soon fit snugly into our routine.'

'Yes, of course, Mr Sharma,' Tabitha said. She smiled at Kathryn and her eyes twinkled.

Is she laughing at me? Kathryn wondered.

She spent most of the morning trying to guess what sort of a person Tabitha was. She worked with an air of businesslike efficiency that she admired, but there was also something else there, something in her eyes, a trace of mischief? She couldn't put her finger on it.

At lunchtime, Mr Sharma left the shop, saying he would be back in half an hour. As soon as the door had closed behind him, Tabitha turned to Kathryn, smiled broadly and said: 'Me name's Tab, not Tabitha – no matter what he insists on calling me. And shall I call you Kat or Kathy?'

'I like Kathryn, if you don't mind,' she replied.
'Are you saying your name isn't actually Tabitha?
I thought it was a bit unusual for around here.'

Tab laughed. 'Not just for around here – you
don't find any bloody Tabithas anywhere. Except
cat rescue centres, maybe.'

'So what's Tab short for? Apart from cigarette?'

Tab looked sheepish. 'Well, it *is* short for
Tabitha, which is why old Sharma-shanks calls
me that, even though I've asked him not to,
because I bloody hate it. You see, me mam was
obsessed with a ridiculous sixties sitcom called
Bewitched. Do you know it?'

'I think so,' Kathryn said, although it didn't
ring a bell.

'It's about this housewife who's secretly a witch
and wiggles her nose to do spells, and her bairn's
called Tabitha, which is how I got lumbered with
the name. I tried shortening it to Tabby, but that
sounded like me neighbour's kitty. So it's Tab.'

'Right, I'll call you Tab from now on.'

'And I'll stick with Kathryn for you. Nice,
sensible name – your mam clearly wasn't a nut
job like mine.'

Kathryn looked away. 'Not really,' she said. 'I'm
hungry. Can I pop in the side room and eat my
sarnies?'

The shop door beeped. 'Hang on for a minute
and serve the customer,' Tab said. 'I'll be back in
a mo.' She slipped into the bathroom at the back.

A man wearing a cap and tweed jacket ambled
towards the counter. With his rosy cheeks and
whiskery face, he looked like fat old Farmer Giles

from a childhood story book, except that there was brown residue around his nostrils, which could have been dirt, pepper or God-knows-what. Kathryn didn't like to think.

She gave him a nervous smile. Where's Tab? she thought, feeling panicked. What if he needs something for his piles?

'Alreet, hinny?' the man said.

'How can I help you?' she replied in her best friendly manner.

He leaned into the counter conspiratorially. She smiled. 'Hev you summick for the weekend?' he asked.

She racked her brains, trying to imagine what sort of elderly health problem might arise at a weekend. 'What do mean exactly?' she asked, tilting her head. It was clearly nothing urgent, because today was Monday, but...

He started winking furiously. 'You know...'

She decided that honesty was the best policy. 'I *don't* know,' she admitted. 'I've only just started working here, you see. I'm still learning the ropes.'

Tab came out of the bathroom. She had her hand in front of her mouth and Kathryn's first thought was that she might be feeling sick. Then she realised that she was trying to stifle her laughter. 'He means blobs!' she hissed, ducking behind the pharmacy screen.

'Oh, blobs, why didn't you say?' Kathryn blurted out, before she could stop herself.

She showed the fat old farmer their limited selection of condoms, trying not to giggle or look disgusted as he posed general questions about texture and size. 'I don't know much about them.

160

I'm new in the shop,' she kept saying, by way of deflection.

She soon realised that he was an old perv having a bit of fun at her expense. 'If you could hurry up and make your purchase, please,' she urged him, crossly.

He went for a packet of ribbed, extra large, which she handed straight to Tab like a hot potato. 'Good choice, sir,' Tab said approvingly, as she rang them up on the till. 'Please make sure you use them correctly.'

Clearly unsure of what to make of this comment, he shuffled out of the shop clutching his small chemist's bag.

'Barf!' Tab said with a laugh, after the door had closed behind him. 'He comes in at least once a week, the cheeky bugger.'

Kathryn turned to her, eyes wide. 'You knew he was going to say that? You set me up!' she said accusingly.

'Trial by fire.' Tab smiled apologetically. 'At least you'll know for next time.'

'But I don't understand why he wanted them for the weekend.'

'My mam says that's what blokes used to say a really long time ago, when no one talked about sex.'

'But why "for the weekend"?'

Tab shrugged. 'Perhaps they were too tired the rest of the time. Or maybe it's when they went out and got lucky. Who knows?'

'Did you see his nose?'

'I *nose!*' Tab said. 'Mam says it must be snuff.'

'What's snuff?'

'Ground-up tobacco.'

'Really? How weird.'

They giggled about it for the rest of the day. 'Ribbed and extra large? Good choice, sir,' they kept saying when Mr Sharma was out of earshot. 'Perfect for a teeny weeny todger like yours. Why not pop some snuff in it while you're about it?'

As the days and weeks passed, Kathryn found she rubbed along well with Tab and Mr Sharma. The shop was busy and she was on her feet all day, so she had achy legs for the first week, but she found the work interesting and enjoyed interacting with the public.

'Think about it,' Tab often ruminated. 'Everybody needs a chemist, so if you work in one, you meet everyone.'

Kathryn started looking forward to going to work. There was never really time to chat in much depth, but she liked hearing snippets about the others' lives. Mr Sharma had a wife and four children who ran circles around him, by the sound of it. Tab was hoping to have a baby with her partner, Robin, whom she constantly referred to as 'me other half'.

It hadn't taken Tab long to discover that Kathryn was new to Chester-le-Street, or that she had no friends there. 'I don't mean to be nosy, but why did you come here, then?' she asked.

'I'd heard it was nice,' Kathryn said.

'Where were you before? Why did you leave?'

'Just outside Newcastle,' she said. 'I was looking for a complete change of scene.'

'And you chose Chester-le-Street?' Tab was incredulous. 'Instead of Cullercoats, Whitley Bay, Durham, even bloody Consett ... lord, I'd choose almost anywhere above this shithole, to be honest.'

'Would you? Honestly?'

Tab tutted. 'I suppose not, although I quite fancy moving down to the Sussex coast. In the meantime, better the devil you know, and all that. But what made you come here?'

'I had my reasons,' Kathryn said, hoping the conversation would end there. She didn't feel ready to open up about the past and wasn't sure she ever would.

'Ooh, Kathryn Blake, International Woman of Mystery,' Tab teased.

A couple of weeks later, Tab asked her if she'd like to join her and Robin on a night out in Newcastle. 'It's a gig at a really good club called Zami's and there's a crew of us going,' she said. 'So don't worry, you won't be stuck with me and Robin all night.'

'Sounds good, I'll let you know,' she said.

She couldn't remember the last time she'd been to a club; she wished they were meeting in a quiet pub in town instead. But I need to get out and meet people, she thought – otherwise I'll turn into a weirdo.

'How will we get back?' she asked, a little later.

'One of me mates is borrowing a people carrier from the school where she works. She doesn't drink, so she can drive us,' Tab said.

A lift there and back made it feel less intimidating. 'OK, I'll come,' she blurted out before she overthought it. 'What will you wear?'

'Black satin,' Tab said with a laugh, and Kathryn couldn't tell if she was joking or not.

Kathryn wore a green halter top, navy velvet jeans and strappy, open toe sandals, even though it was a cold night in March. And no coat, of course.

It is illegal to wear a coat in the north-east, she thought with a giggle. I'd probably get bloody arrested if I wore one.

On the dot of eight-thirty she heard a horn honking and the sound of Abba blasting out from a set of speakers. Taking a deep breath, she ran down the stairs of the block and burst out of the building. 'She made it!' Tab whooped, as she got into the people carrier. 'Everyone, this is Kathryn, not to be shortened to Kathy, on pain of death. And Kathryn, these are my mates.' She went through them, one by one. 'Shelley, Jem, Al, Vicks, Han and, of course, me other half, Robbie the Rob.'

'Hello, Kathy!' they chorused.

'Hi,' Kathryn said, unsure she'd heard correctly. She thought Tab had said, 'me other half' as she'd gestured to the pretty blonde in a silver mini-dress sitting next to the driver. Was that right? Or had she muddled her up with the stocky, boyish driver, Han? Although Han didn't look much like a man, either...

She grinned nervously. Out of the corner of her eye, she saw Jem put her hand on Al's knee and give it a squeeze. It was a suggestive gesture, rather than a reassuring one, and everything fell into place.

Tab's gay, she thought.

She couldn't blame herself for not guessing earlier, yet on the other hand it seemed so obvious now. Tab was clearly not interested in men, so there had been no chitchat about boys between them in the shop, and that suited Kathryn, who was happy to discuss TV programmes and celebrities' lives instead. Maybe it was partly why she and Tab got on so well – they talked about safe things, nothing probing or personal. Or was it because they both had something to hide? They'd got to know each other by discussing people and events, anything from the Spice Girls and Monica Lewinsky to the digital age and the millennium. 'Within fifty years, robots will be doing this job,' Tab was keen on saying. 'I'll have one to do the housework, and all. I hate doing housework.'

Kathryn told herself that it was understandable to assume that Robyn was a man, because of her name, and the fact that Tab was hoping to have a child with her. And yet she felt she should have realised, all the same. Just on instinct.

'Everything all right up front?' Tab yelled at her from her seat in the back.

She turned round to face her. 'Great!' she said. 'I haven't been out in ages, so I'm glad it's a girls' night. It makes it easier, somehow.'

Next to her, Shelley winked and crossed her long legs, which were sheathed in Lycra. 'We'll ease you back into the groove.'

'Bring it on,' Kathryn said, and then felt self-conscious, because she'd only ever heard someone say, 'Bring it on,' on TV.

Shelley handed her a flask. 'Vodka.'

165

Kathryn shook her head. 'No thanks, I don't touch spirits. I love my wine.'

Shelley raised her perfectly plucked eyebrows. 'Each to their own,' she said, taking a swig herself. She gave Kathryn another wink. 'Red or white?'

'White, I suppose,' Kathryn said.

'You like a drop of Pinot Grigio, I bet,' Shelley said.

Kathryn shrugged. 'I don't really mind, as long as it's cold.'

They pulled up outside the club twenty minutes later. Tab led them inside and managed to get them all in free by jabbering about a friend of hers who worked at Zami's during the week. 'In we go!' she announced, bursting through the double door that led into the main club space, which was bathed in red and yellow light and exploding with music. The DJ was teasing Britney, Whitney and Lauren Hill samples over a funky R&B instrumental track. 'Oh, baby, baby...' the Britney sample went.

'...how was I supposed to know?' Kathryn sang to herself, but the DJ had already moved on and started playing the first bars of 'It's Not Right But It's Okay'.

She quickly offered to buy Tab a drink, and Shelley and Han too. As she headed to the bar at the back of the room, she passed huge numbers of women chatting, laughing, drinking and dancing with other women. There were men too, but it was mainly women and the atmosphere was joyous. What struck her was how gorgeous they all were, how feminine. Lesbians weren't supposed to look like that – they were dykey and blokeish, weren't they? The vision she had in her mind was of women with short hair and no breasts who wore blazers and dungarees. But either she had the wrong idea completely or the women in the club weren't actually gay.

She looked around at the crowds of women snogging, dancing close or touching each other affectionately. Not gay? She laughed to herself.

Maybe it's a good thing, she thought. I'm safe. I can have fun without worrying.

She bought the drinks and took them back to Tab and the others. 'Which side of the fence do you fall on?' Shelley asked, sipping her vodka and tonic.

'I'm pretty sure I'm straight,' Kathryn said. 'But I absolutely love this place.'

Shelley smirked. 'Just imagine how phenomenal it would be if you were a dyke,' she said, taking Kathryn's hand and leading her to the dance floor.

12

September 2000, Chester-le-Street, County Durham

Kathryn had a lot of time for Mr Sharma. He could be eccentric at times, but he was kind and considerate, and not at all old-fashioned. 'I'm a progressive,' he liked to say. 'I look to the future, not the past.'

This was especially true when it came to technology. He was gadget mad; he had every cool device imaginable, including a flip phone and a camcorder, and he was constantly leafing through magazines that showed the latest digital widgets. Soon after she started working for him, he had installed a video surveillance camera high on the wall above the shop counter and put a sticker in the window saying, 'This shop is protected by CCTV.'

'Does it actually work?' she'd asked, peering up at it the day after it was installed.

'It's about ninety-two per cent reliable, which is good enough for me. But it's mainly there as a deterrent,' he said. 'I'm hoping it will give us all an increased feeling of security.' He didn't have to add that there had recently been a spate of hold-ups in town. They were all very aware of it.

In the days that followed the camera's arrival, Tab waved at it regally and blew a lot of kisses. Eventually, Mr Sharma asked her to desist. 'It is not a paparazzi lens, Tabitha,' he said.

'I don't know why he's so bothered,' she said to Kathryn when he went for his lunch break. 'The cassette's on a loop, so it keeps taping over itself.'

'Maybe his wife watches it at the end of the day,' Kathryn replied. 'She might think you're blowing kisses to her.'

'You mean it could trigger her inner lez?'

They laughed. 'I wonder how "progressive" Mr Sharma would feel if that happened,' Tab said. Suddenly she looked thoughtful. 'She's lucky having four bairns though, isn't she?'

Tab was desperate to have children, and as the

months went by, her longing for kids started to border on obsession, it seemed to Kathryn. Every day she complained about the fact that Robyn still didn't feel ready to have a baby. 'She's got that many arguments against it, I'm starting to wonder if it will ever happen,' she told Kathryn. 'She doesn't want to lose her freedom, or her figure; she's worried about sleepless nights and feeling bored. The list is endless. "Is it me?" I asked her on Saturday. "Because if it is, tell me now, so I can meet someone else before it's too late." But she said, "Tab, I've told you, I love you and I want a baby with you – only not just now. Be patient, please. It will happen when the time is right."'

'You'll just have to wait, then,' Kathryn said, hovering outside the stockroom. She had been through the list of options with Tab a hundred times in recent months. 'Unless you give her an ultimatum, leave or get pregnant yourself,' she added.

Wary of taking sides, especially now that Robyn was also a good mate, she turned to pick up a box of body lotions.

'You know what kills me?' Tab went on. 'When I hear about women leaving their babies in dustbins and doorways. I mean, how can they live with themselves?'

Kathryn went still.

Mr Sharma popped his head over the pharmacy screen. 'Don't judge them too harshly, my dear,' he said. 'Giving birth sets off hormonal changes that can precipitate mental illness in a small percentage of women. Some of them literally have no

169

idea what they're doing.'

Lining up a row of plastic bottles and tubs on one of the aisles, Kathryn wondered how he knew so much about post-natal depression.

'Well, what about the scumbags who give their bairns up for adoption?' Tab said. '*They* know what they're doing. It makes me want to cry.'

Kathryn tensed. She had learned to switch off her feelings when the topic of adoption came up, but it wasn't easy.

'Often they're teenage girls, or drug addicts, Tabitha,' Mr Sharma said. 'And don't forget that adoption offers hope to childless couples,' he went on. 'A child is a blessed gift – and I'm convinced that the law of karma leads each spirit to its destiny.'

'I'm just thinking about the bairns,' Tab said. 'You'd have to be heartless to give a baby away, and the poor kid has to live with that rejection for the rest of its life.'

'I think you're being a little heartless yourself,' Mr Sharma chided. 'There are many reasons why a teenage girl might not be able to look after a baby.'

Kathryn felt like hugging him, although of course she would never do anything of the kind. But she was dismayed to hear Tab's views. She had half-hoped that one day she would feel able to confide in Tab about her past, about giving baby Ross away, about Nana and her mam. But how could she fess up now that she knew that Tab considered people like her to be 'scumbags'? She would never be able to face her friend's disapproval.

Mr Sharma broke into her thoughts. 'How was your class, Kathryn?' he asked. 'Did you like the new teacher?'

'She seems really nice,' she said, picturing the friendly tutor who had supervised her seminar the evening before.

It was now more than a year since Mr Sharma had encouraged her to take up a hobby. Thinking she was lonely and didn't have enough going on in her life – she guessed – he had given her a leaflet about yoga and craft-making classes at the local community centre. He had done it with the best intentions, correct in thinking her alone in the world, even though by then she had a group of mates – mainly Tab's mates – to go out with. He couldn't know that her loneliness stemmed from the secrets she held and would not tell, but maybe he sensed her grief or, at least, something untold, and realised how isolating it might be. Being alone with it was sometimes all she could cope with.

So it was a good idea of his to suggest doing an evening course. And although he'd probably done it in the hope that she might make more friends, maybe even meet someone special, for her part she had leapt at the chance to distract herself without having to get too close to other people. She loved Tab and the gang, but there were moments in their company when she felt like a complete fraud: she was constantly dodging questions and being deliberately vague, and sometimes she felt resentful of the way they probed into her childhood, even though it was completely normal of them to want to share and compare memories. After all,

171

they couldn't know how dark and messy her past was, how shameful. But how much easier it would be at college, a safe space where you didn't have to get too personal, where you chatted about coursework and then went home.

It made her smile to recall how surprised Mr Sharma had been when she told him she'd signed up to do a diploma in computer studies and business in Durham, instead of pottery at the local community centre.

'It sounds like a lot of hard work,' he said, frowning.

'But it's going to be really useful – and I need this sort of qualification to widen my employment opportunities,' she explained.

'I see.' She watched his face as it dawned on him that she didn't intend to work at Sharma's for ever.

'I might not have thought of doing evening classes if it hadn't been for you, so thank you,' she added, hoping he wouldn't feel put out.

He grinned. 'If you ever need time off to study for exams, don't be scared to ask,' he said. 'I am a hundred per cent behind this scheme of yours.'

She had definitely landed on her feet when she got the job at Sharma's, she thought. Not only had she made a friend for life in Tab, but Mr Sharma had become a bit of a father figure, and she was fond of him. He put a lot of trust in her and thought nothing of asking her and Tab to hold the fort for him or to close up shop when he had to dash off to help his wife or extended family. Occasionally, when Tab was also off some-where, he left Kathryn in sole charge, although never for more than an hour or two. It was mad, considering her history, but of course he knew nothing of her past and she didn't plan on telling him, or betraying his trust.

Until the day in mid-September when everything changed.

It was late afternoon on a Tuesday and Tab had an optician's appointment. Mr Sharma was suddenly called home to deal with a crisis involving a broken boiler and a bairn with a tummy bug. 'I dearly hope the two are not connected,' he said. 'Either way, I'm going to have to leave you on your own and go and sort it out, I'm afraid. Can you manage alone until closing time?'

'I'll be fine,' she assured him. 'It's not for long.'

He put a box of pills in a Sharma's paper bag and placed it in a small wicker basket on the counter. 'This is Mrs Cuthbertson's repeat prescription. She telephoned earlier to say she would be picking it up before the end of the day. Please inform any other customers that the pharmacy is closed until nine o'clock tomorrow morning. Remember to say that we're very sorry for the inconvenience.'

'Yes, of course, and I'll lock up at five. I hope everything's OK at home.'

'Thank you, my dear. Don't forget to go through the checklist before you leave. You know the alarm code, don't you?'

'Seven-five-four-seven-two-three,' she recited.

'Very good, please phone me once you've left.'

'Right you are,' she called after him. 'Don't worry about a thing.'

Calculating that there was an hour and ten

minutes until closing time, she crossed her fingers and hoped, firstly, that this wouldn't be the day the shop was held up by armed robbers and, secondly, that Farmer Giles wouldn't come in mumbling about buying French letters or summick for the weekend. He was harmless enough, but she still didn't like the idea of being alone with him.

Relax, she told herself. The shop is not going to be raided. Plus, the old perv only ever comes in at lunchtime, when he knows Mr Sharma isn't around.

The shop was quiet and so she immersed herself in counting stock to help pass the time. At a quarter to five, the door beeped and a mother came in with a little boy. 'Let's see if they've got your favourite toothpaste, shall we, Jack?' she coaxed.

Kathryn darted behind the counter and smiled as they approached. 'We've got a tutti-frutti flavoured one that tastes pretty good,' she said.

The boy's eyes lit up. 'Tutti-frutti!' He looked up at Kathryn. 'I'm five,' he said with pride.

'Are you?' she replied automatically.

She had learned to detach herself from the succession of sweet little boys who came into the shop chattering about their birthdays, daddies and toy cars. But these last few days it hadn't been so easy – in fact, it had been downright painful ever since Ross's fifth birthday, nearly two weeks before. Where was he, her bairn? Was he happy? Had his parents thrown him a big party to celebrate his special day? She had marked the occasion by making him a chocolate sponge cake, which she'd cut into the shape of a car and decorated with blue icing and Smarties. It was the first time she had made anything like it and to her surprise it had turned out quite well, but it had felt unbearably sad to have her lost bairn's untouched birthday cake in the flat and an hour later she'd put it out on her window ledge for the birds.

Now, faced with this happy little thing standing in front of her, her sorrow returned. She couldn't help thinking that her bairn would probably be every bit as beautiful as this boy was. The outline of his features was so perfect, so simple, his eyes so clear and wide, that she wanted to reach out and pull him close, squeeze him tight, never let him go. Instead she smiled and said, 'Well, you're a big boy now, then!'

'Hello there, it's Kelly – isn't it?' said his mother, stepping forward for a closer look.

Kathryn stared at her in surprise, taking in her friendly smile, pretty face and slim, balletic figure. An instant before she recognised her, she said, 'Actually, it's Kathryn.'

'Kathryn? Why did I think it was Kelly? I'm usually so good with names,' the woman said. 'Do you remember me? Zoe? You bought a cot off me when we were both expecting.'

Kathryn swallowed hard. 'Oh, yeah, hi!' she said with an enthusiasm she did not remotely feel. Her body tensed. 'How are you?'

'I never saw you again,' Zoe said. 'I often wondered how things went for you. Your little boy must be the same age as Jack now.' She frowned. 'You were having a boy, weren't you?'

She had no idea what to say. She could feel her

blood pumping in her ears. 'That's right, Ross is just five. They grow up so fast, don't they?' she managed to babble, echoing the words she had heard people say when they talked about their children. 'Bundle of fun and trouble,' she added, and then forced a laugh. 'I wouldn't have it any other way, of course, but sometimes he runs me ragged.'

She felt feverish all of a sudden. She dreaded answering any more questions and wished they would leave the shop.

'Is he at school in town?' Zoe asked.

'Yeah, just around the corner,' she replied, perhaps too quickly, she thought. Was there even a school round the corner?

'Someone else picking him up today?'

'He's with his nan,' she said abruptly, barely able to hear her words for the whooshing in her ears. She looked up at the clock on the wall. 'Now, that toothpaste...' she said. 'I don't mean to hurry you, but I'm closing at five.'

'Oh, yes, I'm sorry. You'll be wanting to get off and pick up your boy,' Zoe said. 'We'll have some of the toothpaste you mentioned and a box of Nurofen, please.'

Little Jack beamed at her. 'At my party, there was a magician. He had rabbits!'

'Wow, what a lucky boy you are,' Kathryn said, unable to resist looking at his gorgeous face again. She recalled that she and Zoe had been exactly the same number of weeks pregnant when they met – so Ross would be Jack's size.

Jack could be Ross – standing in front of her, looking up at her eagerly, just as she'd always longed for him to.

'Nice to see you again,' Zoe said, once she had paid for her purchases. 'We should try getting our two together one day, maybe,' she added hesitantly.

'Yes,' Kathryn replied, but she didn't offer to give Zoe her phone number. She looked at the clock again.

Zoe guided Jack towards the door. 'Right, well, see you,' she said.

'You can come to my party when I'm six,' Jack called to her. 'I'll put you on my list.'

'Thank you!' Kathryn called back, using up her last bit of breath.

The door beeped as they left. She walked unsteadily over to a chair on the other side of the counter and collapsed into it. 'Oh,' she whispered, putting her head in her hands. She could almost feel her heart ripping in two. Her sense of longing for her boy was too much for her to cope with. It was physical, like a fire blazing through her body, sizzling every nerve and synapse in its path.

She pushed her fingers through her hair despairingly. I should never have baked a cake for his birthday, she thought. I should have shut him out of my mind.

She felt an urge to drink something, take something – anything to numb the pain she was feeling. Which pub? Any pub. Vodka, pure. Looking up at the clock, she saw that it was past closing time. She needed to go through the checklist, put on the alarm and let herself out, locking the door behind her. She couldn't forget anything.

She locked the till and grabbed her coat and

backpack. Then it was a quick check behind the pharmacy screen to make sure that there were no medicines left out. At the last minute, she remembered Mrs Cuthbertson's uncollected prescription. Better put it away, she thought mechanically, recalling that Tab had said Mrs Cuthbertson was on heavy tranquillisers. 'Enough to flatten a zombie,' according to Tab.

She went to put the box of tablets on the shelf under the counter, and hesitated. *I* need tranquillising, she thought.

Slipping Mrs Cuthbertson's prescription pills into her backpack, she set the alarm, turned the lights off and left the shop.

A few minutes later, Kathryn was sitting in a corner of a pub trying to blank out the memory of little Jack's face – his upturned nose, his sunshine smile, so eager, so lovable. But she couldn't erase him. Her mind would not let him go.

I was getting better, she thought. Now I'll have to begin all over again.

She felt like a counter in a children's board game, undone by the roll of the dice, sliding down a slithery snake, back to the start of the game.

Halfway through her second glass of cider, she took one of Mrs Cuthbertson's pills. At last, the little boy's image in her mind's eye began to dissolve. Feeling calmer, she bought another cider and popped a second pill, just to be on the safe side.

The world smoothed out. It was still light when she left the pub and headed home, passing two lads sitting on a wall next to the church. 'Nice tits! Can I come back to your place with ya?' one of them called out. He jumped off the wall in readiness.

A jolt of fear went through her, overriding the calming effect of the tablets. She kept her eyes fixed on the pavement ahead and strode purposefully on.

'Nah, mate, dog,' said his friend, pulling him back. 'You wouldn't want to do *that*.'

She walked the rest of the way home in a shadowy dream, terrified that depression was about to engulf her again. She could feel it at the edge of her mind, like a spider waiting to pounce. She hoped the anti-depressants she was still taking would keep it at bay. She couldn't endure the darkness again. She would rather die.

Once inside her flat, she sat at the small table in the lounge and watched the sun set through the branches of the trees outside the window. Streaks of pink and orange lit up the sky and then faded into the twilight. Why is life so unfair? she wondered. Why do I always lose?

An image of Mo flashed into her mind – unbidden, unwelcome. Mo, with a fag hanging out of her mouth, cackling at the sight of seven-year-old Kelly's bloody knees after an accident on the swings in the playground. She pulsed with hatred at the memory, which soon merged into others: Mo locking her in Bobby's bedroom with a packet of shortbread; Mo shoving Nana's belongings down the rubbish chute; Mo blowing smoke in her face and telling her to get rid of the baby.

She went to the fridge and took out a half-bottle of vodka that Tab's friend, Shelley, had left there a few weeks earlier. She poured herself a double measure and added orange squash and water. Unzipping her backpack, she took out the stolen packet of pills and stared at it, wondering if she would die if she took them all at once. She tried to remember how to ensure that an over-dose was fatal. Timing was crucial, she recalled. You had to be careful you didn't vomit and sober up again.

She took a third tablet and washed it down with the vodka and orange mix.

Returning to her seat by the window, she tried to imagine what it would feel like to pick Ross up from school. To walk him home in the sunlight and give him fish fingers for tea, with a bowl of strawberries and ice cream for dessert. After tea, she would run him a big splashy bubble bath and watch him play with the foam; she would dry him with a soft towel and help him into Batman pyjamas.

She ached to read him a story, to kiss him goodnight and tuck him up in bed. 'My little one,' she murmured, as she tried to picture his sleeping face. 'My angel.'

What did he look like now, her boy? Was he blond or dark? What colour were his eyes? Had he started getting wobbly teeth? She fetched a pad of paper and tried to sketch him, but the re-sulting portrait was amateurish and crude. Still, there was a likeness in the eyes, she decided – a vague hint of something she recognised. Not that she had the faintest idea, of course. It was just a guess. But still.

She wrote 'Ross' underneath the drawing, kissed

his lips and folded it up. Rummaging through a drawer, she found a tea light candle and holder; she lit the candle with a match and placed the folded picture under the candle holder.

Pressing her hands together in prayer, she lowered her head and shut her eyes. 'Come back to me, one day, my love, my little boy,' she whispered. 'Until then, please God, may you be happy and safe.'

Her cheeks wet with tears, she stumbled over to the sofa, where she curled up into a ball and softly sobbed herself to sleep.

13

Kathryn was woken by the sound of her doorbell buzzing insistently. Looking out of the window, she saw Tab stepping back from the doorway, and went down to let her in.

Tab lurched at her with outstretched arms. 'Thank God you're alive!' she said, panting for breath. 'Mr Sharma was convinced you'd topped yourself.'

'What are you on about?' she asked, blinking in the light. 'What's the time? I must have overslept.'

Tab followed her back upstairs to the entrance to her flat. 'He says you twocked Mrs Cuthbertson's tablets!'

Kathryn's cheeks flushed pink. 'I didn't! I left them under the counter.'

'Stealing controlled drugs is a serious crime,

you know,' Tab said, putting her hands on her hips. 'What the hell were you thinking? I told him you don't take drugs, but then I thought, 'What's she doing with those tablets? You put the fear of God in us.'

She dug into her coat pocket and pulled out her phone. For a moment, Kathryn thought she was calling the police. 'What are you doing?' she asked.

'Ringing Mr Sharma, to say you're still alive!' Tab said, impatiently. 'He's that worried, the poor man. He's beside himself.' She dialled his number. 'Shit, he's busy. I'll have to send him a text message.'

'But I didn't take Mrs Cuthbertson's tablets!' Kathryn said.

Tab gasped. 'That's a lie and you know it. Or are you joking? He saw you do it on the CCTV footage.'

Kathryn stared at her wordlessly.

'Don't tell me you forgot about the camera! Christ, you're a prize idiot,' Tab said angrily. 'What got into you? Mr Sharma says someone came into the shop and upset you. Who was it?'

Kathryn's mind swirled. Everything was moving too fast. She didn't have her story straight. She didn't know what to say. 'Just someone I used to know.'

'What's that supposed to mean? "Just someone I used to know,"' Tab raged. 'Why are you so secretive? What have you got to hide?'

'I'm sorry!' Kathryn yelled. 'She's called Zoe and I knew her in my old life. The life I've been trying to leave behind.'

'Yes, your secret life that you never talk about,' Tab snapped. 'What the hell did you run away from, if you don't mind me asking? What was so terrible that you can't even talk about it? Come on, I'm your friend. It does my head in that you won't tell me.'

'Please don't make me,' Kathryn begged. 'You don't want to know.'

How could she tell the truth after what Tab had said in the shop about despising people who gave their kids up for adoption? But what other excuse could she give? She started to panic.

Tab grabbed her by the shoulders. 'I do want to know. You have to tell me,' she insisted. 'How can we be friends if you're not honest with me?'

'I know, but...'

'Come on!'

She covered her face with her hands and burst into tears. 'I had a little boy and he died,' she whispered through her fingers. 'That's what I ran away from. That's what I'm trying to forget.' She let her hands drop from her face. 'Now do you understand?'

Tab waited for her to bathe and dress and then they walked to the shop together. Kathryn prepared her story on the way. Keep it simple. Say as little as possible, she told herself.

Mr Sharma's eyes flickered with anxiety when he saw her.

'I'm sorry, Mr Sharma,' she said.

He put his hands together, as if in prayer, and bobbed his head. 'I'm glad to see no harm has come to you. Now, I need an explanation.'

She hung her head. 'Yes, of course.'

He flipped the sign on the door from 'open' to 'closed' and asked Tab to make some tea and put out three chairs in the room off to the side of the pharmacy. Despite his obvious concern, Kathryn sat down feeling as if an interrogator's spotlight was on her. She hoped that her Body Shop bubble bath had got rid of the smell of stale alcohol that had clung to her skin for most of the morning. She was sure Mr Sharma wouldn't approve of binge drinking.

He had his clipboard on his lap. 'You know from Tabitha that I've watched back the CCTV footage from yesterday afternoon,' he said gently. 'You are a valued and trusted employee, but I'm afraid the footage has raised some serious issues that I need to clear up with you. May I ask you some questions related to what I saw?'

She nodded, steeling herself.

He started fiddling with his pen. 'How do you know the woman who came into the shop yesterday, after I left?'

'I don't really know her,' she replied, chewing her lip. 'I bought a cot from her about five and a half years ago.' She glanced up at Tab, then looked away. 'When I was pregnant.'

Mr Sharma stared at her for a moment and then referred to his clipboard, as if searching for inspiration. She couldn't blame him for being flummoxed. She had never mentioned having a bairn.

'Did she tell you something that upset you?' he asked finally. 'You seemed very distressed after she left.'

184

She nodded. 'She asked me how me bairn was. And I said he was fine. But...'

'But?' he prompted gently.

She swallowed, willing herself to say it. 'He's not fine. He's dead.'

A shadow passed over Mr Sharma's face and he clasped his hands together.

There was another long pause. Well, he may as well be dead, Kathryn thought. He's gone, and I may never see him again. Just like Nana.

'Me bairn and me mam passed away in a car crash,' she went on, her voice cracking. She conjured up an image of Nana's face and held it in her mind. Within moments, tears were running down her cheeks. 'I lost them both.'

No one spoke for what felt like an eternity. To stay focused, she alternated memories of newborn Ross's little face and Nana's pink lipstick smile – until her brain felt like it was crumbling inwards.

'I am so sorry, Kathryn,' Mr Sharma said. 'I had no idea.'

More silence ensued, broken only by the muted ticking of the electronic wall clock.

Am I doing the right thing? she asked herself as the seconds ticked by. Maybe I don't need to be telling such a massive lie. They'd understand if I told them the truth, wouldn't they? Tab wouldn't blame me for giving Ross away if she knew about Nana dying, and my illness. Mr Sharma would understand, I know he would.

But would I have to say I was raped? I just couldn't. And what if Mr Sharma finds out I was registered on a drug rehabilitation programme in

Newcastle? He definitely wouldn't be able to keep me on, surrounded by controlled medicines. Anyway, if I contradict myself now, I'll look even more untrustworthy – totally dodgy, in fact.

'Do you want a hug, love?' Tab said softly. 'Or would you rather...'

She kept her head down. It was too late to turn back. 'You see,' she began. She wanted to say how grateful she felt – to Mr Sharma for taking her on in the shop and to Tab for being her friend. But her thoughts and words weren't synchronising.

'After the accident, I left everything behind,' she said. 'I didn't want any reminders. I tried to forget. But seeing Zoe yesterday brought it all flooding back. She doesn't know my boy died and I couldn't tell her. I couldn't talk about it. Especially not in front of her ... little one.'

Tab came over and crouched by her chair. She gently put her arm around her. It was less a hug, more of a hold, and felt comforting.

'Ross would have been the same age as her bairn,' she went on. 'He would have been five a fortnight ago.'

'And you lost your mother in the crash, as well?' Mr Sharma asked, after another long pause.

She nodded dolefully. Well, it was almost true. Nana had passed and Mo was dead to her, so there was no one approaching a mother in her life any more.

He shook his head in disbelief. 'I don't know what to say. I can't even imagine the dark times you must have been through.'

She said nothing.

'But, my dear,' he continued, after a pause, 'I'm

afraid that I cannot just overlook the theft of Mrs Cuthbertson's medicine.'

She looked at him in horror. Was he leading up to saying that he would have to report her to the police? Mr Sharma was a law-abiding, upstanding member of the community. He might feel it was his duty to bring charges against her.

'I'm sorry!' she said. 'It was a moment of madness. I needed something to take away the pain.'

He held her gaze and leaned towards her. 'Are you a drug addict, Kathryn? Please answer me truthfully.'

As she shook her head, she felt a sharp pain behind her eyes. 'No, I'm not,' she winced. 'I just didn't know where to turn or what to do. The tablets were there, right in front of me, by pure chance, so I took them. It was a one-off, I promise. Please don't go to the police. I'll never do it again.'

'Hush, there,' he said, gesturing her to calm down. 'Don't worry, I am not treating this as a police matter. But some sort of action needs to be taken to ensure that this – or worse – doesn't happen again. Your grief and sorrow will only fester if you don't find an outlet for it.'

Tab took her hand and gave it a squeeze. 'Do you need a couple of days off, maybe?' she asked.

'I don't know. Yes, maybe.'

'Do whatever you feel is necessary to get back on your feet,' Mr Sharma said. 'In the meantime, I will think over what would be best for you. Would you agree to bereavement counselling?'

She gave him a worried look. 'What would I have to do?'

'Let's just see,' he said. 'I feel it might help you

187

to talk to someone about what has happened. Not a friend, but someone professional, who knows about these things.'

She nodded, knowing she would have to comply, even if it meant telling more lies. Oh God, she thought. What have I got myself into?

14

By the time Kathryn joined the bereavement group Mr Sharma found for her, she had mentally rehearsed her story so many times that it almost felt true. She knew the type of car her 'beloved' mam had been driving – a blue Vauxhall – and she knew on which notorious curve of which B road it had crashed into a barrier. She had visualised where the child seat had been, invented a reason for the journey and accident – and added a small coffin to her memories of Nana's funeral, along with a vicar who had openly wept during his address. She even knew the injuries incurred and time and cause of death. And yet she felt terrified as she walked through the doors of the community centre at six-thirty the following Tuesday. She only had to make one mistake to be rumbled.

She was glad of the shot of vodka she'd knocked back before getting the bus there.

She dug her nails into her palms as she entered the room with the sign on the door saying, 'Bereavement Group' next to the outline of a dove. There were about ten chairs arranged in a circle and only one of them was free.

A middle-aged woman with shoulder-length blonde hair stood up and gave her a friendly smile. 'Are you Kathryn?' she said, in a voice that quivered with sympathy.

She nodded, fighting the instinct to wheel around and walk away. She moved towards the empty seat.

'You're very welcome here. I hope you find it helpful,' the woman continued warmly. 'I'm Sandra, and I'm a bereavement counsellor. Sitting on your left is Eddie, who has been coming to the group for more than a year.' She motioned to a man with a long, sad face. 'It is about a year, isn't it, Eddie?'

'That's right,' he said.

'I wonder, Eddie, would you be prepared to share with Kathryn – with all of us – how you were feeling the first time you came here? And even, perhaps, what effect coming to the group has had on you? To give Kathryn a sense of who we are and what to expect.'

Eddie coughed and shifted in his chair. 'Yes, thanks, Sandra. Hello, Kathryn, and welcome to the group. My name is Eddie – as Sandra just said – and I probably know how hard it was for you to come here today.'

He let out a despondent chuckle. 'As I remember, I was trembling from head to toe when I walked through that door fourteen months ago. My sadness about my mother's passing had reached critical mass and I couldn't function any more. I wasn't getting up in the morning to go to work. I kept bursting into tears – at home with my

189

wife, in meetings with clients, and even on my own, while I was having lunch in a café. Eventually, I went to my GP in desperation, and he recommended this group. I found that being able to talk to people who understand what you're going through makes all the difference. Well, it does for me, anyway, and I'm very grateful for it.'

Kathryn turned and gave him an awkward smile. I shouldn't be here, she thought. I'm a fraud.

She comforted herself with the thought that she would never be coming back. Instead she would pretend to Mr Sharma and Tab that she had found a one-to-one counsellor through another bereavement support organisation. She was sure they wouldn't probe too hard – as long as she didn't show any signs of going off the rails again.

As Eddie continued to talk about sadness and acceptance, she stole intermittent glances at the rest of the people in the group, who were mostly female. There was only one other man apart from Eddie, in fact, and he looked to be about thirty, maybe younger. She glanced at him a second time. He had a round, friendly face, the opposite of angular. His brown hair was cut short and he was clean-shaven. Even though he was sitting down, she could tell he was tall and lean.

He's actually quite attractive, she decided, and was surprised by the pang that accompanied this observation. A pang of – what was it, exactly?

I want a boyfriend, she thought. Someone to hold me tight. Someone who loves me.

Just then, he looked up at her and held her gaze. His eyes were a deep blue, the colour of a holiday sky in summer – the sort you saw in a travel agent's brochure, a paradise sky, completely cloudless. She hadn't realised; she'd expected him to have brown eyes, and it was a shock; she felt a jolt in her stomach. Oh my God, she thought, he's completely gorgeous. She looked away. It was ridiculous. She couldn't fancy a bloke at a grief group.

Why was he here, though? She felt curious about him. Was it because of his mother, his brother, a friend? She waited for him to speak, but the group was dominated by women talking about their dead husbands, some of whom were sorely missed – and some, perhaps, less so.

About halfway through the meeting, Sandra instructed them to pair off and talk about how they were dealing with their bereavement, one-on-one. 'I suggest you start by each summing up how you're feeling, and why, in a couple of sentences. And then you can take it in turns to ask each other questions. There isn't really a set way to do it, but the key to the exercise is to listen to what the other person is saying. More than anything, it is meant to be a listening exercise.' She smiled, and there was something so kind and nice about her face that it seemed to radiate goodness.

The next thing Kathryn knew, the gorgeous thirty-year-old was standing in front of her, asking if she would be his partner in the exercise. 'OK,' she said with an embarrassed smile, because she couldn't think of anything else to say.

He moved their chairs close to one of the walls and they sat down, facing one another. 'I'm Brett,' he said, putting out his hand to shake hers.

She knew that something amazing was about to happen the moment their hands touched. It was a form of magic, she realised later. It was a glitter snap, a sparkle, a handful of enchantment that just happened to be thrown up into the air, like confetti, by an invisible agent of love, right at the moment their hands met. A tremor of excitement shot through her.

She was about to say *I'm Kathryn*, when she realised that of course he already knew her name. She laughed nervously, scratched her head and sat on her hands. Then she mumbled, 'Kathryn,' in case he'd forgotten.

'Would you like to go first?' he asked, and there was something in his voice that gave her confidence, and an unexpected feeling of calm.

She took a breath and then changed her mind. 'No, you go first,' she said. 'Show me how. I've never done this before.'

'OK,' he said, leaning forward, his hands clasped on his lap. He grimaced. 'I'm here because I lost my wife, Sarah, about a year ago. And I miss her, and the children miss her...' His voice cracked and he looked away for a moment. 'I keep going over what happened in my mind,' he continued, after a short pause, 'and wishing I could turn back the clock and bring her back. I need to accept that she's gone, but I can't.'

He sat back in his chair with an expression on his face of such complete misery that she forgot about the thrill of their handshake. Her heart went out to him. The weight of his sadness made her want to weep.

'That's ... really sad,' she said.

'Yes,' he said, looking tired. He rubbed his eyes. 'Now it's your turn.'

She bit her lip. She wanted to say, 'I should leave now. I'm an awful person. I gave away my baby.' But if she admitted she was there under false pretences, she might never see this magical man again.

'I got pregnant by mistake when I was seventeen,' she began, 'but me mam said, "Don't worry, we'll bring the baby up together."' She stared down at her lap. 'So we did, and we managed fine, until eighteen months and three days ago, when me mam and me little boy died in a car crash.' She paused, pretending to gather herself. 'Basically, my life ended that day,' she went on. 'Afterwards, I moved away, got a job and tried to start a new life. I didn't tell anyone what had happened. I just tried to forget about it. But last week I bumped into someone from my old life and it all came rushing back. It tipped me over the edge. I felt so much pain. I went on a drinking binge ... and stuff...'

She looked up at him, thinking that she'd probably said too much, and realised with a shock that his eyes were filled with tears. At first she wasn't sure if he was crying for himself or for her, but then she felt stupid, because of course he wasn't thinking of her.

What am I doing here? she asked herself. Suddenly she missed Nana with a pain that seemed to slice right through her. I want someone to love, she thought. I *need* someone to love.

As if sensing her thoughts, Brett reached over and took her hand in his. 'I'm so sorry,' he said. 'To lose a bairn ... is the worst thing ... and your mam, when you're so young ... it's terrible.'

193

She felt a flash of desire as his hand slipped into hers, but then another sensation took over – a feeling of comfort at his warmth and strength. She closed her eyes and knew without a doubt that she would be coming back to the meeting – every week for a year, if need be – to see this man again.

To see Brett.

15

October 2000, Chester-le-Street, County Durham

Kathryn tensed up every time the shop door opened. She dreaded seeing Zoe and Jack again and looked out for them everywhere she went, an excuse always at the ready: 'Yes, Ross is with his nana again,' or 'He's off having tea with one of his little mates from school,' or 'His auntie's taken him swimming.'

A crack had appeared in her new world, revealing the past she had tried to wall up. She lived in terror of somebody else from her old life appearing. Mo's shadow loomed largest. What if Mo came into the shop?

She decided it would be best to pretend she didn't know her. She pictured Mo screeching something like, 'You're not even going to say hello to your own bleedin' mam?'

'Whoops,' she would murmur coolly, catching Tab's eye. 'Care in the Community alert.

Another nut job. I'll just pop out the back.'

Still, the chances of Mo turning up in Chester-le-Street were low, she reckoned, because Mo never strayed far from home. She needed quick and easy access to her drinking den in Edison House, her viper's nest. But there were other people it would be disastrous to meet. Jami, for instance: in the past few months she had written several letters to Jami that she hadn't sent. Cathy, too: she'd been on the verge of phoning Cathy a hundred times. 'I've a new life and a new name,' she wanted to say. 'I'm somebody else now, but I'll never forget how good you were to me.'

Neither Jami nor Cathy would talk about her past in front of other people, of course – and hopefully they wouldn't refer to Mo, either. So they wouldn't give her away on those fronts if they came into the shop – but they would be sure to light up and say, 'Hello, Kelly, how are you? It's been ages!'

It was bound to be awkward – and when they'd gone, she would have to explain to Tab and Mr Sharma that she'd changed her name, which might rouse their suspicions.

She imagined Tab turning to her, eyes narrowed, and saying, 'Remind me, *when* was it that your mam and little boy died? *Which* bend on *which* road was it again?'

She was trapped in her lie – perhaps fatally so, now that newspapers were being published on the World Wide Web. There were databases you could look at, records available. She was learning about it on her course. It wouldn't be long before everyone did everything via the Internet, according to her teacher. And then people would be able to check facts about car crashes and deaths all over the world. Maybe they already could – she hadn't dared to look.

Every day her anxieties increased. She couldn't get through a single evening without alcohol. Consequently, most of her mornings began with a hangover, which she tried desperately to keep hidden from Tab and Mr Sharma, and any time she felt clear-headed, she ached for another numbing shot.

Her best option was to move away, she knew. It wouldn't be hard to go somewhere and start afresh. She hadn't planned to stay in Chester-le-Street for ever, she reminded herself; she still had her savings pot to tide her over in a new town, and her business diploma could wait, or she could redo the second year at an adult education centre elsewhere. As for her friends, she would come back and see Tab and the gang; she would send funny postcards to Mr Sharma. The rest she would leave behind. It wouldn't be hard. She had done it before; she was good at shutting off.

The more she thought about it, the more sense it made. Except for Brett. She would have done another flit, no question, if it hadn't been for Brett. She had to be crazy, she knew, to be in love with a man who was clearly drowning in grief. But now she'd met him, she couldn't live without him. It was that simple, or complicated. Or both.

He wasn't a good reason to stay. He was too caught up in his pain to return her feelings. When he spoke of the loss of his wife, Sarah, at the bereavement group, there were times when he could barely string his words together – even now, fourteen months after her death. And no wonder, she thought, because Sarah had been an amazing person by the sound of it: a fantastic mother, full of fun and laughter; a wonderful wife; a great cook; a talented painter; and a devoted daughter to her parents. She sounded perfect to Kathryn, who could only picture her as a fairy-tale character – someone like Princess Aurora, perhaps – blessed with every gift you could imagine, including kindness and beauty. She had been lucky, too – until the moment she looked the wrong way and stepped out in front of a car.

'She was twenty-seven,' Brett told the group in a choked voice. 'She had so much of her life left to live.'

Kathryn felt desperately sorry for him. For Sarah, too, but chiefly for Brett, who had come out of the house and seen the accident happen right in front of his eyes. 'She was upset,' he explained. 'We'd been having an argument. Just a silly spat, nothing serious, but she was tired out by night feeds. It was sheer absentmindedness. She dashed out into the road without looking where she was going.'

It was the saddest story ever. Sarah had been right at the centre of life, with two small bairns, a baby girl of eight months and a boy of two. 'Beautiful bairns,' Brett said, with obvious pride, 'but now, every time they learn something new or do something for the first time, I think, All these precious moments she's missing! And it makes me weep.'

It was incredibly tough being a single parent, he

197

told the group, who listened in hushed, sympathetic silence. Sarah's mam and dad had stepped in to help, coming from Darlington most weekdays, but after a year of it they were all getting under each other's feet. Worse, the black hole created by Sarah's absence, instead of shrinking with time, seemed to be expanding and tearing them apart. So there was friction all round, and it was fast becoming unbearable.

'We've a nice neighbour who helps out when she can, and my parents bend over backwards to plug the gaps, but it's a constant juggle and the bairns need more stability,' Brett said. 'I don't know. Maybe I'm wrong. Maybe it's enough to have their grandparents muddling through – and when I mentioned to Ralph and Marjorie that I was thinking of looking for a live-in childminder, they took it very badly.' He shook his head. 'They're dead against it, in fact, as if it's a rejection of everything they're doing, but it isn't. It really isn't. It's just...'

For a moment he looked as if he would burst into sobs. He bit the skin of his knuckles and quickly gathered himself. 'It breaks my heart to say it, but we all need to find a way to move on and get used to life without Sarah,' he went on. 'It doesn't mean she's not important to us any more, or that we'll forget her – believe me, we'll never, ever do that. But we need a routine that we can stick to, so that we all know where we are – Ralph and Marjorie, my folks, the bairns, all of us. It's unhealthy not knowing what's happening from one day to the next, and having to work around Ralph's bowling matches and dental treatment and the like. We need a set routine. I wish they understood that.'

Poor Brett. Kathryn's heart twisted up when she thought of the pain he was in, which seemed so much worse than her own. She wondered if he also drank to dull his grief, but decided that he most likely didn't. An estate agent working for a busy company by day, he was often up with the bairns during the night, so he probably didn't have time to do anything but get on with life before he flopped into bed, exhausted.

But he did always manage to ask her how she was, either before or after the meeting. 'I've been thinking about you,' he'd say, looking intently at her with his summer-blue eyes. 'I hope you're coping. It's so hard, this grief thing, isn't it? It never lifts, never ends.'

She would nod sombrely, trying to disguise the fact that a rainbow was arcing inside her head, splashing colour through the gloom. She couldn't help it – the feeling was always the same when she was near to Brett. There was light, glitter and magic; somehow she knew everything would turn out all right. What exactly she meant, or thought of, as 'everything', she wasn't sure, but he gave her a sense of safety, of love and understanding, even though they barely knew each other.

Stop it, she told herself. Don't go getting crazy ideas.

She herself didn't say much in the meetings. She had leeway, she sensed, to hold back and be reticent, because to have a bairn that had died was understood to be practically unspeakable. There was a taboo around it – people couldn't even bear to imagine it. And she was so young. No one expected her to be able, at the age of twenty-three, to begin to express the agony of losing her bairn and her mam all at once. Sandra, the counsellor, always made sure there was room for her to speak, but didn't gently cajole her when she seemed reluctant to open up, as she did with the others in the group.

Then something odd began to happen, a couple of months after she started going to the meetings: she realised that the story of the car crash was implanting itself in her memory. She noticed it one evening in early December, when she poured herself a drink alone in her flat – and told herself she deserved it because, after all, she had lost her mam and her bairn in a terrible accident. It was only a split second of delusion, but it was a sign that her lies were tangling up her mind. She was beginning to believe something she knew wasn't true.

It was weird, but it was useful, because it gave her more courage to speak in the meetings and she could see that Sandra was pleased that she appeared to be moving forward and confronting her loss. The truth of the matter, she told herself, was that she *had* suffered a terrible bereavement. So what was the harm in expressing it in symbolic terms? Looked at this way, it didn't really seem like a lie any more, which made it easier to live with, and gave her a way to work through her grief about what had actually happened.

It helped that the group really seemed to care about her. It wasn't only Brett who made a point of asking how she was, either before or after the meeting – everybody did. Her sadness began to lift and she began to feel more at home, even starting to forego her shot of Dutch courage before she got on the bus to the community centre.

'It's definitely helping,' she confided in Tab. 'But I can't stop thinking about one of the men I see there every week. I know I shouldn't, but I can't help it.'

'You definitely shouldn't,' Tab said, with a twinkle in her eye. 'It's a lot more fun being gay – I would have thought you'd worked that out by now.'

'Maybe it is,' she laughed. 'But I'm just not.' She shrugged. 'Nothing I can do about it, is there?'

'I'm sure I could find someone who could turn you,' Tab said with a smile.

'Yeah, well, you had your chance. I gave it a year. Now I'm back on the lads.'

'Yeuch!' Tab shuddered. 'I don't know how you straight girls do it, what with all those gibletty dangly bits!'

'Gross!' Kathryn laughed. 'When you put it like that, neither do I.'

Tab winced. 'It's enough to put a lass off her dinner.'

'But you were the one who brought it up,' she protested.

The following week, there was an empty chair at the meeting when she arrived. It's OK, though, she thought – Brett often turned up out of breath, at the last minute. He always seemed to be in a rush.

As she waited for him to appear, she recalled how carefully she had chosen her outfit earlier in the day, with him in mind: bootleg jeans, a pale blue jumper and a butterfly clip in her hair. She had spent all week dreaming about Brett, counting down the days to when she would see him again. He was constantly on her mind. So when he still hadn't appeared by the end of the meeting, she felt herself going into a tailspin. Possibilities whirred in her head: he'd been sacked; he'd killed himself; he'd met another woman; he felt better and no longer needed or wanted to share his sorrow.

I've lost him! she thought, and went home in a panic, where she drank two cans of extra strong cider and fell asleep in her clothes.

He returned to the group two weeks later, looking sadder and wearier, after a ten-day dose of the flu, followed by a week off work looking after the kids when his mother-in-law went down with shingles. A shiver of wonder went through Kathryn when she saw him walk into the room, but she felt too shy to acknowledge him or look him in the eye. Even though he could have had no idea that she had been thinking about him obsessively for three solid weeks, her anxiety around his absence had left her feeling vulnerable.

Thank God he can't see into my mind, she thought. He would run ten miles and jump into the cold winter sea if he knew half of the dreams I've been having about him.

But maybe he did notice something over the course of the meeting, because when it ended he offered to walk her to the bus stop.

It was a crisp, near-black December evening

202

and the sky was full of stars. She felt lost for words as they walked along the quiet street that led away from the community centre. 'How've you been?' she asked eventually, unable to bear the silence.

'This is going to sound crazy, but I've missed you,' he said with a low laugh.

She swallowed, her mouth suddenly dry. 'I was wondering where you'd got to,' she replied, not daring to say more.

'Look, I'd like us to go for a drink, if you wanted to...' He looked at his watch. '...but I'd better get back. Flora's been waking up at ten for the past few nights, and she cries out for her daddy, so I need to be there.'

'Yes, go home,' she said, flooding with elation. 'You get back to her; she needs you. I'll be fine. The bus will be along soon.'

He took her hand and squeezed it. 'I knew you'd understand,' he said.

Her heart sang all the way home. He loves me back, she thought. I just know it.

16

April 2001, Chester-le-Street, County Durham

Kathryn started meeting him in the park of a Saturday afternoon. The bairns quickly got used to her, and George took to yelling, 'I want Kathwyn to push, Kathwyn!' when he asked for a go on the swings. George was a headstrong little lad, always wheedling for a lolly, and when he got one he'd roar like a lion and frenziedly circle the playground to run off the sugar rush.

Flora, at just two, was the sweetest and toddliest any bairn could possibly be, as adept at clownishly slipping over as she was at walking. Brett called her 'Whoopsa-Flora' and 'Inspector Clouseau', which made Kathryn laugh. Yet Flora was far less straightforward than George – she wasn't keen on being held or carried by anyone apart from her daddy, which made Kathryn feel awkward at times, if not positively unwanted.

'Are you OK?' Brett would ask. 'I hope it's not too painful for you to spend time with my bairns. You would tell me, wouldn't you?'

'I'm all right,' she assured him, although it wasn't always true. 'It brings back memories, but I've learned to cope with them. Your bairns are lovely. It's magic spending time with them.'

She took to going back to their house with them for tea. It was daunting to see framed photos of Sarah on every spare inch of wall and shelf, but she paid attention to them as naturally as she could. 'Oh, this is a lovely one! Where was it taken – Whitley Bay or Cullercoats?' And she took comfort from the realisation that, although nice looking, Sarah was no Princess Aurora, as she had imagined. Her face was a little too pointed, a little too queenly for a princess, she thought.

'Will you show me a photo of little Ross, one day?' Brett asked.

Her heart pounded guiltily. 'I threw them all away when I left my old life behind,' she lied. 'I wish I hadn't. It was a stupid thing to do.'

'Someone else must have some,' he soothed. 'Friends, relatives?'

'Yes, maybe,' she said, and left it at that. She had a photo of Nana, nothing more.

She began to stay on after tea for bedtime. When the bairns were finally tucked up and sleeping, she and Brett would sit on the sofa, holding hands, and he'd pour his heart out about Sarah, trying to make sense of her random, shocking death. In turn, she spoke of her own loss and loneliness, mourning the life she would have had if her son had lived.

'It feels safe talking to you,' he'd say. 'We're in the same boat. You understand how hard it is. Nobody else could, or would.'

She began to accept that she would never tell him the truth. It was a crying shame that she couldn't be honest, but she was in too deep now. There was too much at stake.

One evening in April, while his nice neighbour babysat the bairns, he came to her flat and they made love in her bed, without pictures of Sarah overlooking them. It felt very different from the sex she had known before – the puppyish passion she had shared with Michael and her heated clinches with Bern. It felt grown up and fully fledged, altogether more complete.

Brett knew exactly what he was doing in bed. His kisses were dizzying, his touch tender and thrilling. She'd felt unsure of herself at first – her inexperience left her quivery and inept with desire. But once she had relaxed and lost her inhibitions, their connection felt easy and right, their bodies a natural fit.

'I never thought...' he said, holding her in his arms afterwards. She buried her face in his neck. 'I just didn't know if...' he tried again. Tears dripped off his chin onto her cheeks.

'Neither did I,' she whispered. 'I'm glad, though. I'm happy...'

By the time he left to go home at midnight, she knew that her future lay with Brett.

Over the next few days, she kept breaking down, overwhelmed by relief and happiness. It was hard to believe that her luck had turned again – and she did her best to forget that it had turned on a lie. A month later, she gave notice to Mr Sharma, who took her and Tab for a farewell meal at The Raj in Durham, along with Mrs Sharma. 'You are an inspiration to us all,' he declared over chicken korma and Cobra beer. 'Let us raise our glasses to Kathryn, who has moved on from personal tragedy to find happiness again. It's proof of my theory that good things happen to good people.'

'Thanks to you.' Her lip trembled as she raised her glass to Mr Sharma and Tab. 'Here's to friendship.'

The following week, she said her final goodbyes and moved in with Brett and the bairns. It was a leap into the unknown, and a huge one, she realised, as it hit home that no amount of childcare books could prepare you for the reality of looking after bairns. Although she tried to plan for every eventuality, and a lot of it was common sense, the screaming meltdowns, teeny-tiny foibles, bath time floods and long-drawn-out bedtimes often brought her to her knees. The shadow of Sarah hovered – the perfect mother, who took everything in her stride – and she often felt as if she was halfway to failing. But Brett was incredibly patient with her. He never made comparisons with his dead wife or picked up on her ignorance and lack of experience. He wasn't the suspicious type. He was just supportive.

His parents were brilliant. 'You're doing a sterling job,' Peggy told her one teatime, just after Flora had hurled her bowl of pasta and peas on the floor. 'I read somewhere that mams shouldn't get hung up on being perfect. "Good enough" is what you should aim for, and you're a lot more than that, love, don't worry.'

From the start she and Brett agreed that the bairns would call her Kathryn – and that they would make a constant effort to keep the memory of Sarah alive in their minds. She did the best she could, especially when Ralph and Marjorie were visiting, but as her maternal bond developed with George, she started wishing he would call her mam. He was out-of-the-world adorable, was George, and she had the strongest feeling that they belonged together. He was always ambushing her for cuddles, plastering her face with kisses and telling her she was pretty, even when he wasn't angling for a lolly.

Flora was different – she remained anxious and focused on her dad, and asked a lot of questions about Sarah. Sometimes, when Kathryn went to hug her, she would say, 'You're not my mam.' It wasn't an accusation or a criticism – Kathryn realised – rather a statement of fact, because Flora needed clear definitions and boundaries to make her feel safe. But sometimes she couldn't help feeling rejected.

'That's right, love, I'm not your mam. I'm Kathryn, your Daddy's girlfriend, and I love you,' she'd reply.

Privately, she felt that it was not in the bairns' best interests to have their focus trained towards their mam the whole time, and decided to leave that job to Brett, Ralph and Marjorie. She hadn't ever met Sarah, after all; she began to mention her less, and then barely at all, and was glad that Brett didn't seem to notice. He still needed to talk about her, though – for hours on end. He had frequent flashbacks to the accident and tormented himself constantly by running through the moments that had led up to her death, always asking himself the same question: Could I have done something to stop it?

'If only I hadn't...' 'I wish she hadn't...' he'd mumble. He'd wake up in the night shouting, 'Stop! Watch that...!', clapping his hands over his ears as her screams echoed in his head.

She grew anxious that he was stuck, somehow paralysed by the shock of seeing his wife die so violently. She worried that he wouldn't be able to move on and felt fearful of the impact it might have on their future together. Eventually, she had a word with Sandra, who referred Brett to a trauma counsellor, whose effect on him bordered on the miraculous. After being diagnosed with post-traumatic stress disorder, he had therapy to help him combat the flashbacks and started going to the gym to pound out his anxiety on the treadmill. Slowly he began to emerge into the light again.

They had been living together for a few months shy of a year when he came home from work carrying a large bunch of red roses. She was washing up, wearing a pair of yellow Marigolds, as he came into the kitchen. 'For you,' he said, stepping forward to give her the flowers.

'Wow, is it Valentine's Day again?' she joked.

'Well, I was wondering...' He looked at the floor.

'What?'

'Can we get married? I mean, would you like to?'

She stiffened. 'You w–want to marry *me?*' she stammered. A tremor went through her. 'Are you sure?'

He grinned. ''Course I am. I love you! And I think you love me, too. Am I right?'

'Yes, but...'

He waited, his smile fading. 'What is it?' he asked. 'Should I have gone down on one knee? I was going to, but...' He broke off, searching her face for a reaction.

It shouldn't have been a surprise, and yet she felt stunned. She had often wondered if they would get married; she had hoped they would, but imagined the wedding taking place in the fullness of time, at an unspecified moment in a hazy future after she had finally come clean about her past. Now, all of a sudden, that hazy future was imminent. It was right in front of her, beckoning her. She had to make a decision.

What were her options? She was tempted to blurt everything out – there and then, on the spot – but now was definitely not the right moment to make a clean breast of things. It would mar the romance of Brett's gentle proposal; it would ruin a special memory in years to come.

But would this be her last chance to confess? If she said, 'Yes, I'll marry you,' without telling the truth, would she ever be able to unpick the lies she had told? Would she get another opportunity?

Maybe now *was* the right time – the only time, in fact. Because what if he found her out before she got round to confessing? She pictured Mo turning up during the wedding ceremony and screeching, 'She's a liar! I'm her mam. I'm not dead and neither is the bairn.'

Anything could happen. Taking such a big, legal step felt very risky. And she had personal standards – she would want to say her vows with a clear conscience; she couldn't imagine getting married on a lie. It wouldn't be fair to Brett; it would be fraudulent and hypocritical to walk down the aisle in the shadow of such enormous deceit. Anyway, she wanted to be loved for herself, despite everything, not the half-invented woman she was to him now; she wanted them to be truly intimate.

Or – and maybe this was grasping at straws – could it be possible that none of it really mattered? Lie or no lie, one name or another: was any of it really important as long as they loved each other?

Her mind see-sawed back and forth until she felt dizzy with indecision. Tell, don't tell – which should it be? Ripping off her rubber gloves, she ran into the lounge, flung herself on the sofa and buried her face in her hands. He dashed after her. 'What's wrong, love? This is terrible. I didn't mean to upset you.'

'I'm sorry, it's too much,' she said, stifling a sob.

'Look, don't worry, then,' he pleaded. 'We don't need to get married... You won't leave us, will you? You're not going to leave?'

'No!' she said. 'I love you and the bairns. But I just can't believe... I mean, is that what you really want?'

He sat down next to her and gently touched her shoulder. 'You love us? Really? That's all I need to know, I promise. I'd like us to get married – maybe it's a bit old-fashioned of me – but if you're not comfortable with it, it's fine–'

''Course I want to!' she said, suddenly unwilling to give up the idea of marrying Brett. Here was her dream come true, her chance for lasting happiness. How could she turn it down? She needed to reach out and take it while she could. 'It's not that. I'm sorry. It's such a shock – a bloody fantastic shock, but a shock. I just can't believe you love me ... or that you'd want to marry me. Are you sure you really do?'

'Yes,' he said, looking slightly scared, 'and I wanted to give you this as well...' He took a small blue ring box out of his trouser pocket. 'But if it's going to make you cry, we can talk about it another time, and–'

'What is it?' she whispered.

'It's, you know, a ring,' he said, trying to sound casual.

She stared at him. 'Can I see?'

He opened the box to reveal a plain solitaire. It glittered under the overhead lights in the lounge. She gasped. 'It's the most beautiful thing I've

211

ever seen.'

For me, for me, for me, she thought insistently, trying to banish her doubts.

'Will you try it on, at least?' he asked.

She put out her hand and he slipped it along her ring finger.

He knelt down beside her. 'Will you marry me, Kathryn?'

She smiled shyly, not daring to say anything, trying to override the voice in her head that said, 'It's not even your real name!'

But it's the name I've chosen, she told herself firmly, making her decision once and for all. And this is the life I've chosen. I've reinvented myself; it's not a sin; Brett loves who I have become. So the past doesn't matter. Who I was doesn't count. Kelly/Kathryn: what's in a name? This is who I am now – I mustn't even think of it as a lie any more. I'll find a way to make it work; I'll tell him another time – or I won't tell him. Everything will be fine.

She looked directly into his kind, blue eyes and felt that familiar fizz.

'Please say yes,' he said.

'Yes,' she replied.

As he leaned in to kiss her, a shout came from the kids' playroom. 'Kathwyn, can we have another episode of *Octonauts?* Kathwyn? Kathwyn! *Kathwyn!'*

They had a quiet wedding in June and took the bairns to Skye in August for a 'family honeymoon', where they were blessed with sunny days and clear, starlit nights. By then Kathryn was five months gone and had started to show, her pregnancy garnering smiles and indecipherable blessings wherever they went on the island. 'It's nice to see a young mam, for once,' said a grey-haired lady in the bucket-and-spade shop, eyeing her bump and the 'wee' bairns approvingly. 'The mams are leaving it so late these days, especially down there in England, and it's not right.' She shook her head. 'No, it's not right having a bairn when you're forty.'

'Oh well,' Kathryn said, conscious that a 'mature' mother had just entered the shop, carrying her baby in a complicated-looking papoose. 'You can't really plan for these things, I suppose.'

That evening when the bairns were asleep, she and Brett sat looking out to sea on the terrace of their cottage, contentedly sipping wine. As she watched the horizon darken, she vowed to herself that she would go back to her business course after the baby was born, and one day work in tourism.

This is a new beginning, she thought, and it felt like the right time to say something that had been on her mind for weeks.

'I've been thinking,' she began.

'You haven't!' Brett teased.

'I'm being serious, hear me out,' she went on. 'This is important.'

He smiled. 'I'm all ears, sunshine.'

'Well, it's just that when we move house next month, I think we should move forward in other ways too.'

'How do you mean?'

She glanced at the horizon again. 'I mean, it's a new adventure, a new start, and maybe we need

213

to move on and not look back. I'm not saying we should forget anyone – it wouldn't be possible anyway – but although the people we've lost will always be in our hearts, let's not take them into our new home, love.'

A shadow crossed his face. 'What do you mean? No pictures of Sarah? But she's George and Flora's mam!'

Is she? Even now? she wondered, but knew better than to say anything.

'I'm not talking about the pictures,' she said. 'We can have pictures, although maybe not *everywhere*, but it's not as concrete as that. I just think it would be best for us to say, yes, we've had some terrible times – some really, really bad things have happened, and we won't ever totally get over them – but we're making a choice now, to go forward and live the rest of our lives out of the shadows, to be happy. If we're going to make the best of the future, we need to leave the past behind.'

She swallowed hard, acutely conscious that she wasn't being altogether truthful about her reasons for wanting to shut off the past.

He reached down to the bottle of wine on the floor by his chair, picked it up and refilled his glass.

'I just want us to be happy, love,' she added. 'So let's try and give it the best chance we can.'

'I see,' he said thoughtfully. 'I expect you're right.'

She sensed it was a good moment to change the subject. 'Anyway, did you see George's little face when I gave him that plastic dolphin he wanted?'

214

she asked.

He laughed. 'He's still got a bit of a soft side, hasn't he? When he's not being a shouty little tyrant, that is.'

'He's growing up so fast now,' she said ruefully. 'I'm glad a toy dolphin can still make him jump for joy.'

Brett stared out to sea with a smile on his face. He would think over what she'd said in his own time, she knew. She only hoped he would see the sense in it, so that she could bury her lies. She longed to be free of the deceit she had spun, one way or another – and of Sarah, too, if possible.

Steven was born on a frosty day in December. It was an easy birth in the early hours of the morning and she was given her own private room after the delivery, a tiny, tranquil haven on the fourth floor of the hospital. 'You're lucky, love,' Vicky the midwife said, with a wink. 'For once, we're not very full, so it's all yours. Enjoy your baby.'

The hours she spent in that hospital room were among the best of her life. Brett went home to help his mother with George and Flora, so she had baby Steven all to herself, in blissful, toddler-free peace and quiet. Feeling fluid and completely at ease, she whispered and sang to him almost without a pause, consumed by feelings of tenderness, as if drunk on some potent elixir that stopped every emotion except love.

It was the nearest she had ever come to heaven, and so very different to the other time she had given birth. Since she hadn't known whether having Steven would make up for the loss of Ross or make the pain even worse – and she was aware that Brett, thinking Ross dead, had his concerns about this, too – she was truly relieved to find that her feelings for her new baby overruled everything else, even her most painful memories. I'm doing well, she thought.

Her euphoria lasted three days. Then the baby blues arrived, blanketing her in weepy sadness, and the memory of Ross's pale, newly formed face made her want to cry out in despair. 'Don't worry, it's normal,' she tried to reassure Brett every time he went to comfort her – while in her mind's eye, Ross's dark, questioning eyes merged and grew into a great, gaping hollow with a baby falling into it.

She struggled desperately, terrified that she would be engulfed by darkness again. Steven was two weeks old and she was on the verge of going to her GP when she felt it starting to lift. Then something strange happened. As the fog cleared from her mind and her perspective returned – as family life came into view once more – she realised that in having Steven she could somehow get Ross back, rather than feel his loss even more deeply. Through baby Steven, she realised, she could experience both their lives – both his and Ross's – in reality and in her imagination. So, every time Steven did something new in real life, when he gurgled, walked, talked or had his first day at school, she could picture Ross doing it too, and partially retrieve her missed life with him.

She felt happier then, and more at peace than before, feeling she had in some way regained the son she had lost. To anyone else, it might have seemed a weird way of dealing with her grief, but it made sense to her. Ross would be present as Steven grew up; he would live beside them without anyone else knowing.

17

September 2014, Chester-le-Street, County Durham

As it turned out, she probably needn't have said anything to Brett about putting the past behind them. What with the house move, the new baby and coping with three bairns under six, they didn't have time to tie their own shoelaces, let alone dwell on the past. Brett's job was busier than ever. There was never enough money. Like millions of parents before them, they put their heads down and trudged through five o'clock wake ups, tantrums, nightmares, fevers, infections, problems at school, teenage love trouble and spots. One thing came after another, leaving them barely a moment to think about anything but the here and now, which contained equal measures of joy, tiredness and worry. They had the occasional weekend away, when they flopped, vegged and laughed about feeling old, got outrageously drunk, mainly on freedom, and limped home. But by the time they'd been together for ten years and the children were becoming more independent, the past seemed like another life. Somebody else's life, even – a story they'd read in a book, or seen in a film.

It still came up, of course. Sarah remained ever-present, although not much discussed, except when Ralph and Marjorie came for a visit, when she was pretty much the only topic of conversation. Sarah, the domestic sorceress, who could transform household dirt into gold, with enough left over to make cupcakes.

'I'll never forget when Sarah...' was Marjorie's favourite opener.

'She was so vivacious,' Ralph was fond of saying. 'She lit up a room like nobody else.'

Kathryn had to bite down the urge to ask them to stop. She understood that they needed to talk about their child, poor things. Losing Sarah defined their lives; it was tragic that she had died so young and full of potential, and she felt for them in their never-ending sorrow. Yet sometimes their constant recollections grated, and she'd think, irrationally, Why can't they talk to someone else about it? When will they realise that this is my family now?

Brett of course joined in, recounting stories they had all heard before. Brilliant Sarah, wonderful Sarah; all round fantastic wife, mum and daughter. It got Kathryn's hackles up, even though she knew she was being childish. It was silly being jealous of a dead woman, but she couldn't help herself.

Increasingly she felt as if she were acting out a charade during these long afternoons of reminiscence. Instead of smiling and handing out tea and biscuits, she sometimes felt like screaming. Sarah wasn't Brett's wife any more, and neither was she the children's mother! She, Kathryn, was at the centre of the family now. She was the one who snuggled up with Brett at night, the one who fussed over the bairns and looked after them. George and Flora called her mam now. They were hers.

Sorry, but Sarah was gone.

She felt bad when she had these thoughts; she felt selfish and guilty. But she'd found herself growing ever more protective of the family she and Brett had made together – the family she had longed to be a part of when she'd been a child – and when Ralph and Marjorie kept harking back to Sarah, she felt territorial, too. To pass the time as they indulged their memories, she'd picture herself as a tigress, leaping at them with her claws out, knocking them out with her heavy paws, silencing them.

Thankfully, their visits dropped off as the years went on and Brett, George and Flora mostly went to see them at their house instead. It was a cliché, but almost everything seemed to get better with the passing of time. For her part, she felt less and less troubled by her past, and Brett very rarely probed.

Family life, being mostly lived in the present, seemed to consume great chunks of their previous existence, leaving only snippets behind – TV programmes they'd enjoyed, songs their mams had sung to them, childhood accidents and teenage cringes. In the main, they learned about each other's lives, the lives they'd lived before they met, through speedily related anecdotes.

'Did you ever see that episode of *Murder, She Wrote* where she was hired by a toy company to develop a new board game?' he'd ask as they sat down to play Monopoly on a rainy day.

Typically, one of the kids would interrupt – perhaps Flora, wailing, 'Mam, George hit me!'

Wrapping her arms round Flora, she'd say, 'I loved *Murder, She Wrote!* I watched it religiously every week with my mam. George? Stop that now!'

She was able to recount a lot of her childhood memories to Brett by switching 'Nana' with her mythical 'Mam'. She didn't even think of it as lying any more, not really. It was just a name swap. The bigger falsehood – that Ross had died – wasn't so much of an issue, because Brett always left it to her to bring it up, and she rarely did. Yet, as much as she would have liked to erase it completely, she couldn't stop it being woven into the fabric of their family. There was nothing she could do; it was always there – in Brett's sensitivity to her feelings about certain topics, in the way he tiptoed around stories of motorway pileups, funerals and the like. On the very rare occasions that he complained about his mother, he would always apologise first, saying, 'I shouldn't be moaning, because I know how much you miss your mam, but...' and he had once said, 'I could kill those bairns!' and immediately clamped his hand over his mouth. The children had come to learn of it, of course – the fact that, 'Mam's baby and mam died in a car crash; she doesn't like to talk about it.' It was seldom mentioned, but it was always somewhere; she couldn't escape it. To her shame, it was a fact of her life – of all of their lives – even though it wasn't true.

Occasionally Uncle Al's name came up, prompting Brett to ask why they weren't in touch any more, but she didn't have an answer because she wasn't sure herself. Devastated by Nana's death, Al had struggled to understand her depression and hated seeing Mo, so hadn't come to the flat more than a handful of times in the years before she'd won on the bonds and left for Chester-le-Street. That was as much as she remembered, anyway. So much of that time had been spent in darkness.

'I think he might be gay,' she told Brett. 'He kept himself to himself and seemed to have a bit of a secret life. There was a girlfriend, but I never met her, so maybe "she" was a lad. Either way, we drifted apart a bit, and then ... after the crash ... I left without saying goodbye.'

'Why not give him a ring now?' Brett suggested.

She pretended to think about it. 'No,' she said eventually, shaking her head.

'Go on,' he urged.

'No,' she said firmly.

'But it would be great to meet someone from your family.'

She sighed. 'I just want to leave the past behind,' she said. 'Will you let me do that? Please?'

'Sorry, love, I didn't mean–'

'I know you didn't,' she said, going over to kiss him. 'The fact is that the people I'd most like you to meet are dead.'

'I understand,' he said.

She was lucky. Brett always understood. At a Christmas party one year, she'd heard him saying to George's mate's mum, 'I can't imagine Kathryn going to an old school reunion. She isn't one for looking back; she's always saying you should forget the past and live in the present.' He shrugged. 'Which is good, I suppose. It's what the Buddhists say you should do, isn't it?'

Bless him, she thought. Trust Brett to find a reasonable explanation for why she'd shut off her past with such finality. To anyone else it might have seemed weird – even taking into account the effects of the trauma that the invented car crash might have triggered. But he didn't question it. He was so accepting, so trusting.

'Sort of like mindfulness?' the mum had said, gulping down her mulled wine.

'Not exactly,' Brett replied. 'Truth is, she hasn't kept up with any of her old schoolfriends, and never sees her family, either. She doesn't even see her mates from her old work in Chester-le-Street! So it's more like, "Out of sight, out of mind-fulness," I suppose.' He laughed, pleased with his joke.

'Very good,' the mum said approvingly, taking another swig.

Life rushed on, leaving memories in its wake. Before she knew it, Steven was nine and she'd finally passed her diploma in Travel and Tourism. Mr Sharma was the first person she phoned with the news. 'Congratulations, Kathryn!' he said, clearly delighted. 'I only wish I could tell Tabitha, but I don't have her number in Brighton. Do you?'

'I'm afraid not,' she said, wishing they hadn't lost touch when Tab and Robyn moved south.

A few weeks later, she got a part-time job at

Janus Travel, a small, independently owned travel agent with three members of staff dealing mainly in package holidays to Spain. It wasn't quite the glamorous rep job she had dreamt of as a teenager, but she enjoyed sorting people out with their two weeks in the sun. It suited her there and they had been very flexible about her hours: after going full time for a few months, they'd had no problem about her scaling back down to three days a week and then up to four, where she'd stuck.

And then suddenly Steven was twelve. Her baby. How did that happen? she asked herself. How did little Flora get to sixteen without me noticing? And cheeky, gorgeous George, eighteen!

It was crazy – and it meant that Ross was now a grown lad of nineteen, of course. She never forgot to count him, never left him out; he was on her mind every day. She wondered about him endlessly: what he looked and sounded like, the clothes he might wear, the colour of his eyes and hair. She was constantly trying to picture him, trying to imagine how he would react to the situations she saw her other children facing. Would he be brave when a football hit him in the face, or bawl his eyes out? Did he stick to his mam, or have an independent streak? Would he be quiet on his first plane trip, as Flora had been, or loud and boisterous like George? Had he struggled to learn to read, like Steven? Was he one for the girls?

She had carried on making him a birthday cake every year. Chocolate chip, coffee cream, Victoria sponge... If she concentrated hard, she thought she could probably remember every different flavour, in the order she had made them. Brett and the kids never noticed a thing. She enjoyed baking; it was something she did whenever she was in the mood, so they weren't to know that every 3 September she was picturing candles on the cake and a growing boy blowing them out. They didn't see her shutting her eyes and making a wish when she cut the first slice. Please may you be a happy, bonny lad, healthy and strong.

No one realised that whenever she took the children clothes shopping, she mentally chose outfits in the next size up for her other bairn. At the fair, she wondered if he liked rollercoasters as much as her other boys. Ross was like an invisible friend from childhood, unseen by anyone else, her secret companion. Sometimes she left him behind the curtain at home, though. It was exhausting to take him everywhere.

It was just a few days after she'd baked a Black Forest gateau for his nineteenth birthday that the letter arrived from an agency asking if she would be interested in meeting Rory Borthwick, the child she had given up for adoption in September 1995. Ross hadn't written it, but he had initiated it. As she later discovered, he had hung his hopes on it. By then she had given up wondering whether she would hear from him. It had been a whole year since his eighteenth birthday, when he'd been legally entitled to trace her – a year in which she had fretted and agonised over whether she should see him or not, if the chance arose. Finally, after countless sleepless nights, she had come to the painful conclusion that she just couldn't do it, however much she longed for him. Brett and the bairns would have to know; it wasn't worth it; she couldn't risk it. She didn't dare jeopardise her family's happiness – or her own.

She hadn't imagined that words on a page could fly in your face as you read them, like tiny winged daggers. Words, that's all they were – and yet she had come out in blotches across her cheeks within minutes of reading them. It shouldn't have been a surprise and yet it shook her to her core just to know that Ross was still alive. That he thought of her. Wanted to meet her. Even, perhaps, dreamed of her, as she did of him. Frequently. Vividly.

For the best part of his life – and hers – she had thought about him and yearned for him. But now, confronted with the chance to be reunited, she felt only a dark, creeping panic. She wished she had come clean to Brett about what had happened to her as a teenager. But she hadn't, and now it felt as if it was just too late. So, meeting Rory was out of the question.

With a heavy heart, she had written back to say, 'Sadly, my current circumstances make it impossible', shattering nearly two decades' worth of wistful dreams in a couple of sentences. But there was nothing for it – she had to protect her family. And in order to do that, she had to reject her first-born child – her baby, her bairn – for the second time in his short life, however heartbreaking it felt to do so.

A month later, sitting at her desk at Janus Travel, Kathryn had just popped a sneaky Malteser in her mouth when James put a call through to her. 'New client,' he told her. 'Interested in going to Mallorca for Christmas. I said I wasn't sure you'd have anything.'

'OK, put him through,' she said, popping in another Malteser.

'Hello,' said the voice on the end of the line. 'Am I speaking to Kathryn Casey?'

She frowned, instantly sensing that it wasn't going to be a standard client inquiry. 'That's right,' she said. 'How can I help?'

'My name is Rory Borthwick,' the caller said. 'I'm your son.' He paused. 'The one you gave away, remember?'

'Rory Borthwick?' she repeated. Her heart began to race. 'Erm, yes?' she said.

'I need to see you urgently,' he said.

'Urgently?' she whispered.

'Today. I need to see you today,' he insisted. 'Please...'

'Today? I'm sorry, I can't today, but–'

'Then I'll go to your house, later,' he cut in. 'I know where you live.'

She gasped. 'Don't do that!' she whispered. 'All right, let's meet. Where, though?'

'The back room of the Lamb and Flag, in half an hour? Can you make it?'

'I'll be there,' she said, suddenly feeling nauseous.

'Thanks, Mam,' he said. The line went dead.

She sat motionless at her desk, frozen in shock, watching herself fall apart from the inside. What do I do? she screamed into the chasm leading back to her past.

She scribbled a note for her manager, Samantha, grabbed her bag and rushed headlong into a nightmare.

PART THREE

18

Saturday 18 April 2015, Chester-le-Street,
County Durham

Kathryn walked into a dark, musty pub on the other side of town and ordered a vodka shot. Vodka, because it didn't smell – undiluted, because it worked faster.

She downed it in one. 'It's shock treatment,' she told the guy behind the bar, conscious that he probably didn't see many flustered mums in his pub knocking back spirits of a Saturday afternoon. The entire place seemed to be occupied by old men nursing pints.

He nodded and smiled. 'Shot treatment,' he said in an accent she couldn't identify.

She wasn't sure if he had made a joke or just misheard her, but it didn't matter. Nothing mattered – except what she was going to do next. Rory had come back. At this very moment, he was in her kitchen drinking beer with Brett and George. What was he planning? What did he want? Was it love – or revenge? She shivered.

She cast her mind back to their first meeting at the Lamb and Flag. He'd chosen to meet her in a smart gastro pub, nothing like the dive she was in now. She recalled her pounding heart as she'd walked through those varnished swing doors to meet the bairn she hadn't seen for nineteen years. She had picked him out the moment she'd hurried inside – he was standing by the bar, ordering a drink – and although he was taller and broader than Steven, and several years older, it was easy to tell that he was her youngest son's brother, even from afar.

It had stopped her in her tracks to finally set eyes on the son she'd imagined so many times. It didn't seem possible that they were finally going to meet. Oh my love, she thought, remembering the baby in her arms at the hospital, the bairn she had given away in a daze. She strode forward, heart thumping.

As she reached the bar, he turned towards her, and she saw his face in close up for the first time. It was a shock. Something about him was familiar in a way that reached deep inside her, to her core – and yet his was a stranger's face, marked by features she couldn't easily place. The sight of his green eyes disconcerted her – and by the curve of his mouth she sensed that he might laugh at things she wouldn't understand or find funny. But then he smiled and she saw herself and Steven beaming out of him.

A flash of desire zigzagged through her, and she shuddered, repulsed. This was her son, her flesh and blood. What kind of weirdo would fancy their own bairn?

'Wow, you're beautiful,' he said, looking her up and down.

'Steven?' she blurted out.

His smile disappeared. 'It's Rory,' he said, clearly stung by her mistake. 'Was I Steven once?'

She shook her head. 'I'm being daft – I meant

Rory, of course,' she stammered. 'Steven is ... someone else.' She extended her hand. 'I'm Kathryn. But of course you know that. Look, I didn't want to meet you like this, love – I mean, in these circumstances, but you see...' Her voice trailed off.

He regarded her coolly, ignoring her hand. 'Did you even bother to give me a name before you handed me over to social services?' he asked.

'Yes, I called you Ross,' she said guiltily. 'That's what you've been to me until now. It's on the birth certificate, isn't it?'

He raised his eyebrows. She imagined him thinking, So she did choose my name, after all. It struck her that it must have been one of the questions he'd always wanted to ask, because he seemed momentarily appeased, as if he'd ticked it off a list.

Would he have been surprised to know that she had her own list of questions? 'Have you been happy?' she asked eagerly. 'Were you taken in by a nice family?'

He scowled. 'Nice enough,' he said with a shrug. 'But no replacement for the real thing.'

'Oh,' she said, bitterly disappointed. She had hoped for an ideal mam and dad for him, a life of warmth, laughter and cuddles. 'I always imagined...'

He turned his head away, as if to hide his reaction. 'Can we go into the back room where it's quieter?' he asked.

She ordered a lime and soda and followed him to a small table in the back, set against the wall. She needed to explain why she wouldn't be able to see him again, but she felt lost for words, totally confused. It was enough of a struggle trying to bridge the divide between the son she had loved in her imagination and the stranger she was looking at now.

She examined him more closely as he sipped his pint and felt oddly pleased that her baby had grown into such a good-looking lad. He had an air of confidence that she sensed had been bred into him; he had definitely been well brought up.

'Where did you grow up?' she asked.

'Why did you do it?' he said plaintively, his words clattering into hers.

'I didn't want to,' she said. 'But I was seventeen and on my own. My nana had just died and my mam...'

'Yes, why couldn't your mam help out?'

She inhaled deeply. 'She was poorly,' she said, which felt like the truth in a way. 'You have to understand, I had no support or money. I wanted to keep you, but I couldn't give you a good life, so I gave you to somebody who could. I did it for you. I changed my mind later – too late – and tried to get you back. But by then the adoption had gone through and they said it would be wrong to uproot you from a stable home. I just had to hope you were happy and get on with my life. I had no other choice. I never stopped thinking about you though.' A sob caught in her throat. 'I thought about you every day.'

His face relaxed. 'Well, here I am. Why can't we be together now?' He gave her a pleading look and suddenly seemed far younger than his nineteen years. Her heart went out to him.

She lowered her head. 'It's complicated,' she mumbled, feeling deeply ashamed of what she was about to say. 'I went on to have a family; they don't know about you and I can't tell them now. They'd find it hard to forgive me for lying to them all these years.'

'I'm sure they'd understand,' he pressed. His eyes brightened and pink spots appeared in his cheeks. 'It's not lying. You just didn't tell them. It's on the telly all the time, on programmes that re-unite people like us. The women tell their families and it's all right in the end.'

She shook her head. If only it could be that simple. 'This is different. I lied and I changed my name. In fact, I'm amazed you were able to find me.'

He smiled again and she was reminded of the smile that lit up Steven's face when he'd done well in a school test. 'I hired a private detective,' he said proudly.

She caught her breath. 'You did wha'?'

'I asked my dad for the money for a new bike and spent it on a detective instead.'

Her heart leapt. His family's got money, she thought. He'll be fine without me.

'You'll be pleased to know that your mam's still alive and well,' he added. 'The detective found her first.'

She stiffened, electrified by fear. Had he seen Mo? If Mo had anything to do with this, it was time to leave. Mo was a force for evil, a destroyer.

'She says she hasn't seen you since the day you disappeared, which makes two of us,' he continued.

235

She thought of Brett, of the bairns, of how much she loved them. She had to protect them from Mo, from her past. She had to protect herself.

'Don't believe a word she says,' she said hotly.

She felt hostile towards him, all of a sudden. What else had Mo told him? I have to end this, she thought. I'm not that person anymore. I'm not Kelly. I'm Kathryn. My family comes first.

'I'm sorry, Rory, but I can't see you again,' she said quietly. 'I tried to make it clear when the agency wrote to me. It was wrong of you to contact me after that.'

'Why was it wrong? You gave birth to me. You're my real mam.'

'It was illegal.' She looked down. Do I love him? she wondered. She felt guilt and pity, although it felt like pity for a stranger – and a little scared. 'I'm your birth mother, but I haven't brought you up,' she said, trying not to falter. She hoped she wouldn't break down. 'Look, I wish things could be different, but I'm going to have to ask you not to contact me again. Don't come to my house. Whatever you do, don't do that. It would only make things worse. If you leave me alone now, there might be a chance for us in the future, but if you force me to tell my family, I will never, ever forgive you. Do you understand?'

He sat back in his chair, his lower lip jutted. 'Why are you being so cruel? I'm your son. I didn't ask to be born – or to be rejected by my own mother.'

'I know, love. It's not your fault. It's just ... circumstances.'

His eyes flashed. 'Fuck that! You have no idea

how it feels to live all your life knowing you weren't wanted. And now you're sending me away again. Why? What's wrong with me?'

The guilt was overwhelming. She felt swamped by it. 'Nothing's wrong with you,' she choked. 'You were a perfect baby. You're perfect now. No one's to blame. But I was a schoolgirl, with no money and no one to help me. Imagine if it were you. How would you manage?'

'I would find a way,' he said flatly.

'I tried, believe me,' she pleaded. 'I used to lie awake dreaming of our life together, and how happy we would be. But everything went against me, one thing after another, and it broke my heart. I became very ill; I couldn't cope. Please try and understand.'

'Do you *ever* plan to tell your new family about me?' he asked.

'Yes, love, I hope to, when the time is right.'

'And how would you find me, then? If you wanted to?'

She looked around the pub in panic. 'Through the agency? Or you could give me your details.'

He welled up. 'You're just trying to fob me off, aren't you? You won't tell them.'

'I will! I promise you. I just don't know when. Please don't force it.' She looked at her watch and stood up to leave. 'I must go now – they'll be wondering where I am at work.'

'Wait!' He grasped her wrist. His grip was strong.

'Don't, love,' she said softly.

'Please! I hate my parents. I need...' A single tear rolled down his cheek.

'Let go!' she said, shaking her arm to break free of his clasp.

He released his clutch and pushed her away. 'You're a bitch!' he spat. His eyes flashed with rage.

She jumped back, trembling. 'I'm sorry. One day I'll get in touch. Until then, please stay away from me,' she said. And then, because the words sounded so harsh, she tried to soften them by adding, 'Take care.'

She hurried out of the pub and went home, after phoning Samantha to say she was coming down with a migraine and couldn't go back to work.

Rory hadn't contacted her again – and after a few weeks of terror, she'd put her head back in the sand. That had been a mistake. Yet who could have imagined he would infiltrate her life like this, like a spy, like a psychopath. Suddenly he was coaching the Steelers, George's football team? How had he done it? It was creepy to think he was in her house, her haven, at this very moment. Had Mo put him up to it? Had they plotted it together? It was terrifying. She had no idea what to do or where to turn for help.

Her instinct was to get in the car and drive away, as far away as she could go on a half empty tank, then get out and start walking – anywhere, nowhere – until she collapsed in a heap in a ditch by the side of the road.

When she was discovered by a passer-by, she could pretend she had lost her memory. She wouldn't even know her own name. She'd be taken into hospital, perhaps with hypothermia, and the authorities would start trying to trace her family. She could disappear for a while, maybe even reinvent herself again. Her heart fluttered at the thought. She'd do anything to avoid this crisis.

But it wouldn't work, of course, because the car would be found, they'd trace Brett the same day, and she'd be rumbled if she pretended not to recognise him. Her pupils would dilate at the sight of him. The psychiatrists would catch her out. She'd seen the exact same thing in a TV drama. You had to be so careful. You had to plan everything meticulously.

She racked her brains. She could always try and find out whichever hole Jimmy Fry was lurking in these days, if he was still alive – and ask him to sort her out with a false passport. He'd had all sorts of connections, as she remembered; he would get her a passport, for old times' sake, she was sure of it. Then she could draw some money out of the joint bank account, jet away under a false name, dye her hair, get a rep job and start a new life in the sun. She could disappear entirely.

But what about Brett and the kids? She would shrivel up and die without them.

She ordered another shot of vodka.

Running away wasn't the answer. Realistically, she had two options. The first was to go home, pretend nothing was wrong, get on with her life and wait to see what Rory would do. Rory was clever and seemed well educated, but he was half her age. Surely that gave her the advantage? Surely she could outwit him.

Only, the look in his eyes had scared her. There

239

was something scornful there, a mocking glint. She had no idea how far he would go, or how nasty he could be.

She wondered if he was still in her kitchen, chatting happily to George and Brett, worming his way into the heart of her family. Maybe Steven had come home and they were listening to the football results. Maybe Brett had asked Rory to stay for tea. Then Flora would come in and scuttle off to her room, unsettled by her mother's absence. She stood up. She had to get home for Flora, for all of them.

She caught the barman's eye. A final shot of vodka.

The second realistic option, the alternative to playing poker with her life – against her own son, of all people – was to sit everybody down and make a clean breast of it. Just come out with it and see what happened next.

She tried to visualise how they would react, but all she could picture was their horrified faces. Would any of them feel sympathy, or be able to forgive her? It was too upsetting to imagine. Brett would probably wish he hadn't married her.

She stared at the row of bottles upended above the bar. They looked as if they could fall at any moment.

It's over, she thought. I'm finished. My life is about to cave in.

She sat still and tried to relax as the vodka filtered into her bloodstream. It was years since she had been anywhere near spirits – it was a long time since she'd needed to numb her mind – but everything was going to change now the past had

240

caught up with her. Life had just got serious again.

What am I going to do? she asked herself. She twisted off her bar stool and straightened her shoulders. She'd have to come up with a solution fast, but not now, after three shots on an empty stomach. She gave the barman a quick wave, hoping that he wouldn't notice the car keys in her hand, and left the pub in a lightheaded daze.

To her immense relief, Rory had gone by the time she got home. George was up in his room. Flora was reading in a corner of the sun lounge. 'Did you find the photos, love?' Brett asked. 'Don't worry, I've got the tea sorted.'

She felt like bursting into tears. She knew women who had to get the tea on the table by a certain time, come what may. She knew men who would sulk for hours if they didn't get their tea by six. Not Brett, though. He was a diamond.

She walked up to him and put her arms around his neck. 'I love you,' she said, pulling him close and kissing him. His breath smelled of beer.

She turned her head sideways and pressed it against his chest. I couldn't lose Brett, she thought. I couldn't live without him.

He hugged her back. 'What's brought this on?' There was a note of amused suspicion in his voice. 'Have you just broken it off with your fancy man? After realising what a fool you'd be to throw everything away for the sake of a few nights of passion in a Travelodge?'

Brett was sharp. Nothing slipped by him. She forced a laugh. 'How did you know? And now

I'm off down the Rovers to drown my sorrows!'

He dropped his arms to her waist and rocked her gently from side to side. 'I wasn't thinking of *Corrie*. Remember that drama we saw about the doctor?'

'Oh yes,' she said knowingly, 'you fancied the actress, didn't you, that dark-haired one? Looks a bit like me, but I'm better – wasn't that what you said? I read somewhere that there's going to be a second series.'

He grinned. 'Great news. Let's watch it in bed this time.' He cupped her bum and gave it a light squeeze.

'You're on,' she said, trying to fizz up her smile.

The back door opened and Steven walked in. 'Mam, I'm starving,' he said. 'What's for tea?'

She took a step away from Brett and clicked into parent mode. 'Ask your dad, he's in charge today,' she said, putting her arm around Steven. 'How did it go at the study group, love?'

After tea, the boys went over to Steven's mate Graham's house to play on his X Box. Meanwhile, Brett, Flora and Kathryn settled in front of the TV. 'Glass of wine, love?' Brett asked her.

She pretended to think about it. 'You know, I fancy something different tonight, for a change. Something strong and hard.' She tilted her head coquettishly and winked at him.

He gave her a bemused look. 'You mean brandy or something? Are you sure?'

'Just for a change.' She smiled. 'Have we got any vodka?'

She was too deep in thought to follow the

drama they watched. Her hunches and suspicions about Rory crashed into each other like deadly dodgems. How had he managed to get into the house, into their lives? What was he up to? Could she stop him?

Why have I been so stupid and cowardly? she thought.

The next thing she knew, the end credits were rolling and Brett was saying, 'Well, I wasn't expecting that!'

'I thought it was going to be the husband,' Flora jumped in. 'But he wouldn't have left the letter there, would he? What do you think, Mam?'

She had no idea at all. She'd been too busy fretting. 'Yes, the letter threw me right off,' she said, giving Flora's knee a squeeze. 'Proper fishy.'

Brett turned over and they watched something else, followed by the news – or, the 'Bad News', as they called it in their household. Then the boys came back and in time-honoured fashion she found herself in the kitchen making hot chocolate before *Match of the Day*.

The milk was just about to boil when George walked in, phone in hand, whooping at the top of his voice. 'What is it?' she asked, half jumping out of her skin.

'Come on!' he yelled. 'Rory says I've got what it takes to play up front, Mam!'

Rory. She closed her eyes and put out a hand to steady herself on the kitchen worktop. 'That's great, love!' she said. 'He obviously thinks you're really good.'

George's phone rang. 'Wait, mate, I'll put you on loudspeaker,' he said. 'Yeah, me dad's made up.'

'What about your mam? What does she think?' Kathryn flinched as Rory's disembodied voice echoed in the kitchen.

'Well, me mam's not that keen on football...' George's voice trailed off. He obviously wasn't interested in talking about his mother in this context.

'Did you tell her, though?' Rory asked.

'Yeah, she said it was great,' George said.

'Excellent,' Rory said. 'See you at Wednesday training.'

George hung up, grinning like the Cheshire Cat. Kathryn turned her attention back to the cooker and began to wipe up the milk that had boiled over while she wasn't looking.

Kathryn thought the vodka would knock her out, but it seemed to have the opposite effect. Lying sleepless next to Brett, her whole body was tense. Thoughts raced around her head like mice on plastic wheels. She kept clenching and unclenching her fists, ready to flee at the slightest trigger.

She got out of bed and crept to the bedroom window. Drawing back the curtain, she peered out at the street and scanned the pavement, searching for signs of Rory. A long-haired cat slunk out from behind a parked car on the opposite side of the road. It gave her a start. She saw a shadow flicker under a nearby lamp post. Was it Rory, eyeing the house, waiting for a glimpse of her? What would she do if she saw him there?

Nothing? Her hands were tied. She couldn't tell Brett, or call the police. She couldn't tell anyone. Unless she told the truth first.

She came away from the window and got back into bed. For years she had spent whole nights yearning for her lost boy, but now she dreaded the sight of him. Everything had changed.

19

Kathryn woke up to the sound of shouting. She opened her eyes and sat bolt upright. Is it Rory? she thought. Has he come back?

She heard Brett's voice. 'How many times have I told you not to leave your trainers in here? The whole room stinks! And what are your jeans doing on the floor?'

'They're not mine, they're George's,' Steven yelled. 'Why do I get the blame for everything?'

Not Rory, then. She sank back into her pillow. Her head felt terrible, inhabited by a spiteful little creature that was squeezing and pinching bits of her sleep-deprived, hungover brain. At least it's Sunday, she thought. She checked the foldaway travel clock on her bedside cabinet, a gift from Nana on her eighth birthday. It was a quarter to nine. No need to get up – not for a few minutes, anyway.

She shut her eyes and her mind began to race. What would Rory do next? Was he going to betray her? Silently torture her in front of her family? Murder her?

She heard Brett stomping up the stairs and heading for their bedroom. He walked over to her side of the bed and placed a steaming cup on the cabinet. 'Those boys are the limit!' he said, shaking his head. 'They're literally incapable of picking up after themselves.'

'Thanks for the tea, love,' she said.

He smiled. 'It's coffee. I was thinking you might need a blast of rocket fuel to propel you into the kitchen.'

'Why?' She frowned at him. 'Oh, of course!' She had forgotten that his parents were coming for Sunday dinner. Rolling out of bed, she threw on her dressing gown and headed for the bathroom.

So much to do, she thought, as she flew downstairs twenty minutes later, ticking off a list in her head. Chicken, spuds, veg, Yorkshires, gravy, stuffing – and apple crumble. Had she remembered to buy double cream? Despite her headache, she was glad to have something to do. It would stop her fretting.

'Anyone up for peeling potatoes?' she called out. Normally, she was happy to do the roast on her own, singing along to old pop tunes on the radio as she chopped, boiled and basted. As a bairn she had dreamed of belonging to a proper family and having Sunday roasts; even now she cherished everything they represented to her about love and home, and she enjoyed the ritual of preparing and serving up Sunday dinner, despite the pressure of having to get everything ready at the same time. But today it would be an uphill struggle. She could do with a helping hand, and some company.

George popped his head round the door, his blond hair still wet from the shower. 'Sorry,

Mam, I said I'd help Charlotte's dad move their old sofa out and take it to the dump.'

'OK, love.' George was that mad about Charlotte from the girls' grammar school that he'd do almost anything to ingratiate himself with her parents. But at least he wasn't off to meet Rory. 'Make sure you're back by twelve,' she said. 'You know your Nana and Grandpa like to eat early.'

'Cool,' he said, flashing her a smile.

She crossed her fingers and hoped that Charlotte felt every bit as sunny at the prospect of seeing him.

Five minutes later, Steven appeared and made a dash for the back door, a baseball cap jammed down over his messy brown hair. 'Said I'd meet Orson at the park,' he mumbled, and was gone.

It was Flora who helped out in the end, of course – once she'd been coaxed down from her room and away from her books. 'What are you reading now?' Kathryn asked her, half-wishing she'd say, 'Just an old Jackie Collins,' or even, *'Fifty Shades of Grey'*.

'Crime and Punishment,' Flora replied, smoothing her chestnut hair into a ponytail. 'It's background reading for my module on criminal psychology.'

'That sounds interesting, love.' Her head throbbed as she searched in the cupboard for gravy granules. 'How about you make a start on the batter?'

The kitchen was steamed up by the time Peggy arrived at eleven-thirty. Brett's mum always appeared at least half an hour before his dad, Wilf, who liked to linger over a couple of pints in the pub before Sunday dinner.

247

As usual, Peggy offered to help. 'You know me, I can't sit still,' she said, fiddling with the pepper grinder on the kitchen worktop. 'Never happier than when I'm busy.'

'We're fine thanks, Peg,' Kathryn said. 'Go and put your feet up in the lounge. The heat in here will cause havoc with your hair.'

Flora giggled.

Peggy patted her stiff blonde coiffure as she scanned the stove and worktop. 'Done the gravy?' she asked.

Kathryn stopped in her tracks. 'Oh fudge,' she said.

'Never fear, dear,' said Peggy, clapping her hands in delight. 'Flora, if you can find me a drop of sherry, some orange peel, strawberry jam and a bottle of Worcester sauce, I'll mix up my special concoction.'

'Jam in gravy? That doesn't sound right,' Flora said. 'Mam, can't you make it instead?' she wailed.

Peggy tapped her nose. 'Trust me, love, it's delicious. I saw it on *This Morning* a fortnight ago and now it's your grandpa's favourite.'

Wilf appeared half an hour later, looking as pleased with life as ever. After forty-odd years as a sheet metal worker at the steelworks, every year of his retirement – five, and counting – was one in the eye for the life expectancy statistics. Several of his workmates had keeled over within a matter of months of collecting their pensions, so he knew how lucky he was. He was the exception that proved the rule and he was determined to enjoy every minute of his leisure years.

While Flora chopped the Bramleys and Kathryn

rubbed the flour and butter, Brett took his parents into the lounge for a pre-dinner tipple. Steven came in from the park just as Kathryn's phone started ringing. 'Get that for me, will you?' she said.

It was George. Steven put him on speakerphone and left the room. 'Are you on your way?' she asked eagerly.

George laughed. 'I'm about a minute away – and guess who I've met at the end of the road!'

Her heart did a swoop. Please, no, she thought, clenching her teeth. 'Who, love?' she asked, her voice quavering.

'The lad who was round yesterday – Rory – he manages the Steelers and–'

'What was he doing at the end of our road?' The words tumbled out. Calm down, she told herself. Breathe.

'He's got a mate on Levington Avenue, one road up from Charlotte's house,' George said. 'But his mate was out and now he's got nothing to do for the rest of the day. So I said for a joke, "Come to ours for Sunday dinner! Me nana and grandpa are round." I didn't think he'd say yes, but he actually wants to come – is that all right, Mam?'

She held her breath. How to say no? She usually took these last-minute arrangements of George's in her stride. She never turned away his mates.

But today she had to. 'You see, love...'

What could she say to exclude Rory? No excuses came to mind. Short of announcing that she had a terminal illness and wanted time alone with her family, she couldn't think of a single reason why he shouldn't come to dinner. Except, of course, that she wouldn't be able to eat a morsel of the food she had cooked for fear that he was going to announce to everyone that he was her long-lost son.

'Come on, Mam – I've already said he can come!'

She could imagine George smiling, his blue eyes twinkling. She hated to show him up in front of a friend.

'I'm sorry, love, not today,' she said. 'I'm not feeling well and–'

'Whaa?' She heard a crackle down the line, and then George whispering into the phone. 'Please, Mam! I've already asked him.'

She thought quickly. George would need a good explanation if she went on saying no – and she didn't have one. And she didn't like to think of how Rory would react to yet another rejection.

'Mam?'

Which was more of a risk – to say yes or no?

She winced as she tried to imagine sitting down to Sunday dinner with Rory, the unwanted guest, the phantom at the feast. She felt a twinge of pain behind her eyes. The spiteful creature inside her head was still at work, worrying away at her hangover with its malicious nipping and tweaking.

What's happening? she thought. I just can't cope.

'Is Rory there? Can you put him on the phone, love?' she said.

She heard George mumble something. She heard, '...sorry, mate ... gone mental.'

'Hello?' Rory's voice came on the line, sounding

scarily self-assured. She heard a burst of muffled laughter. 'Is that George's mam?' he asked.

She cleared her throat. 'Yes, Rory, it's Kathryn here, and I'm very sorry, because I know George has already invited you – and as a rule, his friends are always welcome in this house, right up to the last minute.' She coughed. 'His really good friends,' she added, just to be clear. 'But I'm about to serve up – this very moment – and we've got his nana and grandpa here ... do you understand? It's just a bit difficult today.'

There was a pause. She held her breath. It was agony talking to him. She couldn't wait to get off the phone.

'Of course, no problem,' Rory said breezily. 'I'll pass by around three o'clock instead.'

'Fine,' she said, even though it wasn't – and he surely knew it. But she was just too relieved that he wouldn't be sitting opposite her at dinner to say what she was really thinking.

The doorbell went precisely on the dot of three. Ten minutes later, Rory was sitting on the sofa with Wilf and George. It felt to Kathryn like the start of the scariest kind of nightmare, where everything seems normal but an unknowable threat is looming, slowly turning the sky dark.

Brett was in the garden with Peggy, getting advice on the rockery. Flora had bolted upstairs and Steven was revising in his room. Kathryn busied about serving tea, listening in from the sidelines, darting glances at the sofa every couple of seconds, her heart beating double-time.

'So where are you from, lad?' Wilf asked Rory,

with characteristic directness.

Rory looked Wilf in the eye and smiled. Nothing seemed to faze him. 'I was born in Newcastle,' he said. 'But then I was given up for adoption – and my adoptive parents live in Corbridge, which is where I was brought up.'

'Corbridge, eh? Lovely town,' Wilf said. 'Must have been a nice place to grow up.'

'Nice is the word,' Rory said flatly. 'But I didn't have many friends there. My parents sent me away to school when I was eight.'

Wilf exhaled with a whistle. 'Bit harsh, eh? For a bairn. Were you that much trouble, then?' he teased.

Rory's eyes glittered. 'I think my main crime was being a child. My mother didn't particularly like kids, as a rule.'

Kathryn set down a plate of assorted biscuits on the coffee table in front of them. 'Help your-selves,' she said brightly. She turned and walked out of the room – hovering just outside the lounge door so that she could hear what was being said.

'Why would yer mam go to the effort of adopt-ing you if she didn't want you?' Wilf demanded. 'It's not like buying a pair of pants, you know. They make you jump through hoops before they'll give you a bairn.'

It was true, she thought, and the idea that Rory had been adopted by someone who desperately wanted him – who would love and nurture him and give him a better life – was the one thing that had kept her going during all the years she had longed for him.

'Maybe she did it for the wrong reasons,' Rory

said. 'Dad wanted a kid. The grandparents wanted a grandkid. It was the expected thing, so Mum went along with it. They all went along with it. But...' He clicked his tongue. 'Perhaps I didn't fit what they were looking for.'

Wilf tutted. 'They chose you, didn't they?'

'Yeah, but I was a baby. I was cute.'

'And they sent you away when you weren't cute any more?'

Rory laughed harshly. 'It's the only explanation I can think of,' he said. 'My prep school wasn't far from Corbridge, so I could have been a day pupil – but they signed me up to sleep in a dormitory with a bunch of eight-year-old boys instead. They can't have liked me much.'

Kathryn peeped round the door. Wilf was reaching for a piece of shortbread. 'You could be wrong there, lad,' he said. 'They might have thought they were doing the best by you, setting you up with a good education. What sort of folk are they anyway? Yer high-flyer type, like? Because those people send their bairns away to school as a matter of course, from what I've heard.'

'Dad's a partner at a big solicitors' firm in Durham,' Rory conceded. 'The way he saw it, if he went to boarding school, then I had to.'

'There you are, then,' Wilf said.

'Were you allowed home at the weekends?' George asked.

'Yes – when my parents weren't away. They were away a lot, though.'

'It must have been weird to spend your weekends at school,' George said. 'I can't imagine it.'

'I got used to it,' Rory said.

253

'Did you get homesick?'

Rory cleared his throat. 'Let's just say that there was a lot of muffled crying after lights-out. It was the soundtrack we fell asleep to.'

Kathryn imagined eight-year-old Rory, sobbing in the dark. She covered her face with her hands. Oh God.

'Mostly, I used to lie there and wish my real mam would come and rescue me,' he went on. 'That was my dream – that my real mam would turn up at the school and say it was all a mistake and she was taking me home.'

She felt her knees buckle. She took a step backwards and steadied herself against the wall behind her. I had the same dream, she thought. Over and over again. I wanted to find you and take you home with me.

'But she never did,' he said.

Neither Wilf nor George said anything. She prayed that one of them would change the subject. Please don't ask him if he knows anything about his biological mother, she begged silently.

Eventually George asked: 'What did you get up to at the weekends? Did they make you do extra lessons?'

Thank you, George, she thought.

'We did a lot of sport,' Rory replied. 'Saturday was football. Sundays we did fencing, archery, riding, shooting, swimming ... whatever we wanted.'

'Cool!' George said. 'Dad took us clay shooting last year. I only missed one target. But the recoil hurt like fuck! My shoulder was a mess afterwards – purple all over.'

Rory laughed. 'I shot my first clay pigeon aged nine,' he said. 'The rifle kicked so hard that it dislocated my shoulder and I passed out from the pain.'

Kathryn shook her head. Stop it! she thought. Stop making me feel guilty.

'Stuck to swimming after that, I expect,' Wilf said, with a tinge of sarcasm. 'Heated indoor pool, no doubt.'

Evidently Wilf wasn't particularly impressed by Rory's poor-me stance. He had no time for people who felt sorry for themselves. He'd had a hard life – none harder, some might say – but he liked to count his blessings and expected others to do the same.

'What brought you here?' he asked Rory.

'Didn't Dad tell you?' George chipped in. 'He coaches the Steelers now, and we keep winning since he came. He's the next Alex Ferguson in the making.'

'But why choose the Steelers when you're from Corbridge, of all places?' Wilf uttered 'Corbridge' with a plum in his mouth, the way he might say 'Buckingham Palace' or 'Winchester Cathedral'.

Rory didn't seem bothered. 'I'm studying sports management at Newcastle Uni and need coaching experience for one of my modules,' he said. 'I looked around the local areas, applied to the Steelers and was called for a trial about a month ago. I'm glad to say that it's working out great for both sides.'

So that was how he'd done it, Kathryn thought. It still seemed odd, though. Had it been sheer luck that the manager role at the Steelers had

255

come up? Or had he been watching and waiting for his moment to pounce?

'Why did you choose Newcastle?' Wilf asked, rubbing his chin. 'Why not go to a college down south or to Scotland for a change of scene?'

Rory smiled. 'Well, I did get offers from a couple of the southern universities, but I chose to stay here because it was the best course for me.'

'Is that so, lad?' Wilf said, as if he didn't quite believe him. 'Is that so?'

'Hey, this is a great cuppa,' Rory said loudly, as if he knew Kathryn was somewhere nearby, listening. 'Where's your mam? I'd like to congratulate her on her tea-making skills.'

'Don't be daft,' Wilf grumped. 'Next you'll be telling me I'm good at eating biscuits.'

George laughed. 'He's trying to be polite, Grandpa! Anyway, you are a champion biscuit eater.'

Kathryn smiled uneasily. George was a natural diplomat. He had a talent for diffusing tension. He got it from his dad.

'Did somebody say biscuits?' Brett called out. He and Peggy had come in from the garden and were taking off their muddy shoes.

'Pop the kettle on and I'll make some more tea,' Kathryn told Peggy. 'The biscuits are already in the lounge.'

'Not any more! They're all gone,' George announced cheerfully.

'Thanks to Grandpa, the champion cookie chomper,' Rory added, sounding for all the world as if he were one of the family now.

Kathryn shooed the boys off the sofa as she brought in the tea. 'Make room for your nana,' she told George. 'Anyway, I expect you two will be off out in a minute. You won't want to be sitting around chatting about the weather with us oldies all afternoon!'

She laughed as if to say, 'How ridiculous that would be!' – her lightness of tone masking her desperation that they would take the hint and go.

But Rory wasn't playing ball. 'I'm enjoying myself here,' he said, looking surprised.

George stood up. Clearly he didn't believe that Rory could genuinely want to stay. 'Shall we go to the park, mate?' he said.

Rory turned his head to the window. 'Is it raining?' He craned his neck to see outside.

George went to look. Raindrops began to spatter against the window. 'Chucking it down,' he said miserably.

Kathryn's heart sank. 'Oh well, you can always go upstairs and play on your phones, or whatever you young people like to do these days,' she said breezily.

George pulled a face. 'Mam, you sound like an old lady, but you're only thirty-seven. One of the boys in my class is seeing a woman who's practically your age.'

Brett chuckled. 'Is he really? Lucky bugger!'

Kathryn made a face. 'You know what I mean, love – I'm just saying...' She waved her hand at him. 'Oh, off you go.'

George looked at Rory, waiting for him to get up. But Rory stayed where he was. 'Here's an idea,' he said, flashing a smile. 'Remember those long drawn-out games of Monopoly you played as a kid on rainy days?'

George groaned. 'Yeah. "Go directly to jail. Do not pass go. Do not collect two hundred pounds." That was me. Grandpa always won. Don't even suggest it.'

'But, look,' Rory said, 'instead of staring at our phones – instead of disappearing down our individual rabbit holes – why don't we do something old-fashioned like play a game together?'

His confidence disconcerted Kathryn. She couldn't imagine any of her other bairns taking over the room like he did. He seemed so much more mature than anyone else of his age, so fluid, open and chatty – more like one of Brett's colleagues, in fact, than a mate of George's. Was it his education or his privileged background that had given him this maturity? Or was he just a cocky so-and-so – born that way, full of swagger?

'Monopoly?' Wilf sniffed. 'As my union rep once said, "That piece of capitalist propaganda! That wedge of Thatcherite nonsense!"'

Peggy bristled. 'A bit rich, coming from you, Wilf Casey,' she said. 'The man who snaps up the posh properties, leaving poor little orphan Annie here with the utilities – and never once will you let me off a fine!'

Wilf shot her a mischievous grin. 'You see what it turns me into? Capitalist swine.'

'Get away,' she shot back. 'You're a competitive scoundrel and you always have been. It's human nature, and don't try to say it isn't.'

Wilf's eyes gleamed, but before he could say anything, Brett jumped in. 'I suppose you tell your friends *I'm* a capitalist pig,' he said. 'Or do you just say I'm an estate agent?'

Peggy reached out to pat Brett on the arm. 'Yer dad couldn't be more proud of you, love, and you know it.'

That was Peggy all over, Kathryn thought. The best mam you could ever hope for, always ready with a word of reassurance. She bit her lip. It was no wonder Brett lived life on such an even keel. He had never questioned whether he was loved. He took it for granted. She hoped their kids did, too.

Which left her and Rory the unlovables in the room.

A low rumble of thunder came from outside. 'We're not going anywhere,' George said, looking out of the window again.

'So let's play a game. I'm serious,' Rory said.

Kathryn shook her head. 'I hate to break it to you, but our Monopoly set went to the scouts' summer fair last year,' she said.

'Mam!' George said. 'How could you?'

She raised her hands in self-defence. 'I thought you'd outgrown it!'

'Have you got a pack of cards?' Rory asked.

He wouldn't give up.

Peggy beamed and patted her hair. 'I love a game of cards, me.'

Kathryn watched helplessly as Brett rummaged around in a drawer and found two packs of cards. They decided to play Cheat, an old family favourite that called for poker-faced lying. Steven and Flora were summoned from their rooms and everyone budged up to make space for each other. 'You come over by me, love,' Kathryn said to Steven, suddenly realising that he was about to sit next to Rory.

'I'm fine here,' Steven said, plonking himself down.

She shut her eyes for a full second. When she opened them, she found herself staring straight at her two biological sons, sitting side by side on the sofa, looking like a couple of peas in a pod. One of them was the little lad she had poured love into since the day he was born; the other she had given away an hour after she had set eyes on him. She started to panic. Somebody was bound to notice.

Rory met her eye and smiled. She felt her throat constrict. Was it a smile of triumph, or hatred – what sort of a smile was it? I'm going to be sick, she thought. She stood up and hurried out of the room.

'Where are you going, love? I'm about to deal out the cards,' Brett said.

'You go ahead,' she managed to reply. 'I'm just going to...' Her voice trailed off as she rushed away.

'I think me mam's got a hangover,' she heard Steven say.

Outside the lounge she paused. Which was better – to stay and keep some sort of guard or to let go and accept that the worst could happen? She turned to go back and join the others, then changed her mind and went up the stairs, passing a black-and-white framed photo of Sarah on the wall. Wonderful Sarah, forever young, her head thrown back in laughter at something little

George had said.

In the haven that was her bedroom, she fell onto the bed and shut her eyes.

If I'm not there to see it, perhaps nothing will happen, she thought, as her head sank into the pillow for the second time that day.

'Everything all right, sunshine?' Brett had followed her up the stairs to check on her. Of course he had.

'Is it OK if I have a quick snooze, love?' she asked drowsily. 'I just came over a bit dizzy there for a moment.'

'Absolutely, princess.' He sat on the bed and gently stroked her hair. 'You haven't stopped all day. Thanks for the roast dinner. It was top notch.'

She looked up at him. Tears sprang to her eyes. 'I do love you,' she said.

He bent down and kissed the tip of her nose. 'You'd tell me if there was something wrong, wouldn't you?'

She shook her head and smiled. 'Nothing's wrong. I'm just tired. Now, go back to the lounge and deal those cards. I'll be down in half an hour. I just need a cat nap.'

She fell into a tense sleep that was punctuated by the sound of pattering rain and outraged yells of, 'Liar! You haven't got a single spade, have you?'

When she woke up, two hours later, Wilf and Peggy were putting on their coats and Rory and George were gone.

20

Kathryn's jaw ached with tension the next morning. She hadn't slept after her catnap; she'd spent the night staring at the ceiling, fists balled, teeth clenched: ready to fight, ready to run; doing neither. She felt so helpless.

Nana, she pleaded silently. Send me a sign. What should I do?

She scanned the kitchen anxiously, as if looking for clues, and her eyes fixed on a picture by Flora, aged five, that she had framed and hung next to the dresser more than a decade earlier. It was her most treasured possession, the one thing she would save from a fire if she had to choose – a stick family portrait of herself and Brett, George, Flora and 'baby Steven', standing in a row, grinning grins, holding stick hands. In one corner of the picture, the sun was shining. In the other, Flora had drawn a cloud with a smiling face inside it.

'That's my first mam in heaven,' Flora had told her when she'd brought it home from school. 'She didn't want to go, but she's happy now. She likes seeing us all together.'

Kathryn had cried the first time she'd seen it, and the stick figures had danced in front of her bleary eyes. In her mind, forever afterwards, the picture marked the day that Flora, her lovely girl, had finally accepted her.

Her head began to throb. She felt as if she would die if she lost that picture and all it meant to her. She felt ill with love for her family, breathless with it.

The house was empty now, quiet. The familiar Monday morning rush was over. Usually so mundane and frustrating, today it had felt searingly poignant in its unfolding chaos: Steven couldn't find his sports socks; George had lost a crucial textbook. Flora and George had started arguing and Brett had shouted at them to stop.

Normally, she was glad when they'd left the house, giving her a few minutes of peace in which to clear up and gather herself. But today all she could think about was how lost she would be without them. Every sign of affection they'd given her was like a kick in the ribs: Steven's jokey bear hug when she found his precious socks behind the radiator in the bathroom; George's embarrassed apology after she'd searched high and low and discovered his book in his school bag; the way Flora softly told them to lay off their mam and grow up; and Brett's lingering kiss goodbye. It was all so painful – because any moment now, it could be gone.

Her stomach whirled and seethed like a food mixer filled with acid. She left the house in a hurry, not dawdling to watch the last bit of breakfast telly as she often did before she walked to work. She arrived just as the manager, Samantha, was opening up. 'Hello, love,' Samantha said, turning round in surprise. She glanced at the clunky gold watch on her wrist. Her scarlet lips formed an O. 'Good weekend?'

'Lovely!' Kathryn said brightly. Her stomach went on seething. She was dreading the usual Monday morning chitchat with her colleagues. 'We had the in-laws for Sunday dinner. And you?'

'I went to that boring travel conference in Birmingham,' Samantha said with a sigh. 'Deadly, it was. Mind you, there was a right gorgeous lad sitting in the row behind me and I slipped him my number, at the last minute. Pray for me, Kathryn – pray that he rings. I'm going to be forty next year. It's all downhill from there.'

She straightened up and fiddled with her bleached blonde hair, which shone like brass in the sunlight. It was a filmic moment. Samantha loved a bit of drama.

Despite her worries, Kathryn suddenly felt glad to be back at work, among people who didn't tug at her heart strings. She looked forward to being busy; she needed the distraction.

Then again, wasn't it just another excuse to bury her head in the sand?

What is wrong with me? she thought. I'm paralysed.

A car drew up and out sprang James, the office junior, looking as neat and spruce as ever. His hair was slicked back, his eyes keen and bright, his trousers ironed, his shoes shiny. 'Morning,' he said with his usual perky smile as he waved off his lift.

'Christ, look at that!' Samantha gasped, staring at the sign above the door.

Kathryn looked up at the sign. It was supposed to say, Janus Travel Agents in black letters on a red background – Janus being the Roman god of journeys – but someone had blanked out the 'J' with a smear of red paint and given it another meaning altogether. Samantha started to giggle and Kathryn knew that normally she would have giggled along with her. But already a thought had occurred to her. Maybe Rory had defaced the sign, in order to send her a message.

Stop it, she told herself. Stop being paranoid. It was daft to think that Rory would have hefted a ladder to the high street in the dead of night and daubed a splodge on a sign just because she worked below it. He was too clever for that. Turning 'Janus' into 'anus' meant nothing. It was just a little bit rude. It was much more likely that some drunken lout had scaled the drainpipe with a pot of paint.

'Is there a ladder in the back?' she asked. 'I could give it a wipe.'

'I'll do it,' James offered.

Samantha snorted with laughter and staggered about on her heels. '"Give it a wipe!"' she screeched. 'Am I really childish to think that's funny?'

'Oh, I didn't mean it as a joke,' Kathryn said, trying to keep her smile going, wishing she could laugh along. 'Shall I wash it off?' she added. Even if Rory hadn't done it, she felt desperate to get rid of it. She needed things to be normal – on the surface, at least.

Samantha was still laughing as she opened up the front door. 'If you wouldn't mind, love.'

They went into the shop, where they changed into the green and yellow uniforms that the agency owners insisted they wear. For James, this meant putting a thin polyester jacket over his shirt and pullover. For Samantha and Kathryn, it meant easy-care smocks that covered their every bodily semblance of womanhood. Samantha's curves and costume jewellery disappeared, the brightness of her hair and lips dimmed – and, as usual, Kathryn felt like a pound of ageing sprouts bundled up in a pinny. Never mind, it was time to get down to business and sell some holidays.

Two minutes later, on the dot of nine, the phones started ringing with a soft electronic purr. This was perfectly normal for a Monday morning. The weekend had that effect on people: it made them want to escape – somewhere, anywhere. She knew exactly how they felt.

'Can you answer that, love?' Samantha asked. 'I've the new window offers to see to.'

'No problem,' she said, putting down her bag. She sat behind her desk and reached for the phone. Then she hesitated. What if it was Rory?

The phones went on purring. She pretended to drop a pen. She leaned down and scrabbled around on the floor by her desk.

'Can you get that?' Samantha called.

What if he was calling to threaten her? Bully her? What would he say? Was he planning to tell Brett? Would he try to blackmail her?

The insistent purr-purr of the phones kept on. Eventually, Samantha stomped away from the window and picked up the phone on her desk. 'Ye-es,' she said sardonically. She put the call on hold and yelled across the room. 'Are you actually capable of picking up a phone this morning?

266

Because if so, it's for you.'

Kathryn felt herself go pale, even though it was perfectly normal for a client to ring her. 'For me?' She cleared her throat. 'Who is it?'

Samantha gave her a wink. 'Someone who claims to be your son.' She turned to walk back to the window.

Her mouth dried. Her stomach seemed to contract and fold in on itself. What did Samantha mean? Was she joking?

She wasted a few seconds putting on an unnecessary plastic phone headset before she took the call. 'Hello?' she asked unsteadily.

'Mam?'

It was Steven – thank the heavens – it was Steven.

'I forgot I had to take my history project in today and I haven't got my keys. Can you meet me back at the house?'

She waited a moment, to let her beating heart slow. 'I'm at work, you numpty,' she said at last. 'Come here and get my keys from me.'

'I can't, Mam! I haven't got time!' he protested.

'But I've only just got to work!' she said, feeling panicked again.

'You've got to help me, Mam, you've got to. Please don't be narky about it!'

She shook her head and the plastic headset wobbled. Her mind was all over the place. 'OK, OK,' she said. 'Let me clear it with Sam.'

She went over to the window, where Samantha was posting up the latest travel offers. A week in the Costa del Sol for £199, including flights.

'Is it OK if I pop home to let Steven in? He's

forgotten his keys,' she said. 'I'll make up the time at lunch,' she added.

Samantha gave her a mischievous grin. 'I know your game,' she said with a laugh. 'Off to meet your lover. Quick bunk up while the house is empty. Get it while you can, eh?' She winked again.

Kathryn laughed half-heartedly. She was fond of Samantha, but today her strain of nudge-nudge humour was getting her down. 'You've got me there,' she said. 'But it really is only Steven, and if I pop off now, I'll be back before the phones get busy.'

'Right you are,' Samantha said, with yet another wink. 'Enjoy!'

'Thanks for understanding.'

She got her bag and coat and made to leave.

'Anything wrong, love?' Samantha called after her.

She stiffened. 'Just a bit annoyed with the bairn,' she said. 'See you in twenty minutes.'

She made it back in fifteen, having given Steven short shrift outside the house, followed by an apologetic bear hug and an off-target attempt at a kiss – which he rebuffed – before jogging back into town with tears streaming down her face. This can't go on, she thought. I'm a nervous wreck and it's affecting us all. Rory mustn't come to the house again. I don't want him there. I have to stop him.

As she walked into work, Samantha looked up and grinned. What next? Kathryn wondered. Had her gorgeous hunk from the conference called?

'Well, aren't you a dark horse?' Samantha said.

'What do you mean?' she asked with a sense of foreboding.

Samantha crossed her arms and gave her a look of mock accusation. 'A lad called Rory just popped in, asking for you. Oh yes. Charming he was, and young, and very well spoken.' She broke into a smile and started wagging her finger at her. 'You should be ashamed of yourself, Mrs. He's almost young enough to be your son.'

'Rory?' Kathryn repeated. She put on a puzzled expression. 'Do I know a Rory?' She shook her head, as if trying to rattle a memory, and pressed her lips together in concentration. 'Do you mean George's friend from football? Why would he want to speak to me?'

'You tell me, love!' Samantha said. 'The plot thickens.'

'Didn't he say?'

'He said to tell you he'd dropped in to talk to you.'

'To talk to me?'

'That's what he said.'

'Oh dear, maybe something's up with George. Did he leave a number?'

'He said he thought you might have it.'

'I haven't got it! Why would I have George's football friend's phone number?'

'Good question,' Samantha said with a knowing smile. The phones started ringing and she picked up a call. 'Lanzarote?' she said to the caller. 'You've definitely come to the right place. We've some lovely places to stay in Lanzarote.'

Kathryn sat stiffly at her desk. Rory was out to get her. She would have to tell Brett. Tonight.

Kathryn walked home from work, her lips moving silently as she rehearsed what she would say to Brett after she had poured him a glass of wine and sat him down. But of course he wouldn't want wine of a Monday evening; he never drank alcohol on a Monday or Tuesday, rarely even had a beer during the week. Had he said he'd be going to the gym after work? She couldn't remember.

She needed to choose her words carefully. She needed him to understand why she had lied. 'I was so young, Brett,' she whispered to the evening air. 'I was just a baby myself. When I lied that first time, I had no idea of the consequences, and then I got tangled up in the deceit and couldn't see a way out. You've got to believe me, *please.*'

Would the wording make a difference? She had seen politicians spin mud into gold on the news. She had seen celebrities turn scandal into triumph. But would she be able to save everything she held dear? She felt deeply ashamed of herself for keeping the lie going for so long, but also deeply sorry for her teenage self – the seventeen-year-old who'd been in the wrong place at the wrong time; the girl who'd been raped and lost her nana.

Would Brett forgive her? Could he? And what would his parents say? She loved and respected Peggy and Wilf, she couldn't stand the thought of alienating them. She pictured their hurt, disappointed faces. 'How could you have deceived us like this, love? How could you have gone on looking us in the eye?'

It was bound to draw unfavourable comparisons

with Sarah in their minds, and not for the first time, she was sure. Perfect, lovely, talented Sarah, who couldn't have been a better mother if she'd had 'Blessed Madonna' angelically stamped on her forehead, versus unglamorous, workhorse mammy Kathryn, newly branded a liar.

A sob escaped her. Don't cry, she told herself. Don't even think about it. You have to be strong and face this. You have to do the right thing – by Brett, by Rory and George, Flora and Steven. You always knew this moment would come. Now it's time.

She rubbed her eyes. This is your chance to tell the truth at last, she thought.

Grab it. Take it. Free yourself.

Kathryn got home to find Flora in tears in the kitchen, her face crumpled with distress. 'What is it, love?' she asked, rushing over to comfort her. 'Has something happened?'

'Oh, Mam...' Flora burst into fresh tears and fiddled with the turquoise silk scarf falling from her neck. It was her 'lucky scarf' and had once belonged to Sarah.

Kathryn put her arms around her. Flora was a sensitive soul – always had been. She found it difficult to share her problems, no matter how gently Kathryn coaxed her to be more open about them. But with patience it was usually possible to get to the bottom of whatever was upsetting her. Only–

Could Rory have spoken to her? Was she crying because he'd told her who he was?

But Flora wasn't pushing her mam away. She

271

wasn't screaming, 'How could you? I hate you!' So it wasn't Rory.

She went on waiting.

Finally, Flora came out with it. 'It's the pressure, Mam! I can't take it. All the teachers talk about is results, results, results. This is the crossroads, they keep saying. We could be heading to a good job and a successful life, or we could be taking the road to nowhere. They make it sound so serious, so final, like the difference between life and death, and it scares me. And I can't stop thinking, what if I mess up my exams and none of the unis will take me and I land up in a dead end job? I couldn't stand it; I'd kill myself. I would!' Her shoulders shook and she broke into great, heaving sobs.

Kathryn's first thought was that a girl in George's class had suffered a serious nervous breakdown after pushing herself too hard at school, her second that Rory's intrusion in their lives couldn't have come at a worse time for Flora. She gave her stepdaughter a squeeze. 'But you're top of your class,' she said softly, giving her back a stroke. 'What's set this off? You're great at exams and you always get As for your coursework. You, of all people, have nothing to worry about. Everyone's saying you'll breeze through these last years at school. The teachers are expecting you to do really well, love.'

Flora let out a small howl. 'That makes it worse! What if I let them down? They're expecting too much of me, Mam. I'm telling you, I can't do it. I can't go on. I'm starting to get palpitations every time I think about my A Levels – and they're not for ages yet.'

Kathryn pulled her close. 'Perhaps you just need a break, love. Why don't you leave your books alone tonight and do something completely different?'

Flora sniffed. 'Like what?'

'Let's do something nice, just you and me,' she said. 'We could go and see a film. Do you know what's on? We can see anything you like. Let's have a girls' night. I can't think of anything nicer.'

Flora sniffed again. 'Really?' she said.

'Yes, come on! Isn't it half price on a Monday?'

Flora leant into Kathryn, snuggled against her. ''K,' she said. 'Thanks, Mam. You always understand.'

Kathryn held her tight. First things first, she thought. I'll just have to speak to Brett when we get back.

They saw an American teen comedy at the Gateshead multiplex. It was about a perfectly pretty, skinny, spot-free girl who was considered the 'ugly' one in a group of friends at high school, but eventually triumphed by being true to herself. It wasn't the sort of thing Flora would have normally chosen, but it was the only film on offer that didn't feature guns, death and violence, apart from a fatally dull-sounding middle-aged drama starring Helen Mirren.

After predicting the entire plot within minutes of the start of the movie, Kathryn switched off. Her thoughts automatically turned inwards and connected up to her secret life with Rory – the imaginary Rory – as they usually did in moments like these. But that bubble had burst. All she could conjure was the real Rory, terrifying Rory, and she didn't want to think about him.

Whispering to Flora that she was popping to the ladies, she slipped out of the auditorium and ordered a double vodka and tonic at top speed in the bar. She was just about to take her first sip when she realised what she was doing and put the glass down, untouched. She loved Flora too much to risk driving her home over the limit.

Flora was quietly chortling away in her seat when she returned. 'I think I needed to watch something completely brainless,' she said cheerfully, on the drive back.

'I'm sorry there wasn't anything better on,' Kathryn said.

'Don't worry, Mam, I'm glad it was a piece of shite. It was a holiday for my brain.'

They pulled up outside the house just as Brett was putting the rubbish out. Kathryn's heart did a flip when she saw him. 'Hello, you two,' he said, breaking into a grin. 'Good film?'

'Not bad,' Flora said, grinning back.

Kathryn grimaced and mouthed, 'Rubbish.'

Brett held the front door open for them. He gave Kathryn's waist a quick squeeze as she stepped inside the house. She pressed herself against him and nuzzled his neck. In the kitchen she found George making toast, ever hungry – and no sign of Rory.

'Hi, Mam,' George said, munching.

'Fifth meal of the day? Sixth?' she teased. 'Bottomless pit, you are. Eat us out of house and home.'

He made a face. 'This doesn't count as a meal.

It's just a snack,' he protested.

She dangled a packet of bread in the air. Only a few slices remained. 'I give you Exhibit A – unopened until a couple of hours ago.'

'Mam, I'm a Formula One racing car. I need constant refuelling.'

She snaked an arm around him. 'Only kidding, love,' she said.

I love you so much, she thought. Please, never stop loving me.

He flashed her an awkward smile. She could see what he was thinking. Mothers couldn't be funny if they tried – and they tried too hard. 'How's your day been?' she asked, giving him a pat and moving away.

'Yeah,' he said, which presumably meant, 'Fine.'

She decided to leave him to his Marmite. As she was walking out of the kitchen, he said, 'Hey, I forgot. Rory says sorry for coming round your work today.'

She paused. 'Oh, I wasn't there,' she said casually.

'I didn't know he knew where you worked,' George said.

She shrugged. 'I must have mentioned it yesterday when he was round.'

'Anyway, he bumped into Tony and Tony gave him my number instead.'

She turned, eyebrows raised. 'That's the reason he came by? For your number?'

George gave her an impatient look. 'Yeah, why else?'

'He didn't leave a message. I wasn't to know,'

she snapped.

'So-o-rry!' George said grudgingly. 'So, he says not to worry. That's all it was.'

As she went upstairs, she mulled over what George had said. Was this Rory's way of calling a truce? Or was he just reminding her that he was the one in control?

Half an hour later, Kathryn got into bed and closed her eyes. Now's your chance, she thought.

But then Brett snuggled into bed beside her. 'Everything all right, sunshine?' he asked.

He put his arms around her and pulled her close. She sighed and pressed herself against him. His lips found hers and he began to kiss her softly, his mouth moving from her lips along the line of her jaw and deep into the curve of her neck. She savoured every moment of the love-making that followed, feeling grateful for this extra night of love, for the chance to fall asleep next to Brett vibrating with pleasure instead of staying up all night trading hurt and pain.

Every extra second of happiness counted when you knew it was coming to an end. She shut out the darkness and drifted into sweet oblivion, aided by the shot of vodka she had downed before coming to bed.

Kathryn woke up with a start in the early hours of the morning, her face and neck drenched in sweat. In her dream, Rory had been calling to her. 'Help me, Mam, I'm drowning!'

She'd run along a riverbank desperately search-ing for him and saw a head bobbing in the choppy water. 'Rory!' she screamed. 'It's your mam. I'm here.'

With a struggle he turned and stretched out his skinny arms to her. He was gasping and flailing – quickly tiring – a small lad of eight fighting a fierce current. She waded into the river and grabbed for his hands, which were frantic and slippery and almost impossible to hold. He slipped out of her grasp and the current whipped him away, dragging him downstream in the blink of an eye. She raced after him, but the river was too fast for her. He disappeared out of sight.

'Rory, Rory!' she screamed, and then he was suddenly beside her. But he was grown now, no longer a boy.

'Can we be together?' he asked, as they walked along the riverbank. 'Can I come and live with you now that I've found you?'

'I love you with all my heart,' she said. 'But we can't be together.'

'Why not?' His face darkened with anger and he towered above her, green eyes flashing.

'Please don't hurt me,' she begged. 'Don't hurt me.'

The river scene faded. They were in a bedroom. He flung her onto the bed. 'Why not?' He threw his head back and started laughing. 'You deserve it, you miserable, uptight cow.'

21

Is it really only Tuesday? Kathryn thought, as she hurriedly buttered two pieces of toast the next morning. The three days since she'd discovered Rory in her kitchen stretched behind her in nightmarish shadows.

Both George and Steven were eyes down to their screens as they came into the kitchen. 'Phones on the side,' she ordered. 'You know the rule. Not at the table.'

Flora's eyes were pink when she came in. It looked like she'd been crying again. 'What's today got in store for you, love?' Kathryn asked her.

Flora sniffed. 'Mr Potter.'

'Loony Potter?' George said. 'Bad luck. He's a fucking schizoid maniac. One minute he's Bruce Banner, the next he's the Hulk.'

'Mind your language,' Kathryn chided, and George rolled his eyes. 'Hopefully he doesn't burst out of his shirt, though,' she added, hoping to make Flora laugh.

But Flora hadn't heard her. She was staring miserably at her bowl of cereal.

George's phone beeped. He moved to fetch it from the kitchen counter. 'Wait until you've finished,' Kathryn said, but he reached for it anyway, glanced at the screen, swiped, scrolled and put it down.

'Rory says the oven's broken at his student accommodation,' he said. 'Can I ask him here for tea, Mam?'

No! she screamed silently.

'Is that what his text said?' she asked sharply. 'He wants to come for tea?'

George laughed. 'Nah, he's saying at least Maccy D's do salads now. He's really into his healthy food, you know.'

'Oh well, he probably wouldn't want the shepherd's pie and peas we're having tonight, then,' she said.

'Can I ask him anyway? Just to be friendly?'

She gritted her teeth. 'Sorry, love, not tonight. There won't be enough to go round, I'm afraid.'

She fretted anxiously as she walked to work, trying to work out what to do. In an ideal world she would come clean to Brett and the kids, who would understand and welcome Rory as a stepson and brother, giving them all a chance to get to know him. But if that couldn't happen, maybe he could become a Casey by stealth, one of those people who was 'family' without being blood-related. Even though he *was* blood-related.

It's just too complicated! she thought.

Was there an answer? It broke her heart that he wasn't happy with his adoptive parents. She wished he would get himself a girlfriend with a nice family set-up and a mam who would take him under her wing and cosset him. He wouldn't need her then. He would leave her alone. She closed her eyes. Half of her longed to mother him; half of her never wanted to see him again.

He was her son, but he was a stranger to her.

She knew almost nothing about him. She loved the lost Rory of her dreams, but what about the real Rory? Who was the person her baby had become? As much as he repelled her, he also mesmerised her. Perhaps she should call George and say she'd changed her mind about him coming to tea? Maybe it would give her a chance to get to know him a little.

Wait, don't be stupid, she thought. She came to an abrupt halt in front of a kebab shop. I'm totally confused. Rory is playing me like a fiddle, and I'm allowing him to do it.

First he had turned up in her kitchen and frightened the life out of her. Then he had gate-crashed their Sunday. So far he hadn't betrayed her, but she sensed he was capable of changing his tune in a heartbeat.

I mustn't let down my guard, she told herself. He's the enemy.

George wheedled Kathryn all day with funny texts, and eventually she caved in. Rory came for tea. He was polite and charming from the moment he arrived. She tried not to watch him, but her eyes kept moving back to him. He was taller than she remembered, his shoulders broader. He's strong, she thought, and alongside her fear of what he might be capable of, she experienced a swell of pride at being his mother. He stood up straight; he had good bearing. His hair was thick and healthy looking, his skin clear.

He didn't resemble her, though. His green eyes were almond shaped; her eyes were blue and round. His nose was straight and thin, while hers was soft and blobby. His lips were narrow, hers fuller. He looked nothing like her, and yet he was the spit of Steven, who everyone said was a fifty-fifty cross between herself and Brett. It was odd.

'Great shepherd's pie,' Rory said, addressing the comment to George. 'Your mam's a fantastic cook.'

She felt uncomfortable. Every compliment he gave her sounded like a reproach. 'I'm sure your mam's shepherd's pie is every bit as good,' she said.

He laughed. 'Me mam buys ready-made food. She's expert at peeling the film off the plastic trays. That's her speciality.'

'Man, I love ready meals!' George said. 'Mam won't get 'em, though. Says they're full of sugar and salt.'

'I enjoy cooking,' Flora said, out of the blue.

Kathryn looked over at her in surprise. Flora was usually so shy and quiet in front of new people.

Rory sat back in his chair, with a satisfied smile on his face. 'What's your signature dish?' he asked Flora.

Flora blanched. 'Um...'

'She does a great Lancashire hotpot, don't you, love?' Kathryn jumped in. 'And the best spaghetti bolognese this side of Venice.'

'Really? I like a good hotpot,' Rory said.

Flora gave him a shy smile and pushed her chair back from the table. 'Can I go, Mam? I've loads of reading to do tonight.'

'Of course, love. How did it go with Mr Potter today? Did he keep his shirt on?'

'He's a bully. Everybody says so,' said Steven.

281

'Is that right?' Rory said. 'Do you want me to twat him for you, Flora?'

Flora looked down and hurried out of the kitchen.

George laughed. 'Don't mind her. She's a spongebob when it comes to studying.'

'I take my studies pretty seriously, too,' Rory said. 'I want to get a first and impress my potential employers.'

'Right, who's up for dessert?' Kathryn said. She put some fruit and yoghurt in a bowl and took it up to Flora.

When she came down again, Rory and George had gone up to George's bedroom. Only Steven remained. 'I forgot to say yesterday – I need to take a baby photo in to school,' he said.

'Have you looked in one of the albums in the lounge? Otherwise, your dad'll have some on his computer, I expect.'

'Thanks,' he said.

Fifteen minutes later, just as she was finishing the washing up, he waved a photograph in front of her eyes. 'Look at this, Mam, it's so weird!'

She took off her rubber gloves and glanced at the picture. It showed a close-up of Steven, at about six months old, sitting in a high chair – and yet it wasn't one of the photographs she remembered.

He grinned and gave it to her. 'This is me, right?'

She was about to say, 'Yes, so?' but stopped herself. A closer look told her that it wasn't Steven's high chair; the background was wrong; he'd never had a Spiderman bib.

She shut her eyes. No, she thought. It can't be. Her heart started pounding.

She tried to force a laugh, but it came out as a strained 'ha!' sound. 'That's not you, love. Nothing like. Where did you find it?'

'It's Rory!' he burst out. 'He had it in his wallet. Come on, we look the same, don't we? We could be brothers!'

She could see he was chuffed. Rory was nineteen to Steven's twelve. He was George's friend. She didn't want to disappoint him, despite the dread seeping through her.

She snorted. 'It just proves that babies all look like Winston Churchill.'

He pointed at the cowlick curl on baby Rory's forehead. 'Even the hair, mam!'

'I see what you mean,' she said, but her voice was sceptical. 'How funny.'

A wave of nausea hit her. 'Sorry, love, I'll be back in a jiffy,' she said. She hurried to the downstairs toilet, locked herself in and threw up as quietly as she could. As she was rinsing her mouth at the basin, she heard Brett's key in the front door.

'Dad! You've got to see this,' Steven called to him.

Kathryn found herself unable to leave the downstairs toilet: her legs weren't walking; her hands refused to unlock the door. She gripped the basin for support. Her throat felt raspy, her voice whispery. Nothing was working properly.

Brett and Steven had moved out of earshot. How would Brett react to the photo of Rory as a

283

baby? Would it arouse his suspicion?

She had to remind herself that Brett didn't have any suspicions about her, or about her version of the past. He would probably be just as amazed and delighted by the likeness between the baby photos as Steven was, and then start thinking about his tea. Just calm down, she told herself. She steadied her breathing and willed her heart to slow down to a normal beat. I can get through this.

But how? She went through the scene she had rehearsed umpteen times in her head. She would call everyone into the lounge and announce that she had something to tell them. Only... Tears blurred her eyes. She needed to tell Brett first. It wouldn't be fair not to warn him. She started to cry, silently. Brett was such a good man.

I'll do it tonight, she thought. Definitely to-night.

She splashed cold water on her eyes and forced herself out of the toilet and towards the kitchen, willing herself to pretend everything was fine until she could get Brett alone.

Suddenly Rory was standing in front of her, blocking her way. 'Did Steven show you my baby photo?' he asked with a smirk.

'Yes,' she said, not meeting his eye.

'Did you think it was funny?' he asked.

'Funny? No.' She raised her eyes to his. 'What are you doing, Rory?' she whispered. 'Why are you here?'

He looked at her with mock sympathy. 'Did it remind you of the baby you lost, the one who died?' he asked coldly. 'Little Ross? So sad.'

She gasped. 'I–' she began.

Brett and Steven appeared at the top of the stairs. 'Mam!' Steven said, waving the photo. 'I showed it to Dad and he agrees! It's exactly like me.'

She tried to return his smile.

'I'm afraid that photo has upset your mam,' Rory said loudly.

'How come?' Steven asked, bounding down to join them.

Brett looked at her with concern. 'What is it, love?' he said. 'Seen a ghost?'

Kathryn swallowed. Is it now? she thought. Is this the moment of truth?

'Sunshine?' Brett said.

She shut her eyes. Her lies had their tendrils everywhere, she realised. The look on Brett's face and the disquiet in Steven's eyes told her how entwined in the family psyche they were. Brett and the bairns didn't treat her the way they treated each other – she could see that now – and it stemmed from their knowledge of the tragedy they thought she'd suffered. It was heartbreaking.

She looked at Rory and her heart went out to him, too. She needed to come clean for his sake, as well.

'I was just saying to Rory...' she faltered, 'that the photo ... reminded me of my Ross, my little one, and, you see, Rory is–'

'Oh, love,' Brett interrupted, moving towards her.

'How do you know about baby Ross?' Steven asked Rory.

There was silence. Here it comes, Kathryn

285

thought, leaning into Brett's shoulder.

'George told me,' Rory said. He smiled. 'Why, is it a secret?'

'No, not a secret – but a sensitive subject, obviously,' Brett said.

'Yes, it's really sad,' Rory said flatly. 'But I couldn't have known the photo would–'

'Of course, you couldn't, lad,' Brett assured him. 'But let's go into the kitchen and have a cuppa now. Least said, soonest mended, eh?'

'Actually, I'd best be going,' Rory said. 'Thanks for tea, Mrs C. You're a great cook, and I'm sorry if I upset–'

'What do you reckon to the Magpies' chances against Swansea on Saturday?' Brett interjected loudly. 'They'll beat Swansea, won't they? They've got to. I mean, give me a break, man.'

Rory looked from Brett to Kathryn and back to Brett. 'I don't know. They're floundering,' he said. 'But they can turn it around. They're still a few points above the relegation zone.'

'I hope you're right, lad,' Brett said, putting his arm around Kathryn. 'See you at practice tomorrow.' He wheeled Kathryn around towards the kitchen, shutting Rory off. 'Now for that cuppa.'

'Bye,' Steven said.

Kathryn thought she heard Rory say, 'Bye, bro.'

Her head swam. Why hadn't Rory gone for it?

He's torturing me, she thought. He wants me to suffer that little bit longer. As she filled the kettle, she glanced out of the window and saw the neighbour's cat stalking a bird. She rapped on the pane and yelled, 'Get lost!'

The cat froze, arched its back and then bounded

away. But it would be back again soon. It was the law of nature.

Brett was called out to a house viewing after tea. 'Sorry, sunshine, but it's their seventh time of looking and I think they're going to put in an offer at last.'

'No worries, I've got loads to get on with,' Kathryn said. 'I vowed I'd make a batch of fish-cakes and freeze them tonight.'

He put on his coat and pulled her close for a kiss. 'Why don't you put your feet up in front of the telly instead? I'll be home soon.'

She smiled. 'I think I can manage to make a few fishcakes, love. I'm not an old lady ... yet.'

'You don't look a day older than when I met you,' he declared.

That made them both laugh. 'Go on with you,' she said, pushing him towards the door. 'Hope you hook them for good this time.'

'Seventh time lucky,' he said.

Back in the kitchen, peeling potatoes at the sink, she recalled the vengeful expression on Rory's face when he'd asked her about the photograph. He was furious with her that she'd killed off little Ross, to make life easier for herself. It was catastrophic that he'd heard about it from one of the sons she had cherished and nurtured in his place for the past fourteen years.

But he's brought it on himself! she thought angrily. I told him to stay away. He knew I couldn't take him in. I told him so! He shouldn't have come here to see what he was missing.

Yet it wasn't his fault, of course. Poor Rory,

unwanted and unloved.

An image flashed into her head, a memory of the rape that had conceived him. She felt herself tense up. Could he be dangerous?

Stop it, she told herself. You're just trying to justify why you're rejecting him.

But she couldn't help wondering which genes had been passed down to him from his rapist father. Or from his grandmother, Mo, for that matter – that other monster from her nightmares.

Stop it! she told herself again. She thought about what Nana had said about children being a blessing, no matter where they came from. She recalled Mr Sharma's words about the law of karma guiding each spirit to its destiny.

She had to stop Rory hating her. He needed to know how much she had wanted to keep him. She'd tried to explain it the first time they'd met, but he'd been too angry to listen, and she'd been so panicked that she'd just wanted to escape. She should have stayed and had the patience to explain. 'I tried to get you back! I tried so hard.'

I need to talk to him, she thought. But where do I start? Do I go right back to the beginning? How much does he need to know?

As she went over the events leading up to that final, unbearable meeting with the social worker, blaming herself for what she had and hadn't said or done, she broke down and wept at the kitchen sink. 'I wish I'd ... how could I have ... why didn't I...' she whispered, raking together a handful of potato peelings and throwing them into Brett's compost bucket.

'Sweetheart?' a voice said behind her.

She jumped and turned to face him. 'Sorry, you gave me a fright,' she said, smiling weakly.

'Oh, love,' Brett said. 'It's the photo, isn't it? It's upset you.'

She nodded, fresh tears streaming down her face, and moved towards his outstretched arms.

22

It was wrong, she realised later, to begin her confession to Brett without explaining the background first. But, overwhelmed by panic, she didn't start at the beginning; instead she skipped to the end and blurted out: 'I've something to tell you. Rory is my son.'

Brett was ready for bed. He had stripped down to his boxers and pulled on an old T-shirt. 'What do you mean, love?' he said, tilting his head quizzically. 'Is it the photo? It must have been tough seeing it, sunshine. It's grim when things like that happen. I know how much it hurts.'

She loved him so much in that moment that she was tempted to say, 'I knew you'd understand,' and leave it at that. For the umpteenth time, it went through her head that she didn't really need to tell him the truth.

I could talk to Rory instead, persuade him not to tell, she thought. But she had been through this scenario enough times in the previous few days to know that it wouldn't work. In the end, Rory would tell someone. Or she would. It was human nature to spill secrets.

'No,' she said, 'the photograph upset me because Rory is Ross, my son. He didn't die in a car crash, although it often feels as if he did. I gave him up for adoption, because I couldn't offer him the life he deserved. I wanted him to have the best chance possible.'

Time stood still. Now that she had finally come out with it, she felt as if the world might end.

'But how can Rory be Ross, princess?' Brett asked, frowning.

'It sounds mad, I know,' she said, her eyes filling with tears. 'After he was born, I didn't see him for nineteen years. Then he phoned me at work one day, out of the blue, and asked me to meet him. It was a total shock.'

Brett stared at her in disbelief. 'When was this?' He sat on the bed, his shoulders slumped, as she told him about meeting Rory in the Lamb and Flag.

'Ross is alive? Your mam isn't dead?' he asked. 'But this is crackers, love. You must be making it up.'

She hung her head. 'I'm not, love. I know it sounds crazy, but–'

'It's the craziest thing I've ever heard,' he said. 'You're saying that you're someone else entirely, with a son I've only just met and a secret life I've never known about.'

'Yes,' she said. 'I'm sorry.'

'You're saying I don't know you. I don't know my own wife.'

'But knowing someone goes beyond facts, doesn't it?' she pleaded.

290

He shook his head. 'You start with facts. You build on facts. We started with lies. Our marriage is built on lies.'

She couldn't deny it, but it didn't sum up their life together. 'I thought it didn't matter, as long as we were happy,' she said weakly.

She told him everything, trying not to break down as she did, while he stared at her in bewilderment. 'There were so many moments when I wanted to tell you the truth,' she said. 'But I was worried that it would change your feelings for me, that you wouldn't love me any more. Especially as I've always felt second best to Sarah.'

He looked surprised. 'Sarah? What's she got to do with this?'

'I'm sorry to bring her up now,' Kathryn said, rubbing her eyes. 'I know how precious her memory is to you. But, you see, I've never felt I could measure up to her, even at the best of times. I thought that coming clean about my lies would make it even worse.'

'For you or for me?' he said. 'I've never thought of you as second best to Sarah. You're completely different people. More different than I could have imagined, as it turns out,' he couldn't help adding.

'You see?'

I can never be as good as her now, she realised. No matter what I do, she'll always be better.

Brett said nothing. He sat still and gazed blankly at the wall.

'I'm the same person I was before we came to bed,' she ventured.

'You may be the same, but we're not. We shared

something. Now it's gone.'

'It hasn't,' she argued desperately.

He went back to staring at the wall. 'I thought we understood each other, that we were honest with each other,' he said. 'But all these years you've been having secret thoughts. You've practically been living a double life.'

'I haven't!' she said. 'I put the past behind me when I came to Chester-le-Street, even more so after we got married.'

'How could you have done? We talked about Sarah and Ross constantly for months after we met.'

'Yes, you helped me to mourn him, as I hope I helped you with your grief about Sarah. I often thought about Ross in the years to come, as I'm sure you thought about Sarah, and it was always with a sense that I'd lost him, as if he'd died, even while I was wondering what sort of lad he was turning into. I know that sounds contradictory, but...'

He barely seemed to be listening. 'You weren't even truthful about your childhood memories,' he said distractedly. He put his head in his hands. 'You had an unhappy childhood. It's just another thing that separates us.'

'It wasn't so unhappy,' she said. 'It was a bit unstable at times, and we were brassic, but I had Nana.'

'Still, it means you're different,' he insisted.

'How?'

'From me.'

Did he mean from Sarah, too? And why was it suddenly so important? 'Please try and understand!' she begged. 'I was all right up until... I was doing well at school. But one night changed everything.'

He gave her a searching look. 'When you were raped? Did it actually happen?'

'Yes!' she sobbed, falling onto the bed. 'I went to the police. Check with them if you like. You've got to believe me, please.'

'I'll try,' he said.

'And I *was* loved as a bairn. My nana was amazing. I wish you'd met her.' She broke into fresh tears.

Brett didn't attempt to comfort her, didn't put his arms around her. She reached over to touch his shoulder, but he didn't respond. She felt more alone than she had in years.

'So Rory is your son,' he said wearily. 'What are you going to do now?'

'Where's Dad?' asked Flora, as she came into the kitchen for breakfast the following morning.

'He's had to go to work early today,' she said, making an effort to keep her tone even.

Steven followed her in. 'Morning, Mam. What's wrong with your eyes?'

'I think I've picked up an infection,' she said. 'I'll get some eye ointment from the chemist later.'

George was last down. 'Where's Dad?' he asked.

Flora shrugged and made a face. 'He went to work early.'

George peered at Kathryn. 'Have you been crying, Mam? What's up?'

'It's an infection, I think. It's made my eyes puffy

and pink.'

'That rhymes!' Steven said. He could still be such a kid. 'When will Dad be back?'

She sighed. Brett had slept on the sofa and gone off God-knew-where at God-knew-when in the morning. She had no idea whether he had gone for good. But he's got to understand in time, she thought. He *must*.

She tried not to think the worst. He can't leave me, she told herself. We love each other. I couldn't do without him.

The kids hurried off to school. Only George hesitated before he left. 'Sure you're OK, Mam?' he asked.

'A-one!' she replied, grinning at him madly.

It's weird how the lies just tripped off your tongue, for all those years, Brett had said.

All her life she'd had secrets, she thought. She had never told Nana what Mo had put her through. She had kept her home life hidden from her friends at school. She had left her past behind when she'd moved away. Everything had been a secret.

Had she finally broken the cycle by being honest with Brett? She missed him. It was like a physical pain. He rang at midday, while she was hanging out a second load of washing in the garden. 'Please come home,' she said. 'Let's sort this out and move on.'

The wind rustled through the trees by the fence and blew into the phone receiver. She heard a blast of white noise.

'It's not that simple,' he said. 'I need time to

think. We've all got our secrets, you know.'

'What do you mean?' she asked.

'I'll let you know when I'm ready to talk.' He sounded distant, as if he'd already detached from her.

'Will you be coming home tonight?' she asked, hoping against hope.

'No,' he said. 'I don't know when I'll be back.'

'But you will come back, won't you, Brett?' *Please, please say yes,* she silently begged him.

There was a moment's silence. 'I don't know.'

At least he hadn't said no outright. 'What shall I say to the bairns?' she asked.

He sighed. 'Why don't you try telling them the truth?'

He rang off abruptly, and for several long moments she stood on the lawn listening to the joyless sound of pillowcases flapping in the wind.

Kathryn couldn't face telling the children in the evening. Her heart felt too heavy and she was exhausted, so she lied and said that Brett had gone to see an old friend. She cried herself to sleep and slept fitfully, her dreams filled with images of babies with two heads. She cried again when she woke up with an empty space beside her.

Over breakfast, Flora said she was planning to do school work all day. Steven was meeting his mate Orson at twelve and George was still in bed, sleeping off a night on the tiles with Charlotte and her mates from the grammar school. At eleven, she went into George's room to wake him, braving the smell of alcohol-sweat and socks, but he was out cold, completely dead to the world. She opened the curtains, called his name, shouted and yelled to no avail. Finally, she tried to pull him out of bed, but didn't manage to move him more than a couple of centimetres.

'Can you put Orson off until a bit later?' she asked Steven. 'I want to talk to you, George and Flora, but I can't get George up.'

Steven looked aghast. 'Why do you want to talk to us? Has something happened to Dad?'

'No, no,' she assured him. 'Dad's fine, don't worry.'

'Are you two getting divorced?'

'I hope not!' she said, trying to sound light-hearted, but she clearly didn't pull it off because the next thing she knew he'd run into George's room and was wailing, 'Get up, G! Mam and Dad are splitting up!'

'Get lost,' George slurred sleepily.

'It's true! She wants to talk to us. Get up now!'

Fifteen minutes later, George and Steven were sprawled on the sofa in the lounge, but Flora still hadn't come out of her bolt-hole. Kathryn went upstairs to find out what the problem was. 'I'm studying. I haven't got time for family stuff,' Flora said from the other side of her bedroom door.

Kathryn wiped her brimming eyes. 'This is important, love.'

'I don't want to hear any bad news, Mam. It'll interfere with my studies.'

I can't help that, she thought despondently. 'It's not bad news, love,' she said.

'I'm still busy. I've got so much to do!'

'Flora, please! Come downstairs. It's important we face this as a family.'

She heard a sniff. 'Sounds like bad news to me.'

'Well, it isn't, not really. But we need to tackle it together.'

'Still sounds bad.'

She groaned. 'OK, it's bad, I admit it. But only for me, not for you – and I need your help. Will you help me, love?'

A shuffling sound came from inside the room. The door opened. ''K,' Flora said.

Back in the lounge, she started at the beginning – missing out her account of the rape, because she and Brett had agreed the bairns didn't need to hear that part. Instead she made something up about going out with a lad who had moved away before she realised she was pregnant. 'We didn't have the Internet back then,' she said. 'So I had no way of finding him.'

Simplifying the story made it seem a lot clearer. 'I lied because Tab was my friend and she disapproved of adoption,' she explained. 'There was another reason, too, I think – it felt too painful to tell the truth. I desperately regretted letting my baby go and hated myself for it.'

'It must have been awful, Mam. It must have felt like he'd died, even if he hadn't,' George said.

'It did,' she said, grateful to him for making the connection.

Flora's eyes were wide. 'You were only a year older than me when you had him, Mam. It's freaky.'

'I was very young, yes.'

'So he's alive and living with another family?' Steven said.

She nodded. Now came the really hard part.

'Do you know where he is?' Flora asked. 'Or don't you think about him any more?'

'Have you tried to find him?' said George.

'He found me,' she said, her heart beating rapidly. 'An agency got in touch by letter, but I said I didn't want to take it any further because my family didn't know about him.'

'You turned him down? That's harsh, Mam.'

'It seems uncaring, but I did it for the family. The thing is–'

'So where is he now? Do you know what happened to him?'

'He's here, in Chester-le-Street.'

'That's a coincidence, isn't it?' Flora said.

'Well, maybe not, because it's Rory.'

'What's Rory?' Steven asked innocently.

'I mean, Rory is the son I gave up for adoption.'

The room fell into shocked silence. Flora looked dismayed; George and Steven's mouths dropped open.

Then suddenly the boys were laughing. 'Rory is our brother?' George said. 'That's just weird, Mam. Are you joking? You don't even like him.'

'I don't know him,' she exclaimed. 'You've spent more time with him than I have.'

'But you knew he was your son all along? And you didn't say anything.'

'He only turned up on Saturday. It's been a week.'

George guffawed. 'That's a long time to be hiding something this mega!'

'I didn't know what to do. It took a while to get over the shock of finding him in my kitchen last weekend.'

'This is so weird,' Flora said.

'But how did he end up here in the first place, being friends with George and coaching the Steelers?' Steven asked. He and George were staring at each other in amazement.

'Yeah, how did that happen?' George said.

She shrugged helplessly. 'I don't think he did just end up here. I think he planned it as a way to spend time with us.' She filled them in on how she had met him at the Lamb and Flag in October.

Flora's cheeks went red. 'Why didn't you tell us before?'

She sighed. 'I felt forced into a corner, I suppose. It was cowardly of me.'

'And what does Dad say?'

She thought fast: If I win the bairns over, then I've more chance of Brett coming round.

'He's shocked, but he'll get over it,' she said, crossing her fingers behind her back. 'He's gone away to think it through, but he'll be back tomorrow.'

Her confidence seemed to reassure them. 'So Rory is Steven's half-brother. That's cool, isn't it, Steven?' George said.

Steven looked worried for a moment. 'I won't have to share a room with him, will I?'

'No, love, he's not moving in. He's not part of our family – well, not yet, anyway. Let's get to know him first, shall we? We're a happy unit. Let's keep it that way as we move forward.'

'He needs to get to know us too,' Steven said.

'Exactly,' she said.

George was already on his phone. 'Rory, mate!

Me mam's just told us you're our brother and I just wanted to say, "Welcome to the madhouse, bro!". Savage!' He hung up, laughing. 'His phone's on VM,' he said.

As ever, she was amazed by George's generosity of spirit. Everything was simple to him; he seemed to grasp complex issues in a flash. Steven, while perplexed, seemed happy to take George's lead, but Flora looked positively annoyed.

'It wasn't exactly bad news, was it, love?' Kathryn asked her.

Flora scowled. 'Well ... where's Dad?' she said shrilly. 'I want to speak to Dad.'

'Give him a call, then,' she said. 'You know your dad loves it when you phone him.'

Flora left the room and stamped up the stairs to her room. 'I think she might have fancied Rory, you know,' Steven said.

'Oh no,' Kathryn said, but something stirred in her, and she wondered if he was right.

Steven jumped up and ran off to meet Orson in the park. 'I'm hungry,' George said, slapping his hand against his stomach. 'What have you got for us?'

'Burgers in the freezer and I bought some fresh buns yesterday.'

'Awesome!' He rubbed his face with his hands. 'Ow, my head hurts when I jerk it around too much.'

'I get the hint,' she said.

He followed her into the kitchen and played with his phone while she got lunch ready. It was comforting to go on as if everything was normal – and as she cooked the burgers, she sensed herself feeling lighter by the minute.

'Whoah, Charlotte's asked me to her house for lunch tomorrow,' George said, suddenly beaming.

'You can't. You're going to see your grandparents in Darlington,' she said.

'Whaaa? Please no, Mam!'

'Yes, you are.' She pointed to the wall calendar, which had important school and family dates scribbled all over it. 'It's six weeks since you last went. Get your appetite up for Marjorie's Singin' Hinnies.'

He laughed. 'All Grandpa does is sit in his chair and go on about the old days.'

'He's getting older, that's all. People get nostalgic in later years.'

'He won't stop talking about our mam, either. Which is nice, in a way, but it makes me feel sad. No offence to you, Mam, but she sounds really amazing and I would have liked to know her. I wish I could remember her.'

'I know, love. It's hard.'

George and Flora often had a touch of melancholy about them when they came back from Marjorie and Ralph's house. She couldn't blame Sarah's parents for trying to keep their daughter alive in their minds, but she wasn't sure it was helpful for the bairns to be continually told how perfect she'd been. Still, there was nothing she could do about it, especially not now.

Normally she would have said something about death being the hardest thing to cope with, adding that she had learned this the hard way when her mam had died. Instead, she said, 'I wish you'd known my Nana as well. You would have loved her. I miss her every day.'

'Hmm,' he replied, distracted by his phone again. The next time he looked up from his perpetual scrolling, he said: 'The match starts in an hour. I'll see Rory there!'

Her heart skipped a beat. Rory would have heard George's message; he would know she'd come clean to Brett and the children. She wondered how he would react. Would he start to forgive her now that she had publicly acknowledged him? Was she even forgivable?

She tried to talk things through with Flora while George was out at football. 'We're a strange family, aren't we?' Flora said, sitting forlornly on her bed. 'Sort of patched together.'

'There's no such thing as normal any more, love,' Kathryn said, putting her arm around her. 'Love is what's important, not normality.'

Flora sniffed. 'Do you love Rory?'

She considered this. 'In a way,' she said. 'But I don't know him.'

'Do you love him more than me and George? He's your real bairn, after all, blood-related.'

'No, sunshine, I couldn't love anyone more than I love you and George and Steven,' she replied tearfully. 'It just wouldn't be possible.'

Back in the kitchen, she waited anxiously for George to get back. 'Did you see Rory?' she asked when he came racing into the kitchen to refuel.

'He didn't turn up,' he said, with a perplexed shrug. 'And he's still not answering his phone, either.'

'Neither is Dad,' wailed Flora, who had come downstairs when she'd heard George come in.

'I've tried him loads of times, but his phone keeps going to voicemail.'

Kathryn lay in bed, unable to sleep, staring into darkness. She had lost Brett – she was sure of it. There seemed to be nothing she could do or say to bring him back.

She had sent him a text, asking him please to call Flora as soon as he could. He had phoned around seven. 'He says he doesn't know what's going to happen now,' Flora told her when they'd finished speaking. 'He can't understand why you've lied to us all these years.'

'Oh well,' she said, trying to hide her distress. 'Maybe he needs time to think it over.'

'*I* understand, though,' Flora said, filling up. 'And I don't see why it matters now that it's out in the open.'

Kathryn flooded with warmth. 'Thank you, love,' she said, trying not to cry.

Yet despite Flora's kind words, it did matter that she had lied – of course it mattered – and she knew exactly why Brett felt betrayed. They had built their life together on a shared patch of grief that she had no claim to, and now that he knew the truth – now that their foundations had cracked and their house was tumbling down – he couldn't be blamed for thinking that he had fallen in love under false pretences.

His angry words echoed in her head. 'You've lied to me from the day I met you. How can I ever trust you again?'

She understood how he must feel. She had brainwashed him for years into believing certain facts about her past – and then contradicted them in the blink of an eye. It probably seemed to him as if the love he had lavished on her all this time had been wasted on a stranger, as if he'd been carrying around a photo of the wrong person in his wallet all along.

I don't know my own wife, he'd said.

How hard would it be for him to readjust to the real Kathryn, the girl with a difficult background, from the roughest part of Byker? Would he have to learn to love her all over again? Was that even possible?

'Mam, I don't want you and Dad to split up,' Flora had said.

'Me neither, love,' she'd replied, putting her arm around her and pulling her close. She'd wanted to say something reassuring, but nothing came. She hated to think of the pain and confusion she was causing.

Memories of Brett's daily kindnesses and loving gestures glimmered in the darkness of their bedroom. It felt as if she was already losing them to the past. The offerings and gifts he had rained upon her every day: the morning cuppas, cuddles and bedtime kisses; the surprise flowers, cards and secret hoards of chocolate. 'Don't let the kids see!' he'd whisper, passing her a bag or a package when nobody was looking. 'Let's open it in bed tonight, on our own.'

How could she live without him? This tender man, razor-sharp in a crisis, who welcomed life's absurdities and made her laugh at its worst moments. 'Luckily, I've got a thing for Thora Hird,' he'd joked the day she nearly collapsed in horror at the discovery of her first white hair. She thought back to the day they'd arrived home to find the lounge ceiling sagging ominously with overspill from a bath Flora had left running, and he'd laughed at their aghast faces and said, 'Do you think this room would be better as a swimming pool?'

She buried her face in the pillow. Brett was a good man, a funny man.

Maybe he was somewhere nearby, also lying in the dark, sleepless. She wondered what he might be thinking. Brett was someone who pondered problems slowly and coolly, trying to take every aspect into consideration. He wouldn't dismiss the endless love and care she had put in to bringing up the children, all the effort put into making sure they were a happy, well-fed family. Would he judge her accordingly? Could he set aside the 'facts'?

'Brett!' she wanted to call out. 'There's only one fact that matters and we're living proof of it. You know who I am because you've seen who I am: I'm your wife, the mother of our children. I've put love and family first every day for fifteen years. Why can't that be enough to keep us together? Love?'

It's all that counts in the end, she thought. He has to understand that.

She sat up in bed, groped around for her phone on the bedside table and began texting him.

23

Just before George and Flora left for Darlington the next day, Kathryn heard George leaving Rory another message. 'Where are you, mate? Have you gone back to Corbridge? I'm going to see me nana today but I'll check you later.'

'No word?' she asked, unnecessarily.

George made a face. 'Nah. Don't know where he is. But he'll be all right.'

Soon afterwards, Steven left on a day trip to Cullercoats with Orson and his mam. Alone in the house and trying not to fret, Kathryn kept herself busy answering work emails. She put on a wash, mopped the kitchen floor, swept through the lads' rooms tidying just enough to make the surfaces visible and sewed some missing buttons onto one of Brett's shirts.

She was sitting down to a quick fried egg sandwich when the doorbell went. Her heart leapt. Was it Brett? She couldn't help hoping. Against hope.

I must be going mad, she thought as she went to answer it. Brett wouldn't ring the doorbell! He's got a key; his name's on the mortgage document; you don't ring the bell of your own home.

She should have known it would be Rory, and yet it was a surprise to see him standing on the doorstep.

'Hi,' he said, shifting from one foot to the other.

He tilted his head and looked her boldly in the eye.

'Rory,' she said, gulping down a breath. 'George isn't here.'

His green eyes glinted. 'I've missed him, have I?'

'Yes, sorry.'

He shrugged, but didn't turn away.

'Well, anyway...' she added. 'You know I've told them. It's not a secret any more. *You're* not a secret any more. I'm sorry for all the hurt I've caused you.'

He nodded. 'Can I come in for a cup of tea?' he asked.

Something – instinct – told her that it would be better not to let him in. 'Actually, it's a bit difficult just now, love,' she said. 'Another day, eh?' She went to close the door.

'Shut the door in my face, would you?' he challenged.

'No,' she replied unsteadily, trying to do exactly that.

But she was too late. His arm shot out and stopped the door. 'Can't you even make me a cup of tea?' His eyes blazed.

'It's not a good time!' she protested, pushing the door again. His arm didn't give. He pressed forward and stepped into the house.

She thought about making a dash out into the street, but couldn't see a way past him. Retreating into the kitchen, she said shakily, 'I suppose we could squeeze in a quick cuppa, couldn't we?'

He followed her inside and sat down at the kitchen table. She switched on the kettle, pulled up a chair opposite him and gave him as natural a smile as she could muster. He didn't return it.

'Have you told them why you gave me away?' he asked.

'Yes,' she said gently. 'They know how hard it was for me to give you up.'

'Bullshit!' He scowled at her.

'Why do you say that? I told you–'

'Did you tell them that your mam begged you to keep me?' he interrupted. 'That she offered to look after me while you were at college? But you refused because you didn't want to be tied down by a bairn, so you arranged to have me adopted? By complete fucking strangers?'

She winced. 'That's not how it was,' she said, shaking her head. 'Did Mo tell you that?'

'Why would my grandma lie about it?' he cut in again. 'She broke down when we met; she cried over the years we've lost. She even offered me a home! She's a good, kind person, unlike you. You didn't even offer me a drink. You were desperate to get away and be rid of me again–'

'No! That's not right!' she protested.

'*She* wanted to keep me,' he said. '*She* did everything she could to stop the adoption, but you were determined to get shot of me so you could be free to live your party life.'

She shook her head. 'This is madness,' she said. 'Me mam was the reason I *couldn't* keep you. Surely you could tell what sort of person she was when you met her?'

He scowled. 'Yeah, right, just turn it around and expect me to accept your version,' he said. 'She's the bad guy. You're the angel. You've never told a lie in your life.'

'I'm not an angel, but me mam was the devil!' she said. 'She was drinking, taking drugs, having parties; the flat was teeming with lowlifes. It was impossible–'

'Why would she lie to me?' he spat. 'I can see why *you* would – you just want to cover your ass and justify your actions, but what's in it for her?'

'I don't know! I haven't seen her for fifteen years, and I never want to see her again, for that matter. She's evil, she's toxic ... she's that bad I don't even know how to describe her.'

'She seemed like a pretty cool older lady to me.'

Appalled as she was, she nearly laughed. 'Are we talking about the same person here? Mo Callan?'

'*She* wanted me, but *you* didn't. She begged and pleaded with you, but you were determined to toss me away, like a piece of litter.'

She flashed back to the night Mo had pretended to be in mortal danger, with a dealer's knife to her throat and a deadly debt to pay. 'It's not true!' she cried. 'She's a born liar. She must think you've got money to give her.'

His cheeks flushed pink. Standing up, fists clenched, he advanced around the table towards her. 'I don't believe you!' he growled. 'I hate you.'

She shrank into her chair, suddenly aware of how tall he was – how strong, how angry. 'Honestly,' she whispered. 'Has she asked you for money? I'm telling you, she's rotten to the core.'

'You're the rotten one,' he hissed. 'I've spent every day of my life feeling rejected – and it's all your fault, you heartless slag. Grandma told me about my father and what a nice lad he was. *He*

309

wanted me, but *you* didn't, so you dumped us both.'

'What the...? No one knows who your dad was, least of all me mam,' she said. 'I couldn't even tell you his name.'

'Liar!' he said, raising his fist to hit her.

She pushed her chair back, darted sideways and pelted past him and out through the kitchen doorway.

He chased after her, lunging out at her, trying to bring her down as she scrabbled up the stairs. 'Get away from me,' she screamed.

She hurtled into the bathroom and slammed the door, gasping for breath. Her hands trembled and jumped as she fiddled with the lock. It turned in the nick of time, a split second before he arrived.

He crashed into the door and started pummelling it. She pressed herself against the bathroom wall and waited for the sound of splintering wood.

Help me, Jami! she cried silently.

The plea to her old schoolmate was a bolt from the blue. It came out of nowhere, bursting through her blocked memories of the night she had been drugged and violated. Help me, Jami! Help me, Jami! Where are you? Save me, please!

'Do you want to know what you've done to me, you fucking bitch?' Rory yelled, punching the door again. 'You've made me want to kill you and your perfect family.'

'No, please,' she whimpered, cowering against the wall.

'Yes, kill you,' he repeated with a roar. 'I hate you and your happy Sunday dinners. I hate your stupid innocent card games and your lame family

310

jokes. You're just losers, all of you. You'd be better off dead.'

She sank down the wall, curling herself into a ball, trying to take up as little space as possible.

'It's all a lie, isn't it, this happy families bullshit? No one is really happy. You're definitely not, you can't be.'

She whimpered.

'But you all look so fucking happy, especially that wazzock, George. I'm going to kill him first, you know – after I've killed you, that is. He's not your biological son but you treat him like a king. Me, though – you won't even give *me* a cup of tea!' He smashed his fist against the door again to emphasise his point. 'And the rest of them – I'll kill them too.'

She was too terrified to speak. Hot and cold shivers rippled up and down her neck and arms and she started having flashbacks to the trauma of twenty years before. Powerless to stop them, she sat on the floor and endured, her teeth gritted, her body shuddering, while her mind retrieved lost images, unveiling one harrowing scene after another.

Raped, and raped, and raped, again, while waiting for Rory to break in and kill her.

'You didn't want me!' he kept shouting. 'Sandra made that clear. "You should be grateful," she always said.' His voice went up an octave as he imitated his adoptive mam. '"Your mam didn't want you. She took one look at you and sent you away. You'd be growing up in care if we hadn't adopted you. You should be on your knees, thanking us for what we've done for you." But I wasn't grateful. Grateful for what? I was lonely! So lonely!' he yelled.

His threats took on a moaning, wailing quality. 'I'll slit your throat with my butterfly knife from ear to ear, Kathryn ... you'll be sorry, you'll be dead, and I'll be laughing at your funeral... And then I'll go for George, because he doesn't deserve what you give him – I'm your son, not him. He's an imposter! I'm the one you should be living with. Why can't you be my mam? Why?'

She sensed his mood beginning to alter, his aggression breaking down and self-pity taking over.

She seized her chance. 'Rory, love, I understand,' she called to him. She held her breath and waited.

'You don't!' he howled. 'How could you understand?' She heard him slide to the floor with a thump.

'I do, love,' she said gently. 'I didn't grow up with my mam, either. Mo – the woman you met – abandoned and rejected me soon after I was born. I had my nana; I was lucky; unfortunately things didn't turn out so well for you. But if anyone understands how you feel, it's me. That's why I'm sure we'll sort this out eventually.'

She took a deep breath. 'I've taken a big step and told my family about you,' she went on. 'It was a massive risk and maybe my marriage won't even survive it, but I've done what I had to do. It was high time. I'm so sorry, love. Now it's time to pick up the pieces; only let me clear up my own back yard first, love, and then I'll move on to you. I've thought about you every day since you were born, Rory. I've missed you and wished we were together. But I don't know you yet – and we

312

won't be able to get any further if you hit anyone or hurt anyone. Do you understand me? I need you to promise.'

She heard a keening sound through the door. He broke into heavy, racking sobs. 'Why me, though?' he wailed. 'Why did it have to be me? Other kids have happy families. Why was I different?'

'I don't know, love. I can't answer that. I've asked myself the same question a thousand times. Why me?'

'I didn't deserve it. I was just a baby! Why couldn't you have kept me, instead of sending me away?'

Suddenly she felt too tired to speak. 'You'd better go now,' she called out. 'Go home before you do something terrible. I can't talk any more – I'm not feeling well – but I'll see you soon. I won't abandon you again. I promise.'

Kathryn spent the next hour curled up on the bathroom floor, sweating and shaking, reliving the night she had been raped in all its forgotten horror. At some point, Rory moved away from the bathroom door. She had no idea whether he had left the house or was waiting downstairs for her with his butterfly knife at the ready.

Later, she fell into a fitful sleep, punctuated by waking flashes of horror and muscle spasms. Although she knew it was PTSD, it began to feel as if she was going through an exorcism, that she was expelling the hurt and pain of what had happened to her. Eventually, her heartbeat began to slow down, her breathing calmed, her mind shut off and she slipped into a deep sleep.

She woke up to the sound of footsteps coming up the stairs. Rory? she thought, tensing up again.

'Kathryn?' a voice called.

'Brett,' she croaked, trying to raise herself out of the bath.

'I'm sorry, love,' he said. 'I won't leave again.'

'You're back?' She pulled herself up, staggered to the door and unlocked it. Brett was standing on the landing. He was such a good man.

His expression changed. 'What's happened?' he asked urgently. 'You look terrible.' He hurried towards her.

'You're back,' she whispered, as he gently put his arms around her. 'Oh, love, I'm so glad to see you.'

Late that night, long after he had put her to bed and made sure the bairns didn't disturb her, after George and Flora had returned from Darlington complaining that they'd eaten too many of Grandma's scones, after Steven had got back from Cullercoats with a bruise on his cheek from fighting Orson, and once the house had settled into the soft-breathing peace and rhythm of night time, Kathryn woke up to find Brett sitting on her side of the bed.

'What is it, love? Are you all right?' she asked. She braced herself. Maybe he would say he was leaving again – because he couldn't cope with her traumas; because her background was too messed up.

'Well,' he said. Backlit by his bedside light and half-silhouetted, he leaned forward, head down, hands clasped. 'I er...'

'Go on,' she urged. 'Say what you have to say.'

There was a pause. 'I didn't love Sarah,' he said haltingly. 'Not after we were married, anyway.'

'Oh,' she said, sitting up. She wasn't sure she'd understood him. 'You didn't...?'

'I didn't love her,' he said. 'She was a nightmare. Everything had to be a drama. She always had to have her own way. She was vicious and manipulative.'

She stared at him. 'Are you making this up to make me feel better?' she asked.

'No, it's true – I've had my own secret all this time. I'm sorry I reacted the way I did when you came clean about Rory. I think I was afraid, partly. I knew it meant that I would have to be honest, too.'

She fought to contain her astonishment. 'I don't understand. I thought Sarah was perfect.'

He tutted and shook his head. 'Far from it – she was selfish, demanding; there were so many bad things that I didn't find out until our honeymoon. That's when she suddenly switched. I'll never forget the look on her face our first night at the hotel, all twisted and mean. "No, I don't want to hole up in our room and have a cosy dinner," she snapped at me. "I want to get out and have some fun, *for once.*" Everything was different from that moment on. I never knew whether she was disappointed that she'd married me, or whether she felt she didn't need to make an effort once we were married. Before long, we started arguing; she was constantly threatening to leave me.'

Kathryn struggled to readjust her view of Sarah, the perfect first wife. Had she always sensed that

315

Sarah was too good to be true?

'But why have you made her out to be the ideal partner and mother for all these years?'

He looked at her with exasperation. 'What else do you say to your bairns when their mam has died?'

'Yes, I see,' she said.

'No, you don't see,' he countered. 'She walked out into that road to spite me, without a thought for how dangerous it was, or what it might mean to those poor bairns to lose their mam. It was the ultimate act of cruelty.'

She frowned, barely able to follow. 'But you're not suggesting she did it on purpose?'

He dipped his head and sighed. 'We had an argument and of course she turned it into a drama,' he explained. '"You'll regret this," she warned me. It was the usual thing. "You'll be sorry when you come home to an empty house." "Oh, grow up!" I snapped. "I'm sick of these idle threats. I can't live like this any more."' His voice cracked. 'Then, she smirked and said, "After to-day, you won't have to." Twenty minutes later she was dead. Was it a coincidence?' He shook his head. 'I'll never know.'

She was stunned. 'Of course it was a coincidence,' she said. 'But it explains why you can't stop feeling you're responsible. Even though you're not, you know. None of it is your fault.'

He looked unconvinced. 'I was weak. I should have stood up to her. I badly wanted to leave her, but then the bairns ... especially Flora coming along so soon after George ... made it impossible. I couldn't leave her then. The worst thing is that in a way I'm glad she died, because it led me to the bereavement group, to you. It's a terrible thing to admit! I only went because of my guilt, and there you were. But I can't let myself feel glad about it because that makes me feel guiltier, so I try to block it out.'

He buried his face in his hands. She reached forward and gave him a hug.

'I know that feeling,' she said with a regretful smile. 'But this is all too much to take in, my love. Way, way too much – my head is spinning, it's that overloaded. So it's going to have to wait for morning, I'm afraid, and in the meantime, please get into bed with me. I need a snuggle with my hubby. I need you so much, my love.'

He got into bed, his cheeks wet with tears. He was wrapping his arms around her when the phone rang. 'Your parents?' she said.

He reached for the phone and showed her the screen. The display said *Unknown Number.*

'Or some bloody call centre,' he growled, flicking the answer button. 'Hello!' he barked, his voice cutting through the tranquillity of the night.

She waited to hear who it was.

'She's not awake, I'm afraid,' Brett said, 'and you need to know that it's too late to call us, son. No, Rory, I mean it.'

She tensed at the mention of his name, but then her fear quickly faded. Poor Ross. Poor Rory. Poor lad.

'I know what happened today and it worries me a lot,' Brett went on saying, 'so I'd like you to give it a rest for now and we'll get together at the weekend to talk things through. How does that sound?' He waited for Rory's response. 'I mean it,' he said shortly. 'Otherwise I will have to contact the police and report you. I'll be in touch at the weekend.'

He ended the call and put the phone back into its base. 'Well done,' she said, waves of exhaustion flowing through her as he lay down beside her again.

'Are you all right, love? What you've been through... I should have been there to protect you. I should have seen that Rory was dangerous. But I was too busy trying to work out how I was feeling,' Brett said.

She exhaled softly, crushed by tiredness. 'Everything came at once. It was all too much,' she said.

He kissed her and switched out the light. 'That boy needs help,' he said, pulling her into his arms. 'Let's try our best to give it to him, shall we?'

'Tomorrow,' she murmured as she drifted off, feeling safe again, at last.

Epilogue

Wednesday 19 October 2016, Chester-le-Street, County Durham

Kathryn was loading up her trolley with two-for-one pasta twirls when someone nudged her and said with a giggle, 'Hello, sailor!'

She turned in surprise and faced an older,

softer version of her ex-colleague Tab, whom she hadn't seen since she and Robyn had moved to Brighton, a good fifteen years earlier. 'Tab! How fantastic to see you! What are you doing here?' she asked, brimming with unexpected pleasure at the sight of her.

'I come to stay with me old mam every now and then,' Tab said. 'Most of the time she visits us down south, but she had a fall last month, so here I am. How are you?' Tab searched her face for clues. 'You look glowing, love! What's your secret?'

She shrugged and laughed. She avoided secrets these days.

Still, she'd been getting a lot of comments along the same lines recently. 'What is it that's different?' people kept asking. 'You look younger, fresher! Have you done something to your hair?'

'It's my last gasp of youth, I think,' she joked. 'I'm going to be forty next year.'

Tab wasn't having it. 'It's not that, love,' she said, shaking her head. 'Something's changed. You always had a bit of a haunted look about you, but I can tell that you're really happy at last.'

Kathryn smiled at her gratefully. 'You look different, too. Are you still with Robyn?'

Tab's eyes twinkled. She glanced at the phone in her hand. 'Have you got time for coffee and a catch-up? Me mam's not meeting me here for another half an hour.'

They finished their shopping at top speed and met up in the supermarket café, where Tab ordered a super skinny latte and Kathryn plumped for a strong cup of tea. 'So you stayed with the bloke you met at that grief thing you went to?' Tab asked. 'Have you enjoyed being married and doing the stepmother thing?'

Kathryn tilted her head. Although it was accurate to describe herself as George and Flora's stepmother, it felt wrong after all this time. 'Actually, I think of myself as their mother now,' she said. 'And I had a bairn with Brett – the bloke from the grief thing – which helped to bring us all closer, I think.'

Tab's finely arched eyebrows shot up. 'You had another bairn – that's wonderful! After the sadness of...' She looked away, clearly embarrassed to have brought the subject of her dead son so soon into their conversation.

Kathryn looked down at her lap. Maybe she glowed these days because she no longer had to stifle vital information on a daily basis; lying didn't come automatically any more. What's more, she wasn't quietly yearning for her long lost son or wondering if she could ever match up to Brett's first wife. And even if there was still a lot to be resolved when it came to her relationship with Rory, her life was immeasurably better than it had been eighteen months previously – better, in fact, than it had ever been before.

They were all doing their best to make Rory feel welcome and include him in their family life, but it wasn't proving easy. He bristled with resentment and was critical of her whenever the chance arose, even over the tiniest things. He grasped every opportunity to make a caustic remark about her failings as a mother; he couldn't seem to help it. Occasionally his anger erupted and he'd yell something, but then Brett would step in with a warning, and although he had never attempted violence again, Kathryn made sure not to be alone with him. She didn't feel ready to trust him wholly yet.

Aside from his moods, Rory was still a stranger to them in custom and habit, having been brought up differently, by parents with high expectations. He seemed ruthlessly ambitious at times, conceited, entitled even, had a very lax attitude to spending money and Flora was always pulling him up on his high-handedness. Yet they all liked him. Kathryn was hopeful that things would work out. It was a work in progress, though. She couldn't deny that they had a long way to go.

'I'm sorry, I didn't mean to–' Tab said.

'Don't worry,' she replied. 'Actually, there's something I should tell you...'

She told her everything.

Tab listened in amazement, her hand flying to her mouth every time it fell open at a new twist in the tale. 'No!' she kept saying. 'You poor love.'

'So it's a strange mixture of good and bad that came out of it all,' she said, in conclusion, dabbing her cheeks dry with a paper napkin. 'I sometimes think, you know, that if I could turn back time, I wouldn't know which moment I'd go back to. Because if none of it had happened, I wouldn't be where I am now.'

Tab leaned forward. 'I, for one, wouldn't let you turn back time!' she said with a grin.

'Why not?' Kathryn asked, frowning. 'Where do you come into it?'

'Because...' Just then, Tab's mam appeared at the door of the café, leaning on the arm of a pretty teenage girl. 'Here's why not,' Tab whispered conspiratorially, gesturing over at them. 'Robyn and I were really, really upset for you when you told me that your son had died, Kathryn.'

She felt a pang of guilt. 'I know, I'm so–'

'Shh!' Tab interrupted her. 'It made Robyn pause, especially. She thought, Life's too short to be worrying about a bairn ruining your looks or losing your social life, or whatever.' Tab waved her arm impatiently. 'All those concerns she had, you remember,' she added. 'So when we got to Brighton, she said, "Let's do it, let's learn a lesson from poor Kathryn's life." And so we found a sperm donor and ... look! Here's another brilliant result to add to your list.' She stood up. 'Kathryn, you remember me mam, don't you?'

She reached out to grasp Tab's mother's hand in greeting. 'Yes, hello, Maureen, how are you?' she said, wondering what Tab was going to say next.

'And this is my daughter,' Tab went on, turning proudly to the teenage girl beside her. 'This is Rose, named in honour of your little boy, Ross. Isn't she the most beautiful sight you've ever seen?'

Rose looked shyly in her direction.

'She is,' Kathryn agreed. 'She really is.'

The publishers hope that this book has given you enjoyable reading. Large Print Books are especially designed to be as easy to see and hold as possible. If you wish a complete list of our books please ask at your local library or write directly to:

Magna Large Print Books
Magna House, Long Preston,
Skipton, North Yorkshire.
BD23 4ND

This Large Print Book for the partially sighted, who cannot read normal print, is published under the auspices of

THE ULVERSCROFT FOUNDATION